NIGHTCREATURE NOVELS

THUNDER MOON

"Will absolutely rivet you to your chair. Murder, mayhem, humor, and horror form a tale that keeps the reader on edge to the very end. *Thunder Moon* is a well-crafted story that will leave the reader longing to dig into the next Nightcreature book as soon as possible."

—*Night Owl Romance Reviews*

"Handeland is at the top of her game in this taut thriller. Part detective tale, part supernatural chiller, this is a full-on exciting read." —*Romantic Times BOOKreviews*

"Provocative, intense, and rife with creepy beings. The romance is sultry, solid, and very intense."

—*Romance Junkies*

"Handeland has a gift for creating and sustaining a mood throughout her stories that keeps the reader eagerly turning the pages." —*Fresh Fiction*

RISING MOON

"Eerie atmospherics and dark passion intertwine, making this a truly gripping and suspenseful read."

—*Romantic Times BOOKreviews*

"What makes the latest in her Nightcreature series stand out is how Handeland paints such a vivid portrait of the Big Easy and its inhabitants. The city itself is a character, not unlike its real-life counterpart...her gift to skillfully

MORE...

repel and attract commands the reader's attention to the very end and will lure genre readers enamored of paranormal romance or mysteries." —*Booklist*

"Phenomenal...the story, characters and dialogue, and descriptive setting are perfect." —*Romance Reader at Heart*

"Keeps you guessing until the very end...I was awed." —*Fallen Angel Reviews*

"A great plot, wonderful characters and a setting to die for. You gotta pick this one up." —*Fresh Fiction*

"Mmm...mmm...mmm! Get ready for the ride of your life…an intriguing eye-opener...Twists and turns, secrets and shadows, captivating characters, a well-written, well-developed plot, and a romance." —*Romance Reviews Today*

"*Rising Moon* is suspenseful, passionate, and edgy, but it's also a true feel-good read with a message of hope and redemption." —*Eternal Night Reviews*

CRESCENT MOON

"Strong heroines are a hallmark of Handeland's enormously popular werewolf series, and Diana is no exception. *Crescent Moon* delivers plenty of creepy danger and sensual thrills, which makes it a most satisfying treat." —*Romantic Times BOOKreviews*

"Handeland knows how to keep her novels fresh and scary, while keeping the heroes some of the best...pretty much perfect." —*Romance Reader at Heart*

MOON CURSED

Lori Handeland

St. Martin's Paperbacks

This is a work of fiction. All of the characters, organizations, and events portrayed in this novel are either products of the author's imagination or are used fictitiously.

MOON CURSED

Copyright © 2011 by Lori Handeland.
Excerpt from *Crave the Moon* copyright © 2011 by Lori Handeland.

Cover illustration by Aleta Rafton

All rights reserved.

For information address St. Martin's Press, 175 Fifth Avenue, New York, NY 10010.

ISBN: 978-0-312-38935-2

Printed in the United States of America

St. Martin's Paperbacks edition / March 2011

St. Martin's Paperbacks are published by St. Martin's Press, 175 Fifth Avenue, New York, NY 10010.

10 9 8 7 6 5 4 3 2 1

ACKNOWLEDGMENTS

A thousand thank-yous to Jody Allen at Scottish Scribbles for reading the manuscript and making sure I got it right. Jody has a great blog at http://scottishscribbles .blogspot.com/

Any mistakes are always my own.

MOON
CURSED

CHAPTER 1

The first recorded sighting of the Loch Ness Monster was by Saint Columba in A.D. 565. The most recent occurred just last year.

"There'll be a sighting every year," Kristin Daniels muttered as she peered at her laptop. "Wouldn't want to screw with a multi-million-dollar tourist industry."

Unless, of course, you were the host of the public television show *Hoax Hunters.* Kris planned to screw with it a lot.

In fact, she planned to end it.

Kris scribbled more notes on her already-scribbled-upon yellow legal pad. This was going to be her biggest and best project to date. The debunking of the Loch Ness Monster would not only put *Hoax Hunters* on the national radar—hell, she'd probably get picked up for syndication—but also would make her a star.

"Kris?"

She glanced up. Her boss, Theo Murdoch, stood in the doorway of her office. He didn't look happy. Theo rarely did.

Public television was a crapshoot. Sometimes you won; sometimes you lost. But you were always, always on the verge of disaster.

"Hey, Theo," she said brightly. "I was just planning our premier show for next year. You're gonna love it and so—"

"*Hoax Hunters* is done."

Kris realized her mouth was still half-open and shut it. Then she opened it again and began to babble. She did that when she panicked. "For the season, sure. But next year is going to be great. It'll be our year, Theo. You'll see."

"There is no next year, Kris. You're canceled."

"Why?"

"Ratings, kid. You don't have 'em."

Fury, with a tinge of dread, made Kris snap, "It's not like we were ever going to compete with *Friday Night SmackDown*."

"And we don't want to." Theo's thin chest barely moved despite the deep breath he drew. The man was cadaverous, yet he ate like a teenaged truck driver. Were there teenaged truck drivers? "Cable's killing me."

Or maybe it was just his high stress and two-packs-a-day diet.

In Theo's youth, back when he still had hair, PBS had been the place for the intelligent, discriminating viewer. Now those viewers had eight hundred channels to choose from and some of them even produced a show or two worth watching.

In the glory days *Planet Earth* would have been a PBS hit. Instead it had played on the Discovery Channel. Once *The Tudors*—sans excessive nudity of course—would have been a *Masterpiece Theatre* staple. Now it was Showtime's version of MTV history.

"Who would have thought that public radio would do better than us?" Theo mumbled.

To everyone's amazement, NPR was rocking even as PBS sank like a stone.

"Not me," Kris agreed. And too bad, too. Not that she could ever have done *Hoax Hunters* for the radio even if she *had* possessed a crystal ball. The show's strength lay in the visual revelation that what so many believed the truth was in fact a lie.

Hoax Hunters, which Kris had originally called *Hoax Haters,* had come about after a tipsy night with her best friend and roommate, Lola Kablonsky. Kris had always loathed liars—she had her reasons—and she'd been very good at spotting them. One could say she had a sixth sense, if a sixth sense weren't as much of a lie as all the rest.

Why not make your obsession with truth and lies into a show? Lola had asked.

And full of margaritas and a haunting ambition, Kris had thought, *Why not?*

She'd used her savings to fund a pilot, and she'd gotten that pilot onto the screen through sheer guts and brutal determination. She wasn't going to let something as erratic as ratings get her down.

If she debunked the Loch Ness Monster, every station in America—no, in the *world*—would want that film.

Talk about a dream come true.

"Scotland," Lola said. "Does anyone really go to Scotland on purpose?"

Kris tossed a few more sweaters into her suitcase. "Just me."

September was cold in the Highlands, or so she'd heard. Not that she wasn't used to the cold. She was from Chicago.

Cold moved in about October and hung around until June. There'd even been a few July days when the breeze off the lake was reminiscent of the chill that drifted out of her freezer when she went searching for double chocolate brownie yogurt in the middle of the night.

"Are you sure, Kris?" Worry tightened Lola's voice. "You'll be all alone over there."

Alone. Kris gave a mental eye roll. *Horrors!* Like that would be anything new.

Her mother had died of leukemia when Kris was fifteen, insisting to the very end that she was fine. Kris's brother had left for college when she was seventeen, swearing he'd visit often. If "often" was once the following year and then never again, he hadn't been lying. Her father hung around until she turned eighteen. Then he'd taken a job in China—no lie. He hadn't been back, either.

So Kris was used to alone, and she could take care of herself. "I'll be okay." She zipped her suitcase.

"I'd go with you—"

Kris snorted. Lola in Scotland? That would be like taking Paris Hilton to . . . well, Scotland. Kris could probably shoot a documentary about it. The film would no doubt receive better ratings than *Hoax Hunters*.

And wasn't that depressing?

"Aren't you getting ready for the season?" Kris asked.

Lola was a ballet dancer, and she looked like one. Tall and slim, with graceful arms and never-ending legs, her long, black, straight hair would fall to the middle of her well-defined back if she ever wore it down. However, Lola believed that style made her already-oval face appear too oval. As if that could happen.

Kris didn't consider herself bland or average until she stood next to Lola. She also wasn't a washed-out, freckle-nosed, frizzy-headed blonde unless compared with Lola and her porcelain complexion surrounded by smooth ebony locks. The only thing they had in common was their brown eyes. However, Lola's were pale, with flecks of gold and green, while Kris's were just brown, the exact shade of mud, or so she'd been told by a man who'd said he was a poet.

The two women were still friends because Lola was as beautiful inside as out, as honest as a politician was not, and loved Kris nearly as much as Kris loved her. In all her life, Kris had never trusted anyone the way she trusted Lola Kablonsky.

Lola set her long-fingered smooth, elegant hand on Kris's arm. "If you needed me, I'd go. Screw the season."

Kris blinked back the sudden sting in her eyes. "Thanks."

They had met while living in the same cheap apartment building—Kris attending Loyola University and Lola attending ballet classes on the way to her current stint with the Joffrey Ballet. On the basis of a few good conversations and a shared desire to get out of their crappy abode, the two had found a better one and become roommates.

Kris hugged Lola; Lola hugged back, but she clung. Kris felt a little guilty for leaving her—Lola wasn't used to being alone—but she didn't have a choice. She couldn't start over again with another show. She believed in *Hoax Hunters*.

She also believed that the Loch Ness Monster was ripe for debunking and she was just the woman to do it.

Kris gathered the backpack that contained her laptop, video camera, mini-binoculars, and purse. "I'll be okay," she assured her friend for the second time. "It's not like I'm going to Iraq or Colombia or even the Congo. It's Scotland. What could happen?"

* * *

Though it felt like a week, Kris arrived in Drumnadro-chit, on the west shore of Loch Ness, a day later.

She'd been able to fly directly from Chicago to Heath-row; however, unlike the rest of the people on the plane, she hadn't been able to sleep. Instead, she'd read the books she'd picked up on both Scotland and Loch Ness.

Loch Ness was pretty interesting, even without the monster. The lake itself was a ten-thousand-year-old crack in the Earth's surface. Because of its extreme depth—nearly eight hundred feet—the loch contained more freshwater than all the other lakes in Britain and Wales combined and never froze over, even during the coldest of Highland winters.

There had been over four thousand reported sightings of Nessie, which no doubt fueled the $40 million attrib-uted to her by the Scottish tourism industry. With that kind of income at stake, it wasn't going to be easy to debunk this myth. Kris certainly wasn't going to get any help from the locals.

By the time London loomed below, Kris's eyes burned from too much reading and not enough sleeping. However, she couldn't drag her gaze from the view. She wished she had the money to tour the Tower and Buckingham Palace; she'd always dreamed of walking the same streets as Shakespeare. Unfortunately, she was traveling on her own dime and she had precious few of them.

The city sped by the window of the bus taking her to Gatwick Airport, where she boarded a flight to Inverness. A few hours later, she got her first glimpse of the city. Why Kris had thought Inverness would be full of castles she had no idea. According to her guidebook, it had over sixty thousand people and fewer than half a dozen castles. Still she was disappointed. Quaint would play very well on film.

She got what she was hoping for on the road south. The countryside was quaint squared, as was Drumnadrochit. White buildings framed by rolling green hills, the place should have been on a postcard—hell, it probably was—along with the wide, gray expanse of Loch Ness.

The village was also tourist central, with a wealth of Nessie museums, shops, and tours by both land and sea. Kris would check them out eventually. They'd make another excellent setting for her show. The charm of the village would highlight the archaic myth, illuminating how backward was a belief in fairy tales. The excessive glitter of tourism would underline why the locals still pretended to believe.

Kris had once adored fairy tales, listening avidly as her mother read them to her and her brother. In those tales, bad things happened, but eventually everything worked out.

In real life, not so much.

Her driver, an elderly, stoic Scot who'd said nothing beyond an extremely low-voiced, "Aye," when she'd asked if he often drove to Drumnadrochit, continued through the village without stopping. For an instant Kris became uneasy. What if the man had decided to take her into the countryside, bash her on the head, and toss her into the loch, making off with her laptop, video camera, and anything else she might possess? Sure, Lola would miss her eventually, but by then Kris would be monster bait.

A hysterical bubble of laughter caught in her throat. She didn't believe in monsters—unless they were human.

She lifted her gaze to the rearview mirror and caught the driver watching her. He looked like anyone's favorite grampa—blue-eyed, red cheeked, innocent.

And wasn't that what everyone said about the local serial killer?

The vehicle jolted to a stop, and Kris nearly tumbled off the shiny leather seat and onto the floor. Before she recovered, her driver leaped out, opened her door, and retreated to the trunk to retrieve her bag.

Kris peered through the window. They'd arrived at Loch Side Cottage, which, while not exactly *loch* side, was damn close. Kris would have to cross the road to reach the water, but she'd be able to see it from the house. The village of Drumnadrochit lay out of sight around a bend in the road.

"Idiot." Kris blew her bangs upward in a huff. "No one's going to bash you over the head. This isn't the South Side of Chicago."

She stepped out of the car, then stood frozen like Dorothy opening the door on a new and colorful world. The grass was a river of green, the trees several shades darker against mountains the hue of the ocean at dawn. The air was chill, but it smelled like freshwater and—

"Biscuit?"

A short, cherubic woman with fluffy white hair and emerald eyes stood in the doorway of the cottage. For an instant Kris thought she was a Munchkin. She certainly had the voice for it.

"I made a batch of Empires to welcome ye." She held out a platter full of what appeared to be iced shortbread rounds, each topped with a cherry.

Kris hadn't eaten since the flight to Heathrow, so despite her belief that a biscuit should only be served warm, dripping with butter and honey, she took one.

At the first bite, her mouth watered painfully. The Empires were crisp and sweet—was that jelly in the middle?—and she couldn't remember eating anything so fabulous in a very long time.

"It's a cookie," she managed after she swallowed the first and reached for a second.

The woman smiled, the expression causing her cheeks to round like apples beneath her sparkling eyes. "Call it whatever ye like, dearie." She lifted the platter. "Then take another."

Kris had to listen very hard to distinguish the English beneath the heavy brogue. She felt as if she were hearing everything through a time warp, one that allowed the meaning of the words to penetrate several seconds after they were said. She hoped that the longer she stayed, the easier it would get.

"Thanks." Kris took two cookies in each hand. "I'm Kris Daniels."

"Well, and don't I know that." The plump, cheery woman giggled. The sound resembled the Munchkin titters that had welcomed Dorothy to Oz. Kris glanced uneasily at the nearby shrubbery, expecting it to shake and burp out several more little people.

Then she heard what the woman had said and caught her breath. If they already knew her here, knew what she did, who she was, her cover was blown and her story was crap before it had even begun. Why hadn't she used a false name?

Because she hadn't thought anyone in the Scottish Highlands would have seen a cable TV show filmed in Chicago. And how, exactly, would she present herself as Susie Smith when her credit cards and passport read "Kristin Daniels"?

"You know me?" Kris repeated faintly.

"I spoke with ye on the phone. Rented ye the cottage. Who else would be arriving today bag and baggage?"

Kris let out the breath she'd taken. She was no good at

cloak-and-dagger. She liked lying about as much as she liked liars and was therefore pretty bad at it. She needed to get better and quick.

"You're Ms. Cameron," Kris said.

"Euphemia," the woman agreed. "Everyone calls me Effy."

Effy's brilliant eyes cut to the driver, who was as thin and tall as she was short and round. "Ye'll be bringing that suitcase inside now, Rob, and be quicker about it than a slow-witted tortoise."

Kris glanced at the old man to see if he was offended, but he merely nodded and did as he'd been told.

Very slowly.

Kris's lips twitched. She'd have been tempted to do the same if Effy had ordered her around.

Rob came out of the cottage, and Effy shoved the plate in front of him. "Better eat a few, ye great lummox, or ye'll be starvin' long before supper."

He took several. "If ye didnae cook like me sainted mother, woman, I'd have drowned ye and yer devil's tongue in the loch years ago."

Looming over the diminutive Effy, deep voice rumbling like the growl of a vicious bear, Rob should have been intimidating. But there was no heat to his words, no anger on his face. He just stated his opinion as if he'd stated the same a hundred and one times before. Perhaps he had. The two did seem well acquainted.

Effy snorted and shoved the entire plate of biscuits into his huge, worn hands with a sharp, "Dinnae drop that, ye old fool"; then she reached into the pocket of her voluminous gray skirt and pulled out a key, which she presented to Kris. "Here ye are, dearie. And what is it ye'll be doing in Drumnadrochit?"

"I'm . . . uh . . ." Kris glanced away from Effy's curious gaze, past Rob, whose cheeks had gone chipmunk with cookies, toward the rolling, gray expanse of the loch. "Writing."

"Letters?" Rob mumbled.

"Why would she need to travel all this way to write a letter?" Effy scoffed.

"Some do."

"I'm writing a book," Kris blurted.

There. That had even sounded like the truth. Maybe the key to lying was thinking less and talking fast. No wonder men were so good at it.

"A children's book?" Effy asked.

Kris said the first thing that popped into her head: "Sure."

Silence greeted the word. *That* hadn't sounded very truthful.

"Mmm." Rob gave a throaty Scottish murmur, drawing Kris's attention away from the loch and back to him. Luckily for her, it also caught Effy's attention.

"Ye ate them all?" She snatched the empty plate from his hands.

"Ye said not to drop them. Ye didnae say not to eat them."

"And if I didnae tell ye *not* to drive into the water would I find ye swimming with Nessie of an afternoon?"

Rob didn't answer. Really, what could he say?

"Nessie," Kris repeated, anxious to keep their attention off her inability to lie. "Have you seen her?"

"Mmm," Rob murmured again, this time the sound not one of skepticism but assent.

"If ye live in Drumnadrochit," Effy said, "ye've seen her."

Kris laughed. She couldn't help it. "*Everyone's* seen her?"

Effy lifted her chin to indicate the loch. "Ye have but to look."

Kris spun about. All she saw was waves and shadows and rocks.

Not long afterward, Effy climbed into Rob's car, admonishing him all the while: "I need to get home, but dinnae drive too fast. Ye give me a headache. And—"

Rob shut the door on the rest of her comment. "Ye give *me* a headache," he muttered, moving around the rear bumper toward the driver's side.

"Effy lives close to you?" Kris asked.

Rob lifted sad eyes. "The woman lives *with* me."

Kris's eyes widened. "You're—"

"Cursed," he muttered, and opened the driver's side door.

Effy's voice came tumbling out: "Ye can walk anywhere ye like, dearie, but stay away from the castle."

"There's a castle?" Kris forgot all about Rob and Effy's living arrangements—were they were married or living in sin? What did it matter? There was a *castle*.

"Urquhart Castle. Ye must have heard of it."

Kris had read about it. The structure overlooked Urquhart Bay, where many Nessie sightings occurred, and had figured prominently in the history of the Highlands, with many famous names like Robert the Bruce, Andrew Moray, and Bonnie Prince Charlie sprinkled through the tales.

"Is it dangerous?" Kris asked.

Effy's Munchkins-in-the-shrubbery laugh flowed free. "Ach no. But they charge a fee, and the place is naught but a ruin. If ye want to know about Urquhart or the loch or even Nessie come to me."

"Why not me?" Rob climbed into the car. "I've seen her more than you have. I drive this road every day."

"I've seen her twice as many times as you, ye old goat."

Thankfully Rob shut the door on the rest of the argument, then drove away.

The sun was setting, though it was hard to tell considering the gray, gloomy sky and incipient threat of rain. Still, by her calculations, Kris had an hour of daylight left. She didn't want to waste it.

She hurried inside, casting a quick glance around the cottage as she moved to the bathroom to throw cold water on her face and smooth back her wildly curling hair. The damp air in Scotland was going to ruin any prayer she had of keeping it smooth.

The house possessed a living area that shared space with a small kitchen, a bedroom complete with a decent-sized bed, a chest of drawers, a night table, and a teeny-tiny closet. Luckily she didn't need, and she hadn't brought, very many clothes.

The place was warm—Effy must have turned on the heat—and it smelled of cookies.

"Biscuits," Kris murmured, and her stomach growled. Thankfully Effy had also been kind enough to stock the small refrigerator with a few staples to tide Kris over until she could get to the market.

Kris made a quick jam sandwich, slugged a glass of milk, then, armed with her video camera, a *Loyola University* sweatshirt, and her best pair of walking shoes, set out.

The western horizon glowed a muted pink and orange, the tourist boats that had bobbed in the distance now disappeared. Nevertheless, Kris filmed a bit of the loch. She had to start somewhere.

The water slid past, dingy in the fading light and pock-marked by several bits of wood. Kris could see how someone with an active imagination might invent a lake monster, especially when everyone else was doing so.

Just as Kris lowered her camera, something splashed. She froze, squinting into the gloom, but she could see nothing beyond the first several feet of flowing, murky water.

"They grow the fish big here," she muttered.

From the sound of the splash and the suddenly larger swell of the waves, they grew them as big as a tank.

Kris was tempted to return to the cottage. Not because she was afraid, but because she hadn't brought the proper equipment needed to film in the fast-approaching night.

Kris cursed her lack of foresight. She wasn't used to being her own cameraman, and she hadn't thought she'd find anything so soon. But if she wanted to have clear, perfect footage of whatever—make that *who*ever—had made that noise, she'd need the light she'd left in her backpack.

Then she heard another splash, nearer the shore, just past that next grove of trees, and before she could think any more about it Kris plunged into the gloom.

The ground was slick beneath the cover of the branches, and she slid a bit, had to slow down. But it wasn't even a minute before she popped out on the shore of Loch Ness.

She looked left, right, across. The far side was hazy—too far away to really see, and she'd forgotten her binoculars along with the light. But still she was pretty certain she saw—

"Nada." Either the culprit was track-star fast or there really was a fish the size of Cleveland in the loch.

Which would explain a few things.

Kris frowned. One of the theories about Nessie was that an unknown creature lived in the depths. Current cryptozoological speculation set the amount of undiscovered species between half a million and ten million—no one really knew. Which meant—

"There could be damn near anything out there."

And that was fine. That was good. Proving that Nessie was a big, toothy, prehistoric fish would debunk the lake monster theory, too.

Kris emerged from the trees, intent on returning to the cottage, then unpacking and taking a shower until the hot water gave out, before jumping into bed and sleeping until the jet lag went away. She even made her way up to the road and turned in that direction.

Then she noticed the castle below.

Despite the fading sun, Kris lifted her camera. The ruins were too spooky to resist—all Gothic and Jane Eyre–ish—perched on a precipice. She could well imagine locking a mad wife in that tower. Back when it still had enough walls to keep someone in rather than allowing her to tumble right out.

A shadow shimmied at the edge of Kris's screen, and without thought she zoomed in—

On a man slipping through the ruins of Urquhart Castle, the last of the light sparkling in his glistening wet hair.

CHAPTER 2

Someone was following him, and they weren't very good at it.

Liam Grant quickly made his way to the tower house, the highest point of Urquhart Castle. From there he could see all of the ruins, as well as some of the road and a good portion of the water. Since he spent a lot of his free time staring into Loch Ness, Liam was very familiar with the area.

Because of that, he was in good position to observe the curvy blonde as she crept along in what had recently been his wake.

She carried a video camera—didn't everyone nowadays?—so she was probably a tourist. Though why she still hung about long after the last visitor had left Liam had no idea.

He continued to watch as she stepped on every stone in her path and even tripped over a piece of the castle that had cracked off in the last high wind. This time of year, they had a lot of wind. As she tried to right herself, she made more noise than a busload of schoolchildren trundling across gravel.

Liam expected her to blunder around the ruins a bit, then scuttle off when full darkness descended. Except she glanced up and she saw him.

Her face was a pale oval surrounded by glorious shoulder-length curls. He'd hadn't seen golden curls since—

Liam jerked away from the edge. He hadn't thought of *her* in ages.

"You stay right there!"

The woman's order was soon followed by the sound of her scrambling up the steps.

"As if I've got a choice in the matter," he muttered, disgusted with himself. "Unless I fly away on gossamer wings or disappear into the mist like one of the wee folk."

And how often had he wished that he could?

Liam turned as she burst into the tower area. Then he leaned against the cool stone and watched her.

'Twas the gloaming time, his favorite, when the night had just begun and the dawn was still so far away. Difficult to see in the gloaming. At least for her.

The woman's gaze darted around the small space, skipping over Liam without pause. It appeared he hadn't lost his talent for blending into the shadows.

From the way she scanned back and forth, back and forth, a bit frantically he figured she thought him a ghost. It wouldn't be the first time.

But she didn't run; she didn't even call out. Instead her eyes narrowed on the place she'd seen him watching her, the place he yet remained.

Liam kept still and quiet, wondering what she would do if she saw him, or what she would do if she did not.

So he wasn't prepared when she suddenly set down her camera and strode forward—full speed ahead! Damn the torpedoes! Typical American—and nearly slammed into him as he straightened away from the wall.

"You're . . ." She lifted her chin, and the warmth of her breath in the chill of the night sent a puff of mist across his face. She smelled like spun sugar and cherries. He wanted to dip his head and steal a taste.

Frowning, she reached out and placed a palm against his chest. His body reacted with embarrassing swiftness. The last time a woman's hand had touched him he'd—

Liam snatched her wrist and jerked her fingers away. Those large brown eyes widened.

"Ye should not touch a strange man in the dark of the night, lass. Ye may get what ye are not askin' for. Unless, of course . . ." He tightened his grip, drawing her closer. "Ye were askin'."

"You're . . . real?" she murmured.

He couldn't help it. The coming moon, the promise of stars, the scent of the loch in her hair, and that husky, *take me* voice . . . He kissed her. What better way to prove—to her and to himself—that he did yet exist?

She tasted as she smelled—sugar, cherries, and the freshness of the water on the wind. Her lips parted as she gasped, and he would have let her go, except her hand flexed, nails scraping his shirt as she gathered it into her fist and held on.

When her tongue darted out, just a flick along his lower lip, he was lost. He kissed her as he hadn't kissed a woman in aeons, and she kissed him right back.

She was nearly his height; he didn't have to bend even his neck to delve. She continued to cling to his shirt as if he would run away. As if he could.

She should have slapped him. That she didn't only made him crave more.

He tasted her, and she was sweet, warm, and willing. Everything he'd missed in a woman.

He continued to kiss but nothing else, afraid if he let

himself touch, he'd do so much more than that. As he'd been told, as he'd been shown, men were beasts, and right now Liam Grant was all man.

So he let his mouth do the ravaging; she didn't seem to mind. However, he didn't sink his fingers into her glorious hair. Didn't fill his palms with her firm, soft breasts. Didn't open his trousers, pull down hers, and—

Dìteadh. He *was* a beast.

On the loch, something splashed, and she pulled her mouth from his, releasing his shirt at the same time. However, she remained close enough that he was drawn to the heat of her body amid the ever-increasing chill.

She stared at him, brow furrowed. "Why did you kiss me?"

Was she really that naïve? If so, she shouldn't be out here alone. Hell, she shouldn't be anywhere without her keeper.

She continued to stare at him, waiting for an answer. Why had he kissed her?

"Ye asked if I was real."

She shook her head, laughed a little, stepped back. He had to clench his hands to keep from reaching out. "Of course you're real. What else could you be?"

"The ghost of Urquhart Castle?"

She tilted her head. "*Is* there a ghost of Urquhart Castle?"

"In Scotland, lass, there's a ghost of *every* castle."

"Except there's no such thing as ghosts."

Liam lifted a brow. "I ken you're not from around here."

"And you are."

"Always have been," Liam agreed, then sighed. "Always will be."

A sharp scritch from below—shoes on stone—made

her tense and frown. The call, "Hullo!" made her step around Liam and glance over the edge. "What are ye doing up there?"

"I, uh, well, you see, we—"

"We?" The man repeated. "How many of ye are there?"

Liam slipped across the short space and started down the stairs.

"Just me and—" The woman cursed. He heard her hurry after him, but by then Liam had reached the ground and disappeared.

Footsteps pounded up the steps, and a second man burst in. It wasn't until disappointment flared that Kris realized she'd been hoping it was *him*.

However, where the first man had been close to her own height and wiry with muscle, this one, whom she figured to be the night watchman of the castle considering the uniform, was huge—at least six-three and over two hundred pounds, his muscles reminiscent of those she'd glimpsed in the high school weight room during those hours the football team spent grunting and posturing.

Kris had always been too focused on schoolwork to date a football player—hell, be honest she'd been too much of a geek for any of them to notice. But she hadn't been blind or stupid or gay, and she'd looked in whenever she passed the window of that weight room. She'd looked in, and she'd remembered.

Right now, she couldn't think why. When she compared the bulky, overpumped pecs revealed by the guard's uniform with the hard, sinewy ripples beneath the worn T-shirt of the disappearing man, the latter won without question.

The newcomer flicked her a glance. He had blue eyes,

too, but they seemed washed out when set in that pale face beneath hair an unfortunate shade of orangutan.

He trained his flashlight into every shady corner. Kris followed the beam eagerly. But no one was there.

The man turned to her with a frown. "Ye said 'we.'"

"There was a guy here, but now he's . . ." Kris spread her hands. "Not."

The frown deepened. "Where did he go?"

Kris pointed at the stairs, then shrugged.

"I came up directly," the guard said. "I didnae see anyone coming down."

A trickle of unease rolled across Kris's spine, but she quashed it. There *had* been a man. He'd kissed her, for crying out loud! Ghosts couldn't kiss.

Because ghosts did *not* exist.

"Well, he isn't here," she said a bit too sharply, "so he had to have gone down there. Unless you know of another way out."

"Just . . ." The guard made a motion of diving off the edge.

Kris resisted the urge to scurry over and check. She'd have heard him if he'd jumped. There would have been an unpleasant splat. Kris shuddered.

"Getting cool out here now, miss. Best ye go back—" He paused. "Where are ye stayin'? I didnae see a car."

"Loch Side Cottage."

"Ah, the Cameron place. Then ye havenae far to go. I'll walk ye."

"No need." She picked up her video camera, thrilled it hadn't gotten trampled in the commotion.

Or stolen by the ghost.

Kris coughed to stifle the inappropriate laughter that threatened to burst free.

"What kind of man would I be if I let a woman walk about in the night all alone?"

"Don't you have to . . ." Kris waved vaguely at the castle. "Watch things?"

In the glare of the flashlight, his lips curved. "Urquhart has stood since the sixth century. I doubt it'll disappear if I glance away."

Unlike the man who'd kissed her.

"You're sure you didn't see anyone?" she asked.

"You're sure ye did?" He stared at the deep, dark sky. "The night plays tricks."

If all that had happened was that she'd seen a shadow, Kris would agree. But the night wasn't such a trickster that it conjured solid, handsome men, who spoke with a brogue and kissed with their tongues.

"I'm Alan Mac," he continued. "Chief constable of Drumnadrochit."

Kris blinked. "Not the watchman?"

"There is a watchman." Alan Mac looked away. "But it's not me."

Kris followed his gaze, but she didn't see a watchman anywhere. She supposed there were a lot of nooks and crannies. He could be anywhere.

"What's the head cop doing here if there's a guard on duty?"

"Taking a stroll."

Kris found that hard to believe. Then again, did she want to accuse the "head cop" of lying? And really, why would he?

"I didnae catch your name."

"Kris." She held out her hand. "Kris Daniels."

His fingers were as cold as the breeze, and she started. "Sorry." He rubbed his palm on his pants. "Me blood's always been a wee bit thin. It's pleased I am to meet ye."

He indicated the stairway. "And now, if ye'd be so kind as to get off the tower."

"Sure." Kris went down the stairs, grateful for the constable's flashlight, which showed her the way.

Once on solid ground, he insisted on seeing her to the cottage. Nothing she said would dissuade him.

As they walked along, Kris searched for a question, any question, to break the eerie stillness. "Does the watchman run across a lot of trespassers at night?"

"Ach, no. No reason to come way out here in the dark."

"But . . ." Kris glanced at the water. "The loch. The . . ." She had a hard time getting the foolish word out, but she managed. "Monster."

"Nessie?" He shook his head. "No one ever sees her at night."

Kris thought back on what she'd read. Certainly the majority of the sightings occurred in the middle of the day, but that only made sense. Midday meant the light was at its brightest, reflecting off the murky loch and creating mirages. It was also the time when the most people were out and about. The more humans in the area, the more tall tales would be told. Still—

"I know there've been sightings at night," she insisted.

"Sure there are. Just look at the place." Alan Mac waved a huge hand at the lapping waves. "Wouldn't ye be seein' things if ye were out there in the dark?"

Kris narrowed her eyes. "I *did* see a man."

"I didnae say you didn't," he said calmly.

Kris decided to let the whole question of the man she'd kissed in Urquhart Castle fade away. She'd seen him. Alan Mac hadn't. End of story.

For now.

"Wait." Kris stopped, and the constable did, too. "In 1999, Nessie was spotted on land for the first time since

1963. And it was at night!" she finished with a triumphant poke in the direction of his broad chest.

He lifted his flashlight from the road ahead to a spot just above her belly button, then contemplated her in the upward spray of yellow light. "Ye seem to know a lot about the monster."

Whoops.

For an instant her mind blanked. She had a lie in place for situations like this, but for the life of her she couldn't remember what it was. Such was the trouble with lies.

"I . . . uh . . ."

She needed practice. Lying had to get easier the more you did it. Which was probably why the best liars were always the biggest liars.

Maybe by the time Kris came home from Scotland she, too, could stare a child in the face and say, *I'll never leave you, sweetheart. I promise.*

Kris winced as the last words her mother had ever said to her whispered through her mind.

"Yer a Nessie hunter?"

"No!" she said, much too loud. "I mean I don't want to hunt. How could I hunt something that . . ." She paused before she blurted the truth.

You can't hunt what isn't there.

"I'm here to . . ." Why in God's name *was* she here?

"Oh, wait." His confused—or had that been suspicious?—frown smoothed. "Yer the writer woman. I remember Effy talkin' about ye now. Ye'll be writing about Nessie?"

Kris hadn't said what she was going to write about, but that seemed as good a topic as any and would explain why she knew so damned much.

"Sure."

"A children's book?"

Why did everyone think she was writing a children's book?

"Okay."

He nodded sagely. "I've heard how ye writer types don't like to talk about yer work. Curses it, so to speak."

"Right." Kris grasped at the excuse, even though she believed in curses as much as she believed in the fairy tales where they were found. "Wouldn't want to do that."

They began to walk again. The lamp she'd left on inside the cottage seemed to flare like lightning against the night. Behind the house, hills that she knew to be sapphire in the sunlight loomed like the great black humps of a mythical beast.

Kris sighed. One day in Drumnadrochit and she was being drawn into the group delusion.

"Your last name's Mac?" she asked, desperate for a normal conversation.

"Mackenzie," he said. "They call me Alan Mac because my father is Mac, ye see."

She didn't but nodded anyway.

"There are a lot of Mackenzies. 'Tis a Highland name."

"All the Mackenzies are related?"

"Not by blood necessarily. Back in the auld days everyone had a leader. A clan chieftain. And all in that clan would take the chieftain's name as a matter of loyalty. Started back in the eleventh century."

"Eleventh century," Kris repeated. She couldn't imagine. She had no idea when her ancestors had come to America or where they'd even come from. "You've always lived here?"

"I have." He lifted his big shoulders, then lowered them. "Where else would I go? Why would I want to?"

The mind-set was so foreign to Kris, she wasn't sure what to say. He could go anywhere. Do anything. The idea of staying in the same place as her parents and her parents' parents and their parents for all of her days made her twitchy. Sure, she'd been in Chicago since she was twelve, but if she couldn't travel, she'd go mad.

"If you've always lived here, then you must know everyone."

"Everyone who lives in the area. But we get so many tourists or folks who stay awhile, then go." He glanced at her. "Like you."

"What about a guy who's my height, maybe one seventy-five? Long, black hair." Kris indicated a length near shoulder level, then frowned.

She couldn't say if it had been curly or straight since it had been wet and slicked back from his stunning face. And why was that?

She'd never asked. Her tongue had been occupied with better things.

"Blue eyes," she blurted. "Brogue. About twenty-five."

"That describes a good portion of the village." Alan Mac laughed. "Ye'd best give up that ghost."

But Kris never gave up on anything once she set her mind to it. If she had, she wouldn't be here.

A heavy splash sounded from the loch.

"What was that?" she asked.

"Nessie."

"You said she was only seen in the daytime."

Alan Mac returned his gaze to the loch. "Just because ye cannae see her doesna mean she isnae there."

CHAPTER 3

Liam watched from the trees, moving along slowly, silently, nearly parallel to their path.

Though the moon was rising, it was still very dark. But the flare of Alan Mac's trusty flashlight surrounded the two figures in an eerie yellow glow.

Their voices carried in the still, chill night; Liam heard everything. Her name was Kris, and she was here to write about Nessie.

He didn't believe her.

However, he didn't think she was here to hunt the thing. He'd met hunters, and she wasn't the type. For one thing, she was a terrible liar.

She asked about the man in the ruins again. What did Liam expect when he'd kissed her like that? He knew better. His talent at kissing was second only to his talent for everything that came afterward.

Liam had been born for seduction. Seduction was what had gotten him into trouble in the first place.

Kris disappeared inside the cottage. Alan Mac turned and headed right for Liam, pausing a few yards away.

"I didnae think she believed me when I said you were a ghost."

Liam didn't think so, either.

"You should stay away from her."

Liam should, but he wasn't sure that he could.

The constable walked on, leaving Liam to stand in the trees and watch the full moon rise over the loch.

God, how he hated them. People behaved foolishly beneath the bright round moon.

He certainly had.

Kris awoke to sunlight spilling in through her bedroom window. She'd been so tired the night before she hadn't thought to draw the drapes.

After a quick shower, Kris checked her e-mail. She'd promised to meet Lola for Skype sessions while she was here, but the way the Internet behaved—switching off and on at will, as well as crashing completely when she tried to access a large Web site—Kris doubted that would happen.

Instead, she sent her friend a quick note telling her not to worry. She'd be in touch. Since the same thing had happened on other trips, in other places, Lola would deal. She didn't have much choice.

Effy had left tea in the cabinet, but in Kris's opinion tea was for the sick. Coffee was for her right now. Or as soon as she could walk into Drumnadrochit and buy some.

Once outside, Kris glanced in the direction of Urquhart Castle, but she couldn't see the ruins from here due to a bend in the road. She could, however, see the loch. Beneath the brilliant sun it should have been blue and clear. But this was Loch Ness. Due to the high peat content in the surrounding soil, the water was often the shade of wet sand.

Therefore, while the area around the loch was a post-card of beauty—cobalt-tinged mountains, rolling emerald hills, and pine forests—the loch itself . . . eh. Nevertheless, several boats chugged along, most sporting signs that identified them as offering various Nessie tours.

Kris turned in the opposite direction from the one she'd taken the night before and, after crossing a few fields, strolled into Drumnadrochit.

Considering that the area's main business was tourism, she found a coffee shop without any trouble. Americans needed their fix—witness the Starbucks on every other street corner—and the French and Italians were no doubt the same, though never suggest Starbucks to a Frenchman. Kris had learned that the hard way while filming *Hoax Hunters* in New Orleans. Of course when you had Cafe du Monde, what possible reason could there be for Starbucks?

It appeared they had no need of one in Drumnadrochit, either, since the sign with the steaming cup of dark liquid was perched in the window of a place called Jamaica Blue.

The woman behind the counter wore a purple tie-dyed T-shirt and ancient, ratty jeans. She sported sun-streaked light brown dreads, hazel eyes, skin the shade of the loch beneath the sun, and an accent that made Kris long for sand, coconut oil, and a Beach Boys sound track.

"What can I get you?"

"Do you have Blue Mountain?"

"Have you looked outside?"

"I meant in a cup."

"We have dat, too."

In seconds Kris did, along with a bag of ground beans to take back to the cottage.

"You must be de writer woman stayin' at Effy's place."

"Word travels fast."

"Word is all we have here of a misty eve. I'm Jamaica." She offered her hand. "Jamaica Blue."

"That's really your name?"

The woman just smiled.

Over the intoxicating aroma wafting from her cup, Kris smelled a story. "Care to join me?" she asked.

Jamaica's exotic eyes flicked around the currently empty shop. "Don't mind if I do."

She grabbed a bottle of water from the cooler. "I drink my share of coffee before seven A.M.," she explained.

They took a table by the window and watched the crowds stream by.

"Is it always like this?" Kris asked.

"Some days are busier dan others, but . . ." Jamaica took a large swig from the bottle. "Yes."

"Nessie's good for business."

"Nessie *is* our bizness."

Kris took a sip of coffee. "Mmm," she said, the sound a commentary on both the taste and Jamaica's remark. "How long have you lived here?"

"Ye dinnae think I'm a local?" Jamaica replied with a perfect Scottish brogue.

Kris lifted a brow, and Jamaica laughed.

"I opened dis place . . . oh, 'bout five years back."

"Have you seen Nessie?"

"Of course."

"Really?"

"You t'ink I'm lying?"

Kris thought everyone was lying, but that was just Kris. "You said yourself, Nessie is your business."

"Mmm," Jamaica murmured, the sound very Scottish.

How long had Jamaica had to live here to acquire the talent for a murmur that said both everything and nothing? Perhaps it came with the ability to speak in a brogue.

"You are right. Nessie is good bizness." Jamaica gazed out the window in the direction of the loch. "But I *have* seen her."

"When? Where?"

"De day I arrived I drove along A Eighty-two. Sun was shinin' like today. Saw something move on de loch, and when I turned my head, dere she was. Plain as dat sun, swimming along right next to de road."

Kris opened her mouth, but nothing came out. What could she say? The word in her head—*bullshit*—just didn't seem appropriate.

"She welcomed me to my new life. Led me right into Drumnadrochit."

"Have you—uh—seen her since?"

Jamaica shook her head, and her dreads flew. "I don't need to. I know she's dere."

"Mmm," Kris said, the comment not Scottish at all.

"You don't believe?" Jamaica drank some water, but she kept a measuring gaze on Kris.

"I didn't say that."

"You didn't have to."

"I met a man last night," Kris blurted.

Jamaica's perfectly arched brows arched further. "Already? Good for you. What's his name?"

"I'm hoping you might know. He disappeared before I could ask."

"Disappeared? You sure he was dere?"

Kris sighed. Questions like that always gave her a headache.

"I'm sure." Quickly she described her mystery man, ending with, "His hair was wet. Anyone like to swim in the loch?"

Jamaica snorted. "De *experts* say de loch too cold to support a monster. Which makes it too damn cold for swimming."

"*Monster,* by definition, means something beyond anything we know. So how can the experts say the water's too cold for a monster?"

"Experts say a lot of t'ings," Jamaica observed. "Most of it's crap."

Kris laughed. She liked Jamaica more with each passing minute.

"I t'ink in dis case dey talkin' 'bout de plesiosaur principle. You know it?"

"Sir Somebody theorized that the Loch Ness Monster was a plesiosaur, a long-necked reptile that swam through warm inland seas in the days of the dinosaurs."

"But Nessie would have to be a herd of plesiosaurs. Just because dey might not be extinct don't mean dey be immortal."

"Right," Kris agreed. "The shape and size of what people have seen is about right for a plesiosaur, or so this guy said."

"Sir Peter Scott," Jamaica said. "British naturalist. Plenty famous. But a plesiosaur was a reptile and so cold-blooded. Which means it wouldn't survive in de freezing cold of de loch."

"There goes that theory," Kris muttered. "So how cold *is* the water?"

"Average temperature around six degrees Celsius."

"English, please."

"Dat *is* English." Jamaica shook her head. "Six Celsius is . . . oh," she pursed her lips, "about forty-two degrees American. You know, besides de cold, you can only see five feet down, which means you're swimming above a great black maw of nothing."

"Not only cold then, but creepy."

Jamaica lifted her nearly empty water bottle in a toast. "No one swims in de loch unless dey had ten too many local lagers. Maybe dat was de case with your mystery friend?"

Kris shook her head. "He didn't taste like Guinness."

The sudden silence made Kris glance up, then curse. She'd actually said that out loud.

"You kissed him?" Jamaica asked.

"He kissed me. It was—"

Fabulous, she thought.

"Weird," she said.

Jamaica remained silent, in her eyes an expression Kris couldn't read. She seemed both concerned and annoyed, with a bit of afraid thrown in. But none of that made any sense. Unless—

"You know who he is now?" Kris asked.

"Why would now be any different dan before?" Jamaica returned.

Two customers burst in the door, and Jamaica hurried off with a "Nice talking to you" that held the distinct undertone of *Get lost.*

Since Kris had just met the woman, she couldn't say for sure what she'd seen in Jamaica's eyes or heard in her voice. But Kris had done enough interviews to realize that answering a question with a question was almost always an attempt to hide a lie. Although why Jamaica would lie about something so minor as knowing the identity of the man who'd kissed Kris in Urquhart Castle was anyone's guess.

Sufficiently caffeinated, Kris went in search of lunch. Along the way, she became enchanted by the wonder of Drumnadrochit.

Lola owned a large collection of old Hollywood musicals, and *Brigadoon* was one of her favorites. Kris had probably watched the movie a dozen times, and parts of Drumnadrochit had her humming "Almost like Being in Love." She half-expected to turn a corner and find Cyd Charisse twirling and jumping along the sidewalk.

Other parts resembled every small tourist town in America—shops, museums, tours, hotels with catchy names like The Highlander, and restaurants that advertised a "Nessie-sized breakfast." One place in particular caught her eye.

"The Myth Motel," Kris read. "Museum, gift shop, rooms, and eatery. Specialty—Nessie Nuggets." How could she pass that up? Especially since she was by now hungry enough to eat Nessie.

Kris paused with her hand on the door, wondering if Nessie Nuggets were shaped like Nessie, something to feed *to* Nessie, or made *of* Nessie.

She snorted. There *was* no Nessie. Sheesh. If she wasn't careful she'd be sharing the delusion of everyone in Drumnadrochit. Where would *Hoax Hunters* be then? Where would *she* be?

"Out on my ass with no place to go," Kris muttered, and yanked open the door.

A tall, slim man in a kilt stood just inside. His close-cropped dark hair and goatee proved a stunning contrast to his light gray eyes. "Welcome to The Myth Motel."

"You're American?" Kris blurted, both startled by the lack of an accent and thrilled by it. She hadn't heard English without an accent since she got off the plane. Sure, it had only been a day, but she missed it.

"Technically, no."

Kris tilted her head and waited.

"Raised there, born here," he explained. "I'm Dougal Scott."

Kris offered her hand. "Kris Daniels."

They shook. He had nice hands, a good handshake. Not too soft, not too hard, and he looked directly into her face with a smile. "The writer woman?"

Kris rolled her eyes, and he laughed, the sound deeper than she would have expected and very engaging.

"You'll soon learn that everyone knows everything in Drumnadrochit."

Kris certainly hoped not. She might find herself tossed into the loch if they did. She was, after all, planning to expose their livelihood as one of the biggest tourist traps of all time.

"I've never met anyone named Dougal," she said, eager to change the subject before he started posing more questions that would require more lies.

"I went by 'Doug' in the states, but I'm back to 'Dougal' now." He indicated the kilt. "Anything to appease the tourists."

"Yet you don't add a brogue?"

His lips curved. "I come off sounding more like Foghorn Leghorn than William Wallace."

"How long were you in the states?"

"Most of my life. I inherited the motel from my *granaidh*. My grandfather. I added both the restaurant and museum. If I do say so myself, my museum's the best in the area. A combination of scientific facts, cryptozoological theory, and the most comprehensive list of sightings available in this country or any other."

Kris felt a prickle of excitement. She'd never been able to find information on all of the sightings compiled in one place, so it was impossible to compare and discover if some were repeats of others.

Meeting this guy was a golden opportunity. And she'd walked in for the Nessie Nuggets.

"You sound like a true believer." Though Kris wanted

the information, she was kind of disappointed to encounter yet another sheep in the "I love Nessie" flock. Was no one in Scotland a skeptic, like her?

"Don't tell, but . . ." Dougal made a show of looking around, then stepped closer and lowered his voice: "I'm here to cash in. People want Nessie . . ." He swept a showman's hand toward the museum's entrance. "I'll give them Nessie."

Kris smiled. At last. Someone with a clue.

"I'd love to hear more," she began, and the door opened, spilling tourists into the foyer.

Dougal appeared torn. He obviously sensed in her a kindred spirit and he wanted to talk longer, but he needed to deal with all those wonderful customers.

"Are you busy tonight?" he asked.

Kris blinked. Was he asking her out?

Kris hadn't had a date in six months, with good reason. The last had been of the blind variety. Lola had set it up with a friend of a friend of a ticket taker at the ballet.

"He's a nice guy," Lola had insisted.

Apparently his wife thought so, too.

Lying creep.

Such was the way with dates. They looked good on paper. Even seemed to go all right on the phone. But by the third meeting, if not before, the lies started to tumble out.

Dougal patted Kris on the shoulder, already moving toward his unexpected mother lode. "Don't look so deer-in-the-headlights. I was just going to suggest you walk through the museum and if you're still interested in talking, there's a pub where the locals go. MacLeod's. The oldest of its kind in the village."

"How old?"

"Maybe eight hundred years," Dougal answered. "They say Andrew Moray's troops drank there. And there are the usual tales of the Bonnie Prince, Robert the Bruce, and William Wallace all lifting a tankard on their way to the next kill fest. But I think, sometimes, those tales are very much like the American claims that 'George Washington slept here.' If the man slept everywhere they say he did, he wouldn't have had any time left to win the war."

"Where is it?"

"Next street over." Dougal jerked a thumb past his right ear. "I usually get there around sunset." He turned and greeted his guests.

Kris ducked into the eatery ahead of the crowd. Nessie Nuggets turned out to be deep-fried chicken strips shaped like a herd of bumpy-backed dinosaurs.

"Chicken McNessies," Kris commented when they were placed before her.

From the waitress's expression, she'd heard that one before and hadn't found it funny then, either. Kris had done her share of waiting tables in college and understood the sentiment. Everyone was a comedian. Or at least thought they were.

The Nessies came with chips and veggies, she assumed the latter to help clean out the arteries being clogged by the deep-fried former.

She ate everything, washing it down with what had been billed on the menu as "Scotland's other national drink" or Irn-Bru—which tasted like a combination of orange pop and 7UP.

Kris exited the restaurant ahead of a large group of Belgian tourists, then paid the nominal fee for the museum to a young, dimple-cheeked woman who *did* have a brogue and slipped inside.

If the museum were comprised of a few out-of-focus photos of fish fins and some inflatable purple plesiosaurs, Kris wouldn't feel bad about skipping the rendezvous at MacLeod's, although from the description of the place she would need to stop there at some point. An ancient, authentic Scottish pub should not be missed.

However, Kris was impressed by Dougal's museum. He'd done a fantastic job with the displays. He obviously had artistic training or perhaps had hired someone who did. Everything was well lit, colorful, easy to read, and there was a lot here Kris hadn't seen before. She wished she'd brought her notebook so she could write down the questions she wanted to pursue later.

Dougal Scott just might be her new best friend.

CHAPTER 4

After an afternoon wrestling with the Internet, followed by a nice, long nap, Kris retraced her steps to The Myth Motel. As the sun fell toward the horizon, she took the next street to the north, walked a block, and bingo.

Tucked into a stream of newer buildings, MacLeod's stood out like a great-grandfather at a four-year-old's birthday party.

The gray-stone exterior appeared to be original. The structure listed slightly to the right. However, the roof was no longer thatch and the windows, which had no doubt begun as mere holes in the walls, now sported sparkling glass and red shutters.

Inside the floor was polished wood, as was the bar. The ceilings were lower than Kris was used to—a testament to how much shorter men were back when the pub had been built. Through timbered archways several smaller rooms were visible, which made her think that once upon a time MacLeod's had hosted both a public drinking area for the unwashed masses and private areas for the privileged few.

The place was three-quarters full—both men and women of all ages sat in booths, at tables and the bar.

Their attire was testament to their occupations—cook, waitress, parking valet, farmer—very few had bothered to change clothes after work. In the corner sat Rob and Effy Cameron, a pint in front of them both.

They were arguing, or at least Effy was. Her mouth moved; her hands waved; she slopped ale over the edge of her glass and onto the table in an effort to make her point. Rob just sat there and drank.

The conversation dimmed when Kris walked in. She almost walked back out. MacLeod's was for the locals, and she wasn't.

Dougal stood, waving her to the bar. As she crossed the room, whispers followed. It wasn't until she took one of the several empty stools surrounding him that the voices started up again.

"I wasn't sure you'd come."

She hadn't been, either, but even after the whispers and the strange looks she was glad that she had. She was in Scotland. She should see Scottish stuff as much as she could before she ran out of money and had to go home.

"You look like you could use a drink." Dougal's concerned expression made Kris realize she'd been frowning at the thought of her rapidly dwindling bank account.

She made herself smile. "Yes. Thanks."

Dougal lifted his hand and the bartender, an extremely large man in every way—height, breadth, belly, chin; make that chins—grimaced. Strange behavior for a business owner, but it was quite busy. Eventually, after waiting on every customer down the line first, he made his way to them.

"Johnnie, this is Kris Daniels, the writer woman staying at Effy's place."

Kris's offered hand disappeared in Johnnie's when they shook. His smile for her was warm, and his voice when he asked what she'd like friendly. She must have been mistaken about his annoyance.

Kris didn't think white wine was on the menu or, if it was, that she'd want to drink it, so she indicated Dougal's glass with a finger and said, "Whatever he's having."

Johnnie moved off with a surprisingly light step for his bulk and pulled a bottle from the top shelf.

"Did I just order the equivalent of Scottish lighter fluid?" Kris asked.

"You'll see."

Johnnie brought her drink, about an inch of liquid the shade of burnished sienna; then he waited while she tried it.

Yep, definitely lighter fluid.

Kris managed not to choke. She even managed to swallow the stuff instead of spraying it all over the bar. But what really impressed her was that she smiled and thanked Johnnie in a voice that sounded almost like her own.

The big man left to wait on another customer, and Kris turned to Dougal. "What is that?"

"MacLeod's only serves the very best Scotch."

"Which is?"

"Well, most have their favorites, Glenfiddich, Glenlivet, but in this bar—" Dougal lifted his glass. "Only single-malt whisky from the Highlands. This is called Loch Ness Whisky."

"No way."

He downed it in a single gulp. "They call it the 'monstrously good malt.'"

Kris took a baby sip. Fire trickled down her throat and leaped into her stomach. She coughed.

"You don't have to drink it," Dougal said.

"It's growing on me." Kris took another sip. "Or if anything *is* growing on me, this will definitely kill it."

Dougal signaled for another, and, eventually, Johnnie brought the bottle. He glanced at Kris's barely touched glass, and his lips twitched before he moved off again.

"Is he always so laid-back?" Kris asked.

"Laid-back?" Dougal repeated.

"He takes his sweet time waiting on people." From what she could tell, he took his time only when waiting on Dougal, but she didn't think it prudent to mention that. Turned out, she didn't have to.

"He's just like that with me," Dougal said. "I'm not a local."

"Neither am I."

"Tourist is different. You won't stay." Dougal glanced at Johnnie. "I won't go."

"Why would they want you to go? Your grandfather lived here. Doesn't that make you one of them?"

"Not so's you'd notice." Dougal shifted his shoulders. "I hear it's the same in every small town in America. You could live there for fifty years and you'd never truly belong."

He was right. But it still didn't seem fair. And while Dougal said he understood, Kris didn't think that he liked it. She didn't blame him. Dougal seemed like a nice man. Interesting. Attractive. With those light eyes and dark hair, that well-trimmed beard and tall, taut body, she'd even call him sexy. You'd think every single woman in town would be after him.

Although . . . She glanced again at Johnnie. Maybe that was why.

They remained silent for a few minutes; then Dougal cleared his throat. "What did you think of the museum?"

Kris accepted the change of subject gladly. "You've put together something very nice. Did you do all the work yourself?"

"I planned it. Had some help from an artist woman who came to the village to paint the loch."

Kris's lips curved at the description. How long did you have to live in Drumnadrochit before you were known by your name? According to Dougal, maybe forever.

"Have *you* seen Nessie?" Kris asked.

Dougal sipped his whisky. "Everyone's seen her."

"That appears to be the party line. But . . ." She waited until Dougal looked up. "Have *you*?"

Something flickered in those amazing eyes. He hesitated, then shook his head. "Can't see what ain't there."

The words could have come right out of her mouth. Kris felt again the tug of a kindred spirit. She scooted her stool closer to Dougal's. "For a skeptic, you put forth a pretty good front."

"I don't have a choice. You think anyone would come to a museum that explains all the reasons there *isn't* a Nessie?"

Probably not.

"You're familiar with the history of the loch?" Dougal asked.

She was, but she wanted to hear what he knew. "Enlighten me."

"Twenty thousand years ago a glacier skidded through this area."

Skid might be pushing it. Glaciers moved pretty "glacially."

"Dug quite a few holes and when the ice melted, about ten thousand years later, the land rose and the new waterways separated. Where once Loch Ness may have been part of the North Sea, it was no longer."

"Any proof of that?"

"Remains of sea urchins, clamshells, and the like have been found in the deep sediment of the loch, despite its being a freshwater lake."

"Go on." Kris was intrigued.

"Some theorize that Nessie is a sea creature that was trapped here when the waterways separated and she's evolved, adapting to the freshwater."

"How could a single creature live that long?"

"Couldn't," Dougal agreed. "Unless there was something supernatural about it."

Kris lifted her brows. "You think there is?"

"No." Dougal grinned. "But it makes for a very good story."

"What about the idea that a herd of these creatures was trapped in Loch Ness?" Kris asked. "A breeding population."

"In theory, that would explain the issue of life expectancy. However, a trapped breeding population would end up so *inbred* that they'd eventually be unable to procreate."

"And you're right back to the life expectancy problem," Kris said. "What else?"

"Some say that down where the depths of the water are unknown and uncharted there's a way out of the loch. That Nessie is, in fact, a group of ancient sea creatures that has adapted to live in both salt and freshwater and despite the extreme cold of the loch they thrive here."

"That would take care of the argument that several animals of such size couldn't survive on the amount of food contained in Loch Ness without significantly and obviously depleting it."

"Exactly!" Dougal exclaimed, obviously thrilled that Kris was familiar with all the Nessie factoids. "If there's a way out, there's no need to feed while *in*."

Someone jostled Kris, and she glanced around. The pub was filling up. All the seats were taken. Though Dougal had said this was a local watering hole, quite a few tourists seemed to have found it, too.

Which might explain why Kris had the sudden sensation of being watched. In a crowd like this, someone had to be staring. She took a surreptitious glance around and caught the gaze of an elderly man at the end of the bar.

He was tall and very thin, his once-blond hair faded to white. His skin was lined from a lifetime spent outdoors, and his pale blue eyes shone.

He lowered his chin, an acknowledgment that he'd been staring, then returned his attention to his drink.

Probably lonely, she thought. *He's gotta be two or three decades older than anyone in here.*

"The passage to the sea creates the possibility of a large breeding population, which also gives an explanation as to why the sightings of Nessie can vary from ten to twelve feet in length to other reports of a thirty- to forty-foot creature," Dougal continued.

Kris turned back to her companion. "Baby Nessies."

"Yes!" Dougal punctuated his exclamation by downing the rest of his whisky. Kris had given up on hers.

She cast another glance at the old man, thinking maybe she'd ask him to join them, but he was gone.

"Sounds like a solid theory," Kris said.

"If creatures the size of Nessie can get in, then why haven't others? Sure, they'd die in the freshwater, but then there'd be bodies. Somewhere. Sometime."

"And if Nessies were going in and out, wouldn't someone have observed them in the sea?"

"Well, to be fair, out there they'd be seen as whales or dolphins or squids."

He was right. People often saw what they assumed they'd see, whether it be truth or fiction. Kris had found just that in many of her hoax-hunting cases. If one person saw a ghost or a beast or a monster, everyone else saw one, too. If people expected to see a whale, they weren't going to see a Nessie.

And vice versa.

"For me, it comes down to this," Dougal said. "If Nessie's been hanging out in Loch Ness for several thousand millennia, why hasn't anyone proved it yet?"

Kris played devil's advocate better than she played just about anything. "Maybe she's hiding. Maybe she doesn't want to be captured, then examined and analyzed and—" Kris shrugged. "Dissected."

Which was what would happen if Nessie were actually caught. Luckily she never would, or could, be.

Kris, enjoying herself immensely, sat back and, in doing so, caught a glimpse of the room behind Dougal's head. There, on the other side of at least two dozen people, stood the man who had kissed her last night.

He wasn't looking in her direction, was in fact facing away, but she knew it was him as surely as she knew she really, really hated Scotch whisky.

Kris blurted an excuse to Dougal, shoving her unfinished drink in his direction before making a beeline to the place where she'd last seen the mystery man.

By the time she got there, he was gone. But she hadn't fallen off the idiot tree—at least not lately—and when she saw the rear exit she took it. Unfortunately, if *he* had, he was quick as a bunny—or a ghost—because there was no sign of him.

She considered going back inside but, instead, headed out of town.

The night was clear and lovely. A bit cool, but she didn't mind. The moon, only a day past full, glowed like a silvery sun, which was handy, because once she left Drumnadrochit and walked toward the cottage the moon was all she had to light her path.

She picked her way carefully across the fields, crested a hill, and became captivated by the shimmering bands of brilliant white that topped the waves of the loch. She was drawn nearer by the strange little blips of something darker that bobbed through the moonlit water like—

"Nessie," she breathed.

Kris knew the rolling spots, which appeared very much like the humps of a sea serpent, would turn out to be shadows, a floating tree trunk, a combination of both, or even something else. Nevertheless, she crossed first the road and then the cool grass to reach the shore.

Sure enough, once she was closer those blips weren't so round and humpy. More flat and woodsy, with the sparkle of the moon hitting one just right and causing what was perhaps a knothole to gleam like an unwavering eye.

This gave her the sensation of being watched again, and she turned, scanning the road, then the tree line behind her.

Problem was . . . she kept walking.

And tripped over the body.

CHAPTER 5

Kris flew forward, stumbling, stepping on something that felt like some*one*.

"Sorry!" she exclaimed, an automatic response.

Her first thought was that she'd interrupted a couple reclining on the banks of the loch, smooching and mooning at the stars. For an instant she envied them. She'd never done anything remotely like that.

Her second was that whoever she "felt" watching her had somehow gotten in front of her and tripped her on purpose.

She was from Chicago; she knew better than to walk around alone in the night. But she'd been lulled by the quaint hominess of the small Scottish village.

Maybe she *had* fallen out of the idiot tree and hit her head several times on the way down.

Lurching backward, Kris slid on the damp ground, falling to one knee, but as she did, she brought her arms up in a defensive posture, just in case a blow came in fast or grasping, groping hands reached for her throat.

Instead, she came nearly face-to-face with the dead girl.

Kris would have thought her asleep, her face still and peaceful, except for the moon shining off her open eyes the same way they'd shone off the log in the loch. She cast a glance in that direction, but whatever had been there before was gone.

"Son of a bitch," Kris muttered. She lived in the land of five hundred murders, yet she'd had to come across the ocean to find her first dead body. Not that she'd ever *wanted* to find one, but still . . . at Loch Ness? What were the odds?

She lowered her arms, unclenched her fists, and, even though she knew the girl was dead, reached over and placed her fingertips against the pale, cool throat.

"Sometimes I hate it when I'm right."

Kris had hoped that talking out loud might lower the creep factor. Instead, hearing her voice in the still of the night only increased it significantly.

She needed to call the police. Except she didn't have a phone. She'd planned to communicate with anyone she needed to by computer.

Even if she'd had a phone, Kris had no idea how to call for help in this country anyway. She didn't think 911 would do a damn bit of good.

Kris got to her feet, ignoring the damp patch on her knee, wiping the tingling fingertips that had touched the dead girl's throat against her jeans.

She was going to have to walk into Drumnadrochit. Kris glanced at the empty, winding road, the dark, gaping fields, then again at the body. She really hated to leave the girl alone. She looked so . . . fragile lying there. Although what else could happen to her now?

"I'll be back as soon as I can," Kris said, and didn't even feel foolish for talking to a dead person.

Until she turned and ran smack into someone else.

* * *

Liam snatched Kris by the forearms as she bounced off his chest, caught her heels on something in the grass, and began to fall. She clutched at him, holding on—tightly, desperately—making him remember other women who had held on to him that way. Usually when he was rising above them, sliding into them, his hands braced on either side of their bodies as he gave them what he'd promised.

The memories, when combined with the scent of her hair, the warmth of her skin, the sharp intake of her breath that caused her breasts to rub against the insides of his wrists just once, were so vivid he nearly kissed her again. Then he saw what lay beneath and let her go.

"What—? Why—? *Where,*" Kris managed, "did you come from?"

Liam had watched her exit MacLeod's and followed. Against his better judgment, but now he was glad that he had. She shouldn't be out here alone, and she shouldn't have to deal with this.

Liam knelt next to the girl, put his fingers against her throat, but she was dead. Had been for a while.

"Who are you?" Kris asked.

"Right now we'd best be more concerned with who *she* is."

Liam didn't recognize her, so she was probably a tourist. Which was only going to make things worse.

"I'll go to the village and bring the proper authorities," he said. "Will ye be all right?"

Kris hesitated, peering at his face as if she could see into his head and discover all his secrets. But Liam knew better. No one had discovered his secrets in years.

"Kris," he said quietly when she continued to stare at him without answering.

Her eyes narrowed. "I'll be fine. Much better than she'll ever be again."

"I'll be quick as I can." Liam turned, but she stayed him with her hand on his arm.

"How do you know my name?"

"A ghràidh," he murmured, sliding out of reach. "Some say that I know everything."

Kris kept her gaze on her mystery man until he melded with the darkness. What was it about him that made every lucid thought in her head fly away?

He'd nearly kissed her again. She'd seen the intent in his marvelous blue eyes, sensed it in the slight increase of his breath, felt it in his touch. But even more amazing than that intent was her desire to let him.

She should have pushed harder—for his name, for an explanation of how he had known hers. But it had seemed beyond tacky to do so with a dead girl at her feet. They had more pressing issues than names.

An icy, damp finger seemed to brush her cheek, and Kris glanced toward the loch. A thick haze had formed, hanging above the water, blocking any hint of the opposite shore. The wind pushed the fog in her direction; vapor settled on her skin and in her hair. She saw—

"Through a glass darkly." She'd always liked that phrase but hadn't really understood it until now. Peering at the dead girl through the mist was like peering into a murky mirror.

"First Corinthians."

The voice was firm and commanding. The voice of God.

If God had a thick German accent.

The tall, slim outline of a man wavered in the depths of the haze as the voice continued: " 'For now we see through a glass, darkly, but then face to face: now I know in part; but then shall I know even as also I am known.' "

The old man who'd been staring at her in the pub stepped from the gloom. He bowed slightly, an Old World gesture that seemed completely at home in this old world.

"Chapter thirteen, verse twelve," he finished. "Very apropos. Soon, you will no longer know only in part."

"Know what?" Kris asked. "How did you get here?"

"I walked, Miss Daniels. The same as you."

He knew her name, too. Had it been written in the sky when she wasn't looking?

"You followed me?"

"Why would I do that?"

Kris glanced at the dead girl, suddenly remembering that the old guy had disappeared from the bar *before* she had. He hadn't followed her; he'd beaten her here. What had he been doing before she arrived?

Kris took a step backward, preparing to run, and he snatched her elbow with surprisingly quick and freakishly strong, bony fingers. "You do not want to do that," he murmured.

She tugged on her arm. He didn't let go, instead reaching his free hand beneath his voluminous coat and withdrawing a gun.

"I do not have the patience or the time to argue with you."

He released her but kept the gun right where it was, pointed at her sternum. His coat had caught on what appeared to be a bandolier of bullets strung across his chest. Kris could just make out another pistol stuffed into the loose waistband of his pants.

Who was this guy?

"The authorities will be back directly," he continued, "and I'd prefer not to be here when they arrive."

Rubbing her elbow, which would probably bear the imprint of his claw-like digits come the morning, Kris glanced at the corpse, then at the gun, then at him. "I bet you would."

His bushy white brows lifted. "You think I killed her?" He shook his head. "She drowned, poor thing."

"Drowning doesn't preclude your killing her."

His lips curved. "True. However, I did not."

"I'm just supposed to believe you?"

He shrugged. "It is up to you. But you will learn that many have drowned here of late. I'm afraid more will follow."

Kris frowned at the loch. "Is there some kind of undertow? A heavy kelp growth tangling in swimmers' legs or boat propellers?"

"No boats have sunk; none are even missing. This is not a place for swimming, and the drownings, they are not accidental."

The man was very good at saying *murder* without actually saying it.

"Why haven't I heard about this?" Kris asked.

"Tourist town," he said. "They do not like to broadcast such things."

Kris could see where a serial killer might put a damper on the revenue.

"This girl is only the second to be found." He jerked his head at the water, which had become completely obscured by the mist. "But there are more out there. Many more."

"If you didn't kill them, then how do you know that?"

"When people start to disappear, I am the man they tell."

"Who's 'they'? No, wait!" The better question was: "Who the hell are you?"

He did that half bow again, which seemed much less polite with the gun still in his hand. "Edward Mandenauer."

Maybe that hadn't been the better question. She didn't know him from Adam. So she reiterated the first.

"Who's 'they'? Why do they tell you?"

"Perhaps *tell* was not the right word." He frowned. "Sometimes my English is still not *vollkommen*." A growl of annoyance rumbled in his throat. "Perfect."

Kris thought his English was damn perfect and he knew exactly what he was saying—and not saying.

"I have connections." He rolled the barrel of the gun in a tiny circle. "Good ones. When people disappear, I hear of it. I come to the area, or send someone, and we discover what is making them go . . ." He lifted his free hand, fingers touching the thumb; then he released them toward the sky. "Poof."

"Poof," Kris repeated.

"Or . . ." He stared pointedly at the dead girl. "Not poof."

"You belong to some kind of international serial killer task force?"

His lips twitched. "Some kind."

"*What* kind?"

"We are called the *Jäger-Suchers*."

"My German is worse than your English," she said.

"Hunter-searchers. We hunt monsters." Kris blinked. "As do you."

"I'm not hunting a monster!"

"No?"

"I . . ." Kris paused.

She was pretending to be a writer; no one was supposed to know why she was really here or who she really was. But this guy—with his superior connections and monster-hunting task force—appeared to already know. Of course he could be nuts, probably was, but since he was holding the gun, she decided to tell him the truth.

"I expose hoaxes," she said.

"Which you're very good at."

"Thanks. But I don't believe there's a monster here."

"No?" he repeated, again glancing pointedly at the dead girl.

Kris sighed. "A human monster, sure. But a lake monster? No. And I plan to prove it."

"You do realize it is impossible to prove something does not exist? You can merely prove it has not yet been found."

"I've proved that things don't exist."

"You've proved that certain myths were being perpetrated by what you call a hoaxer. However, just because someone has hoaxed does not mean the myth is not real."

"That's exactly what it means."

"No." He shook his head as if she were a poor deluded soul. "It means that someone has been deceiving others. It does not mean that the monster might not still be there but not yet found."

"I'll prove the Loch Ness Monster isn't real."

"If you can, please do so. It will remove one more creature from my . . ." His mouth curved. "To-do list."

"I don't work for you."

"Would you like to? I will pay you. You can accomplish all sorts of things with that kind of cash."

"What kind?" Kris asked, intrigued in spite of herself.

He reached into his coat again—what all did he have in there?—and removed a plain, white envelope, which he tossed in her direction.

It was full of hundred-dollar bills. They looked pretty real.

"Who do *you* work for?"

"You are a smart girl. If you add one and one, I bet you will get two. Unlimited funding." He waggled his gun. "The best weapons and a lot of them."

She *could* add, and what she came up with was the U.S. government. Who else printed money like it was newspaper, let damn near everyone own a gun, and kept secrets like they were the gold stored at the Federal Reserve?

"Of course the powers that be would not admit to funding a monster hunt."

"Of course." Kris lifted the envelope. "What do I have to do for this?"

"Simply keep me informed of whatever you discover."

"About the un-monster? I don't see how that will help."

"I'm not paying you to analyze the information; I'm paying you to let me do so. I've been in this job long enough to know that where there is smoke there is usually a dragon."

"If there *were* actually dragons."

"They'd call it a *guivre* in this area—serpent body, dragon's head. Venomous breath. Afraid of naked humans. The females have green scales."

Kris opened her mouth, shut it again, then: "Are you for real?"

Confusion fluttered over his well-lined face. "Why on earth would I not be real?"

Kris rubbed her forehead.

"Where there are rumors of a monster," he continued, "a monster often appears—be it human or no. As you research the loch and its most famous inhabitant, I'm certain you will discover information that can be of use to me."

"And then?"

"You will tell me."

"How?"

"I will come to you."

Kris got a little tingle across her spine at that statement. "It would be easier if you gave me your contact information."

"No doubt," he agreed, but he didn't offer any. "I must be on my way. I'm needed . . ." He paused, then gave a tiny twitch of one shoulder in lieu of a shrug. "Elsewhere."

"And the other Yag—" She bit her lip and tried again. "Suke—"

He sighed as if dealing with a slightly amusing but extremely annoying two-year-old. "Jäger-Suchers."

"Yeah, them. No takers on the age-old Loch Ness problem?"

"I'm a bit . . ." He glanced toward the road, then back. "Shorthanded of late. And the monsters are multiplying."

"I don't believe in monsters."

A sudden commotion from the road—voices, a siren— drew her attention. Headlights permeated the hovering haze.

"You will," Edward Mandenauer said.

When she looked back, the old man was gone.

CHAPTER 6

Chief Constable Alan Mac was the first to arrive, but he wasn't alone. Her mystery man, whose name she *still* did not know, appeared to have roused half the village, then sent them ahead without him.

Some came in cars, some on foot, but come they did, and a crowd began to gather.

"Keep them back!" Alan Mac shouted to the other officers as they arrived. "This is a crime scene!"

He shot Kris a quick, unreadable glance before he knelt beside the dead girl and checked for a pulse. Then he sighed, and his big head dipped.

"Were you on duty when the other one was found?" Kris asked.

Alan Mac's head came up so fast he must have gotten a crick in his neck, since his hand went there and rubbed. He climbed to his feet. "Where did ye hear about the other?"

"I . . . well . . . uh . . ." How was Kris supposed to explain that she'd learned the news from an ancient German who'd disappeared into the mist faster than the characters in a Stephen King novel?

Alan lowered his voice: "That information has *not* been released."

Uh-oh.

She was saved from answering when a boatload of police and techs arrived and began to set up a perimeter, pushing her out of it. Alan's attention was captured, but he pointed a large finger at her and said, "Dinnae go anywhere, ye ken?"

"I ken," Kris muttered.

Her gaze wandered over the crowd, searching for the man she'd met at Urquhart Castle, but he wasn't there. She almost asked Alan Mac where he'd gone, but she knew where that would end. With the beginnings of a headache when he insisted that there was no such man. Although if that were the case, the constable wouldn't be here.

Kris's mind whirled. This place was starting to get to her.

And now she had an envelope of cash from a man who'd "gone poof" after tasking her with gathering information on a monster. Or perhaps a serial killer.

"One is both the same," she murmured, a saying of her brother's that had always confused her. Until just now.

People came and went. In the states she would have identified a coroner or medical examiner, crime scene techs, forensic experts—hey, she watched *SVU*—but here she had no clue on procedure or the proper titles for the players involved.

Eventually, Alan Mac separated from the others, took her arm, and led her a few yards from the hubbub.

The fog still floated atop the loch, obscuring the opposite shore, but the police lights illuminated the near side like the grand opening of a used-car lot.

The constable removed a small notebook from his

jacket and poised his pencil over a pristine white sheet. "What happened?"

"I was walking home from the pub—"

"Which one?"

"MacLeod's."

Alan lifted his gaze to hers. "Ye found that already, did ye?"

"Dougal invited me."

He frowned. "Dougal Scott?"

"Is there more than one Dougal?"

"Around here? Aye. So ye had a date with Dougal—"

"No," Kris interrupted. "I met him to talk about . . ." She waved her hand at the now-invisible loch.

"Ah." Alan nodded. "He's a good one for that. But he let ye walk home all alone?"

"Let me?" Kris bristled. "I'm not a child."

"Mmm." The sound made Kris bristle even more. But before she could say anything, Alan continued. "How did ye end up down near the loch?"

"I . . ." She glanced in that direction and hesitated.

"Did ye see somethin'?" Kris gave a reluctant nod. "What was it?"

"A log," she said firmly.

"Mmm," he said again, the sound very Scottish and male. "And then?"

"I tripped over—" She flipped her fingers at the dead girl, whom she could no longer see for all the people.

"Did ye touch her?"

"I fell on her," Kris said, and shivered with the memory. "Then, yes, I touched her to make sure she was dead."

"All right. How long until the boy came by, and ye sent him to the village?"

"I don't think he's a boy. He's probably older than you."

"The lad who came to find me was no more than fifteen."

"No, it was . . ." She paused. This was what came from not insisting on a name. Now she didn't have one to give. "The same man I saw at Urquhart Castle."

"The ghost?"

"He wasn't a ghost," Kris snapped. "I saw him tonight at MacLeod's."

"Did anyone else?"

Kris scowled. "I spoke with him right there next to that body, and—" *Yes!* "He touched her, too," she said triumphantly. "There should be fingerprints."

"Mmm," Alan murmured again. If he kept that up, she just might smack him. "It's rare to get fingerprints off a neck."

"Crap," Kris muttered.

Alan Mac's lips curved. "So ye came down to the loch because ye saw . . ." His smile widened. "A log. Then ye tripped over the body, and the boy came by—"

"Man," Kris corrected. "The man from the castle, and he said he'd bring the authorities."

"Anything else?"

Kris paused. Should she tell Alan about Mandenauer or shouldn't she?

Her hesitation was answer enough.

"Ye better spill it all, lass. Holding back information in a police matter is serious business."

Why had she even considered lying? Truth was her stock-in-trade. Getting to the truth was all she'd ever been any good at.

"There was an old man. He said this was the second body."

Alan's eyes widened. "Tall? Thin? White hair, blue eyes?" Kris nodded, and he sighed. "German?"

"You know him?" Kris imagined Edward Mandenauer escaped often from the local loony bin. And if that was the case, they needed to do something about those guns.

"He's an American agent. Some sort of Special Forces operation. Though I've never been clear on what sort."

Kris's brows lifted. Mandenauer had been telling the truth.

"Comes about now and again. Checks in with us since he never goes anywhere without a gun." Alan's lips twitched. "Or five. Except . . ." Now his lips tightened. "He hasn't checked in lately."

"I—uh—don't think he's staying."

"No? He said as much?"

Kris nodded, and oddly, Alan appeared to relax at the news.

Someone called his name, and the constable raised a hand to them before returning his attention to her. "Anything else?"

Though Edward hadn't said she needed to keep their relationship secret, Kris decided to. She wasn't supposed to be doing anything in Drumnadrochit but writing a children's book about the local lake monster.

And wasn't that a bizarre combination? Children and monsters? Then again, maybe not. Who else believed in them?

"If I think of something, I'll let you know," Kris said.

Since that was true, the words came out sounding sincere. Since Alan was preoccupied—his gaze had gone past her to the thick grove of trees—he didn't notice Kris's tension at omitting the truth. To her, a lie of omission was still a lie, and she didn't like it.

"Ye know where t' find me." Alan inched past but paused when Kris spoke.

"Is this murder?"

His face gave away nothing, but she had the distinct impression he was annoyed. "A drowning is usually an accident."

"Unless it wasn't."

"We'll have t' wait and see." He walked away.

She didn't like withholding information from the police. It made her uncomfortable. But if she was going to find out anything at all about who was perpetrating the Loch Ness hoax, she'd best keep her secrets a secret. If word got around—and it would in a place like this—that Kris was some kind of spy for an American agent, there was no telling what would happen.

Liam watched from the forest as Kris made her way to Loch Side Cottage

"He's here." Alan Mac strode into the cool, mellow darkness of the trees. "He was talking to her."

"There are a lot of *hes* about right now. Ye'll have t' be more specific."

"Mandenauer."

Liam tensed, then narrowed his gaze on the crowd. "I dinnae see him."

"Gone now. But he could still be in Drumnadrochit."

"What did he tell her?"

Alan Mac shrugged. "Didnae seem like much, but with him ye never know."

Liam relaxed just a little. "He'll no doubt visit now and again until the day that he dies, and he often talks to people. He often does much more than talk. 'Tis nothing new."

"These killings are."

"Ye think Edward Mandenauer is drowning young girls? He's in lovely shape for an old, old man, but I doubt he's capable of that."

Alan didn't answer but continued to stare at Liam until Liam sighed and met his eyes. "Ye think it was me?"

"Was it?"

"I havenae drowned a maiden in years," Liam said dryly.

Alan Mac snorted. "Like ye'd tell me if ye had."

The two of them pondered the crowds, the lights, the tarp-covered body at the edge of the loch.

"We aren't going to be able to keep this quiet anymore," Alan Mac murmured.

Liam didn't answer. He hadn't thought they'd be able to keep it quiet this long.

Kris returned to the cottage, hoping she could fall into bed and straight into sleep. Instead, as soon as she closed her eyes, she saw the face of a nameless dead girl.

Still, Kris tossed and she turned and she tried for quite a while, but eventually she sat up and turned on the light. Where was her book?

Kris padded into the living area, where her copy of *Supernatural Secrets*—always a good place to ferret out her next hoax—lay on the couch. She leaned over to pick it up, glancing through the window as she straightened.

Someone stood near the water.

Her heart leaped. The murderer perhaps? How long until he headed for the cottage? Kris wished Edward had handed over one of his guns along with his money.

As if she'd know what to do with a gun if she had one. Though how hard could it be? Long end pointed toward what you wanted to shoot and then—

"Bang," she murmured, still staring at the figure near the loch.

The moon shone down like the beam of an alien spacecraft. If she were fanciful she'd expect him to drift upward, captured forever and gone.

Instead, he bathed in the light, as if the moon were water and he was parched. The sheen sparkled in his hair like dew, and suddenly she realized who it was.

Despite the chill and her bare feet, as well as her night-time attire of T-shirt and flannel pajama pants, Kris slipped out of the cottage and down to the loch.

If he heard her coming, he gave no sign, continuing to stare into the water. The mist had disappeared as quickly as it had come, and the night was clear and cool.

He wore the same thing he'd worn the first time she saw him. Dark jeans, dark short-sleeved shirt—in this climate he should be cold; she was—yet he stood there on the banks of Loch Ness, arms at his sides instead of wrapped around himself like hers were, as if it were the first day of summer in the tropics and not the beginning of autumn in the Highlands.

Kris paused a few feet away, waiting for him to speak, to offer some sort of explanation, but he didn't. Eventually she had to ask: "Why did Alan Mac say a boy had come to tell him about the dead girl?"

He breathed in and out a few times. Kris didn't like the hesitation. In her experience, hesitation meant lies. Of course, in her experience, a too-quick answer meant the same.

Hell, be honest. In her experience, damn near everything that came out of people's mouths was a lie.

"I couldnae find him," he said at last. "So I snatched a lad, sent him one way, and I went in the other."

It sounded plausible enough; however— "You have an answer for everything."

"Shouldn't I?" He continued to stare at the loch as if transfixed.

"Alan Mac thinks I imagined you."

"Alan Mac thinks many things. 'Tis his job."

"Why is it that no one seems to know who you are?"

"I couldnae say."

"Couldnae?" she mocked. "Or wouldnae?"

He took another deep breath and let it out. "My name is Liam Grant."

She waited, but he said no more.

"That's it? You kiss me in the moonlight and all you tell me now is your name?"

"What would ye have me say?"

What would she have him say? She wanted to know both everything about him and nothing at all. She'd had men tell her things before—both lies and the truth—that she'd wished later they hadn't. Perhaps it was better to kiss but never tell.

"You didn't come back." She hadn't meant to say that. She sounded like an abandoned girl. Something she'd been once but had sworn never to be again. Which might be why she had so few dates and even fewer friends. If she didn't care, she couldn't hurt.

"I'm here now." His voice, low and soft, trilled along her skin like a gentle spring breeze, raising gooseflesh in its wake. She rubbed her hands against her arms, but it didn't do any good.

Drawn by that voice on the wind, the moon in his hair, and a promise of warmth, she stepped closer. "*Why* are you here now?"

"D' ye expect me to say I came to kill ye?"

"Did you?"

He laughed, short and sharp. Then he spun, grabbing her shoulders, and she had no choice but to steady herself by reaching for him. Her hands landed on his hips.

His blue eyes caught the light from above and shone like molten silver. "If I'd wanted t' kill ye," he whispered,

"I'd have done it before, then tossed both you and the girl back to Nessie."

She took a single step forward, surprising him, so his hands at her shoulders slid free, encircling her back and turning what had begun as imprisonment into an embrace.

"Then why *are* you here?" she repeated, every breath she took brushing her breasts against his chest in a rhythm as old as the sea.

He cursed in a language she didn't understand—Gaelic most likely—and then he was kissing her as if he'd been denied such things for longer than either of them had been alive.

His mouth was cool, damp, like the loch, like the mist and the night. She opened, drinking him in as he had drunk the bright and shiny moon.

His tongue was warm when it stroked hers, igniting the heat she had craved. He tasted of desire, a flavor like the darkest chocolate; his hair was as smooth as satin sheets, and the way he smelled . . . He could be wearing a cologne called Wicked. Was there a cologne called Wicked?

She pressed against him. He was all sharp angles and sleek muscle, while she was just round and soft. That had always bothered her, being round instead of slim, soft instead of hard. Right now she couldn't think why.

Her mind spun away on sensation. His skin blessedly cool against her hot, hot hands. His mouth so clever—a nip here, a caress there. Who would ever have believed that a bit of pain could bring so much pleasure?

His palm at her waist, his thumb stroked her belly. She arched, wishing he would lift that hand, that thumb, and—

He cupped her breast, the chill of his skin sifting through the cotton, making her nipple tighten even harder.

When he brushed the tingling bud—back and forth, back and forth—mimicking the motion with his tongue against the tip of hers, she moaned.

Her hands in his hair clenched; she tilted his mouth just so. She'd forgotten where she was. She'd forgotten *who* she was. This man—*Liam*—had become the whole world.

Something splashed in the loch—close enough that she felt a hint of spray. An instant later they had both dropped their arms to their sides, disentangled their tongues, and taken one giant step backward.

Kris was trembling—from the cold, the shock, the lust, she wasn't sure. Maybe all three.

"What was that?" she whispered.

"Sturgeon," he said quickly.

She'd meant what was *that* in relation to the strange sense of need that seemed to overtake her whenever he came near. All she wanted to do was kiss him, touch him, and more.

She'd never been tempted by a stranger, seduced as if she had no will to resist a man whose name, until only moments ago, she had not even known.

The splash came again. Ripples spread toward the shore. "That sounds pretty big," she said.

"They are." Liam frowned at the water. "Big. The sturgeons. They can grow t' be twenty feet long. Some have mistaken them for sharks."

"Or lake monsters?" she murmured.

"Aye."

"Do you believe in lake monsters?"

He glanced at her, and his lips, gorgeous, wet, and clever, quirked. "I think they could exist."

"Do you think Nessie exists?"

His smile faded, and his deep blue gaze held hers. "I'll

not lie to ye. I've lived here all my life," Liam continued, "and I have never once seen Nessie."

Usually when someone said they wouldn't lie, it was right before they lied their butts off, yet, strangely, she believed him.

"You'd be the one of the few in Drumnadrochit," she said. "Or one of the few who admits it."

"Aye," he repeated, but she wasn't sure which part of her statement he was agreeing with. Reaching out, he tucked a stray strand of hair behind her ear. "Best get inside before ye freeze, Kris."

Her name, uttered in that low, sexy burr, made her shiver again, and she lifted her hands to rub at her bare arms. "Aren't you cold?"

"Not anymore."

"You could . . ." She paused. "Come in."

He looked at the loch, a quick, sharp glance like he'd heard something, although she hadn't. "I have to go." He turned away.

"Wait." Kris reached for his arm but let her hand fall back to her side before she touched him. She'd never been clingy—had learned long ago that clinging only made people run away faster—and she wasn't going to start now.

Liam turned with a lift of one dark brow.

"Where do you live?" she asked. "What do you do?"

"Do?" he echoed.

Was that expression too American?

"For a job," she clarified.

"Whatever comes along."

Before she could ask what that meant or point out that he hadn't answered either of her questions, he jogged down the shore, disappearing into the sudden darkness caused by the fall of the moon.

The eastern sky had begun to lighten. She should really go inside. Instead, Kris stayed right where she was, hugging herself for warmth and watching the sun rise.

As it burst over the horizon, all red and orange and yellow, a distant splash echoed across the murky expanse of the loch.

This one didn't sound anything like a sturgeon.

CHAPTER 7

Kris had stayed up all night in the past. Studying. Working on *Hoax Hunters*. Talking with Lola. Crying because what was left of her family ignored her.

The latter hadn't happened in quite a while. Neither her father nor her brother ever remembered her birthday; they seemed to have completely forgotten Christmas. After the third time June 8th had passed with no call, no card, no damn e-mail, Kris had snuffled through a bottle of champagne and vowed never to shed a tear over them again. So far she hadn't.

It was a new experience, however, to remain awake all night because she'd found a dead body. She'd have to rank the experience just above the crying-over-Daddy episode.

Kris considered trying to sleep, but with the sun up and the birds tweeting and the loch lapping she doubted she'd have any luck. Instead she made a pot of the coffee she'd bought from Jamaica yesterday and sat in front of her computer to work.

She typed up what she'd learned so far, which wasn't a

helluva lot more than she'd already discovered from books and the Internet. Sure, she'd heard a few Nessie-sighting stories, but there were thousands of them. Besides, she'd come here to *debunk* the myth, not add to the lore that perpetrated it.

How was she going to catch the hoaxer in the act of hoaxing? With all the extra interest that would soon be focused on the loch now that two dead bodies had been found, she doubted anyone would be out and about creating mischief.

Although . . . she wouldn't put it past the hoaxer to attach the blame for these drownings to the monster. What a perfect way to draw attention to their little lie. And if the deaths were later proved to be caused by something else, the doubt would always be there and the publicity would already have been had. The idea that Nessie had pulled a few unsuspecting folks to their deaths in the depths of the chilly water would only increase the whole "monster" cachet.

Kris sighed. She was going to be here a lot longer than she'd originally thought. She'd bet the rest of this fabulous coffee that until the drowning hoopla settled down there'd be no Nessie sightings. Luckily she now had enough money, courtesy of Edward, to remain here until the hoaxing started up again—then she'd pounce.

"Which reminds me." Kris frowned at her computer, considering what she should Google first, hoping the Internet was in the mood to work right now. Thankfully, it was.

Edward Mandenauer brought up very little, and none of it referred to an ancient German man who liked guns. Which was disturbing. Most people had *something* about them *somewhere* on the Internet. That he didn't meant someone had removed it. Which leant credence to his claim of being backed by the U.S. government.

She tried *Jäger-Sucher* and received half a dozen on-line translation sites. *Hunter-searcher* only brought her hunting stores, adventure vacations, search-and-rescue units.

But she kept at it. Kris never would have gotten any-where in life if she'd given up at the first hint of trouble.

She continued to feed words into the search engine. It wasn't until she typed *old German man* with sharp, hard clicks of frustration that she actually found something worth reading.

From the *National Enquirer*:

Werewolves Attack Small Town in Northern Maine

Under siege during a terrible blizzard, the residents of Harper's Landing watched their numbers dwindle as the number of werewolves increased.

They were saved when an old man with a heavy Ger-man accent walked out of the storm carrying guns and silver ammunition. Within days, every werewolf was dead and the old gentleman disappeared as mysteriously as he'd arrived.

"Werewolves," she said. "Great."

But she followed the lead, typing *werewolf* and follow-ing the amazing number of bizarre stories from there. In a helluva lot of them an old German man showed up, kicked ass, then disappeared.

Poof.

There were also several mentions of a white wolf that fought the sudden influx of freakishly smart, incredibly strong, and really pissed-off wolves, all of which seemed to sport human eyes.

That was something she never wanted to see. And she wouldn't, because—

"It's all bullshit. They want to sell newspapers."

None of the stories appeared in any publications of note. No tales of wolf packs in the *New York Times*. No white wolf popped up in the *Chicago Tribune*. There had been a few strange incidents mentioned in the *Times-Picayune,* but Kris had found that when you were dealing with New Orleans strange happened a lot.

However, she did notice that whenever the white wolf showed up a beautiful blond American woman did, too. When Kris traced that lead, she found connections to other weird tales—leopard shifters, zombies, Gypsies, and bizarre accounts of eagles and ravens and crows.

The abundance of scary stories involving Mandenauer and what had to be his *Jäger-Sucher* cohorts would have been troubling. If Kris believed them.

"I'm gonna have enough myths to bust for the rest of my hopefully very long life," she murmured.

Someone knocked on the door. Kris, who'd been reading a report of a Navajo shape-shifting witch who could take the form of any animal whose skin he wore and had actually taken the shape of a man—the explanation for that was just too disgusting to contemplate, though she *had* been contemplating it—jumped to her feet at the sound, heart pounding.

Then she gave a shaky laugh. "Doubt there's a Navajo shape-shifter anywhere around." She moved toward the door. "'Cause first they'd have to exist."

Nevertheless, she glanced out the front window. Dougal Scott stood on the doorstep.

"Hey," he greeted. "I heard you found a body last night. You okay?"

He was dressed in his kilt, and the Scottish outfit combined with his very American way of speaking had Kris fighting back a ridiculous giggle, along with the longing for a man who dressed like an American and spoke like a Scot. She was starting to think that he existed in the same realm as skinwalkers, werewolves, and Nessie.

"Yes." Kris opened the door wider so Dougal could come in, then pointed to the couch. She sat on the single chair to the left. "Didn't get any sleep, but that's happened before."

"Why were you out wandering near the loch in the night? It can be dangerous."

Kris could hardly say she'd been looking for a ghost, then been drawn to the loch by the reflection of the moon off a log and—

"You know someone by the name of Liam Grant?" she blurted.

"No," Dougal said slowly. "There are Grants aplenty, of course, but none named Liam that I recall." He tilted his head. "I think there might be Grants in Dores, which is nearer to Inverness."

"Dores," she repeated. "Okay."

"Does he have something to do with the body?"

Kris contemplated Dougal. He seemed awfully interested in the body. Of course she'd learned over her years in television that a lot of people were ghouls.

To be honest . . . most people were ghouls.

She shook her head. "I ran into him at the castle, and we had a nice chat."

Kris had to struggle to hold back the snort of derision that threatened to erupt from her throat. Since when did a chat involve the exchange of DNA?

Dougal's brows lifted. She half-expected him to chant: *Liar, liar, pants afire,* and she touched her nose to see if it had begun to grow as long as a telephone wire. Her lying skills had not improved.

"Mmm," he said in that way the Scottish had, which could indicate disbelief, sarcasm, or the desire of one speaker for the other to move on. "There was a man asking around the village about you."

Kris frowned. "Liam?"

"As I've never met him, I don't know, but I doubt it."

"If you've never met him, then how can you doubt?"

"I'd expect Liam Grant to have a Scottish accent."

"I'd expect Dougal Scott to have one, too, but there you go."

Dougal touched his fingertips to his forehead and flicked them outward in a jaunty salute. "Touché."

Kris had a thought. "Was he German?"

Dougal shook his head. "American. Said he was from . . ." He paused. "The East Coast."

"Oh, that narrows it down," Kris muttered. "What did he ask?"

"Where you were staying."

Kris started, and Dougal's expression became concerned. "I didn't tell him."

"Good," she said, though eventually someone would. "You didn't wonder why he was asking?"

"Oh, I wondered. But I was busy. Someone needed directions; someone else wanted to know the weekend hours for the museum. When I turned back, he was gone."

That happened a lot around here.

"Would you like to visit The Clansman?" Dougal asked.

"Clansman?" Kris repeated, confused at the sudden change of subject.

"A hotel, near Inverness. They have a wonderful restaurant overlooking the loch, where a great many Nessie sightings are said to occur."

"You're asking me to dinner?"

Dougal cocked a brow. "It appears that I am." He seemed as surprised about it as she was.

Kris hesitated. She liked Dougal. She enjoyed talking to him. It was refreshing to be able to discuss Nessie with someone else who did not believe. But she didn't want him to think there was any chance for a lasting relationship. Even if she were capable of such a thing, she wasn't going to be here that long.

"It's dinner, Kris." Dougal's mouth quirked as his gray eyes observed her dilemma with obvious amusement. "I'm not going to start picking out china patterns and flatware."

Kris laughed. She really did like him. "People still do that?"

"I have no idea." His lips parted in a genuine smile that had her smiling back. "So . . . dinner? Between friends and fellow anti-Nessie-ites?"

"I'd like that."

"The restaurant is called Cobbs after John Cobb. He was killed on Loch Ness in 1952."

"Nessie?" Kris asked dryly.

"Of course."

"Tell me."

Dougal's expression became intent. He appeared to enjoy telling Nessie stories as much as Kris liked hearing them. Probably because he rarely got to share them with someone who agreed that they were hogwash.

"Cobb held the land speed record at the time—just over three hundred and ninety-four miles per hour—and he was trying to break the world water speed record. His boat disintegrated on its first run."

"That's odd," Kris said, though she had no idea if it was odd at all. In her opinion, driving a boat at speeds over *fifty* miles per hour was more stupid than odd.

"They say the boat bumped several times, then disappeared in a spray of water like no one had ever seen. When it reappeared there were pieces of it all over the place."

"And Cobb?"

"They pulled him out alive, but he died before they could get help. They've never been able to prove what happened."

"But they've theorized," Kris said.

"Waves. Mechanical failure. Human error. He could have hit a piece of driftwood."

"Named Nessie?"

"If that were the case, wouldn't the monster be in pieces, too?"

"What is there about *monster* that you don't understand?" Kris murmured.

"And we're back to the concept of a supernatural entity," Dougal concluded. "In my opinion, if the only way to explain something is by magic, that isn't an explanation at all."

The man made a good point. Probably because it would have been *her* point. He was handsome, funny, intelligent, rational. They shared an interest and a point of view.

So why wasn't she more excited about going out with him?

Liam shivered despite the warmth of the sun. He had never become acclimated to the temperature here. Considering he'd always been *here,* every attempt he'd made to leave resulting in disaster, he couldn't understand why.

He watched Loch Side Cottage from the shadows, the lap of the water lulling him half to sleep. If he kept this up, sooner or later someone was going to see him, and then what?

There'd be shouting and pointing and problems. There always were.

Floating on a river of exhaustion, Liam drifted. He dreamed of walking along the loch, hand in hand with Kris in the sunlight. They'd talk of their lives. He'd tell the truth. She'd kiss him and laugh and say it didn't matter.

Talk about a fantasy.

Liam found his fascination with her strange, which only made him more fascinated. In the past, he had been the one who was stalked. Women were captivated by him to the point of ridiculousness. How many had sworn to give their lives for his love?

How many had?

After agreeing to an early dinner with Dougal, Kris had been debating a snack or a nap—deciding on the latter as she remembered she had nothing in the place but coffee, tea, and milk; she'd eaten the small amount of bread and jam already—when another knock came at her door.

"Forget something?" she asked as she opened it.

Her gaze, positioned upward to meet Dougal's eyes, instead met empty air. A Munchkin giggle drew her attention two feet lower.

Effy didn't wait to be invited inside. Since she was carrying a plate of something that smelled like raisin bread, Kris didn't care. The probability of food was worth another visitor so soon after the first.

"I heard ye had a rough night." Effy set the plate on the table next to Kris's computer. "Thought ye could use a bannock." She motioned Kris closer. "It'll cure what ails ye."

Kris couldn't resist Effy's good cheer, nor the scent of the bannocks. She lifted one—a round, flat brown object the size of a dessert plate and filled with raisins—and took a bite.

"Like a fruitcake," she said. "Only better."

Effy beamed for several seconds before sobering. "Ye should not be out in the dark. Didn't yer mother ever tell ye that?"

Kris choked on the bannock. Her mother hadn't had time to tell her much. Not even good-bye.

"I'm fine," she said once she'd recovered, with a little help from Effy's pounding between her shoulder blades.

"Ye call finding dead bodies a few feet from yer doorway fine?" Effy tsked. "Americans. So much violence in yer lives, ye dinnae even realize something's bad when ye trip over it."

Did Effy know that Kris had tripped over the body, or was it just a figure of speech? Only Alan Mac, who shouldn't be blabbing information to anyone, imaginary Liam, and Edward Mandenauer were aware of exactly what had happened on the shores of Loch Ness last night.

"I'd have ye come into the village," Effy continued, wringing her pale hands, "but all my rentals in Drumnadrochit are full."

"That reminds me," Kris said. "Can I keep this place for a month?"

"A month?" Effy's pale brows lifted. "Truly?"

"Yes. I . . ." Kris paused, mind groping for a lie and not finding one. "Hold on."

She went into the bedroom, pulling out some of Mandenauer's cash, stalling for a few minutes while she got all her ducks of deceit in a row. When she returned to the living area, she handed Effy the money before she began her falsehood, hoping the older woman would be too distracted by the multiple images of Benjamin Franklin to hear the lie on Kris's tongue.

"I've sold my book. My—uh—publisher loved the idea so much they want me to write it immediately. And since it's quiet here—" *when there aren't dead bodies washing up on the shores*—"I thought I'd just stay until I finished. Did you want me to get that changed into pounds?"

Effy shook her head, still staring at the bills in her hand. "They sent you cash?" Doubt colored in her voice.

"Uh—no. I had that with me."

"And ye weren't stopped at Customs?" Now Effy was eyeing *Kris* as if she were a Colombian drug lord.

"I didn't have that much." Kris laughed, and it must have been convincing, because the other woman relaxed, folding the bills over and pulling her dress outward so she could tuck them into her bra.

Kris couldn't help but see the edge of a tattoo on her breast. Effy didn't seem the type.

The woman saw where Kris was looking and let her neckline fall back into place before heading for the door. "Ye just be careful out here, ye ken?"

"I've lived in Chicago for years," Kris said. "I'm aware of the dangers that come with the night." In certain areas of the Windy City, they came with the daylight, too.

"I dinnae think the dangers there are anything like the dangers here."

Kris tilted her head, peering into the woman's emerald eyes. She had the feeling that Effy was trying to tell her something. So why didn't the woman just tell her?

Before she could ask, Effy slipped out the door and headed toward Drumnadrochit at an impressive clip for a woman of her age and size.

Kris went inside and shot a quick note to Lola, asking if anyone had called, or even come by, looking for her. She doubted it, but as Lola was the only person Kris had told where she was going, she didn't understand how anyone could be asking for her by name in Drumnadrochit. She didn't like it.

That accomplished, she began to make notes about her show—where she'd film and what she'd say. But her mind wandered to Edward, and when she pulled it back she saw she'd sketched the tattoo she'd seen on Effy's breast.

Just a half circle. Could be anything. That it was there at all was more interesting than imagining what the tattoo could be. Although—

Effy could easily have come of age in the hippie-time sixties. Had there been a hippie-time sixties in Scotland?

Kris doubted they'd been protesting Vietnam, although who knew? And the Beatles, who'd been born down the road about four hundred miles, had been pretty hippie time. Weren't they blamed for the whole long-hair craze that swept the United States? Kris didn't think they'd had any tattoos, but that didn't mean folks who really got into the counterculture hadn't. Maybe Effy was a closet flower child. Stranger things had happened.

Kris glanced at her computer, thrilled to see that the Internet was still cooperating. She Googled *tattoos in the sixties*. Sure enough, before that time tattoos were mostly found in the military or on those who'd been in prison. But later in that decade tattoos had begun to appear in the younger population. What better way to prove you were a rebel than to ink something rebellious on your body forever?

Kris had to wonder how many sagging peace signs graced aging flesh. She frowned at the drawing she'd made of Effy's tattoo. Could *it* be a peace sign?

Hell, it could be anything.

CHAPTER 8

Dougal arrived to pick up Kris right on time. The contrast of charcoal slacks, soft gray cashmere sweater, and shiny black shoes with his usual kilt was so sharp Kris might not have recognized him in a crowd.

Two different men in one easy-on-the-eyes package, she thought. *Not bad.*

Kris had had to search high and low to come up with something that wasn't jeans and a sweatshirt. Luckily, she had tossed a black skirt and clingy red sweater in her suitcase at the last minute. Combined with her least clunky pair of shoes, that would do. Although, right now, Dougal certainly cleaned up better than she did.

"I know it's early," he said, "but I thought after dinner we could head out to the loch and watch for Nessie as the sun sets. It's always good for a laugh when she doesn't show up."

Except, *someone* was perpetrating the lake monster hoax, and according to Dougal, they perpetrated it often in the water near The Clansman. With the current upheaval around Drumnadrochit, perhaps the hoaxers would feel more comfortable north of all the trouble. She would catch them in the act, and the rest would be history.

A history she would be the first to record.

"Sounds good to me." Kris snatched her backpack, which contained her video camera, then followed Dougal to his car—something German; she was no good with makes and models. He held the door. Lucky, since she'd have gone straight to the wrong side of the automobile if left to her own devices.

The drive to The Clansman retraced the route Kris had taken from Inverness along the shore of Loch Ness. The tea brown waters played hide-and-seek as they drove—there and then gone and then there again. All around, mountains of blue and gray battled with walls of evergreen for dominance.

They made small talk. "Nice day." "Beautiful weather." "Do you like salmon?"

Kris relaxed, thrilled not to have to think for a while. Dougal was easy to be around. He didn't ask too many questions she was required to invent answers for.

From the outside, The Clansman did not impress. If Kris had been driving, she'd have gone right past. They came around a curve and bam, there it was—the parking lot directly off the highway on one side, a small harbor on the other.

The building itself was smaller than most country inns in America and consisted of weathered brown wood and sand-shaded bricks. To the rear, towering green trees covered a massive hill, which appeared to flow into the slowly darkening sky.

Inside, however, the place was beautiful. There were cream walls with wood accents in the lobby. The carpet was a little busy, but she'd found that to be the case in many places of business. Kris had a feeling busy carpet didn't show the dirt as clearly.

The restaurant was even more lovely, with windows that looked out on the loch, a polished wood bar, bottles glistening in the setting sun, and lots of tables with comfortable, cushy chairs.

Theirs was next to the window, and Kris found herself captivated by the long expanse of water. From here it almost looked blue.

The waiter appeared before she could comment. "Would ye like something from the bar?"

Dougal tilted a brow. "Whisky?"

"I think no." Kris smiled at the waiter. "Wine. Something white and dry. You choose."

He inclined his head, then turned to Dougal, who predictably ordered their best single-malt whisky.

"Why does the loch seem blue?" Kris asked. "I know the water's brown from the peat."

Dougal glanced in that direction. "In some places the reflection of the sky hits her just right; then you have . . ." He spread his hands forward and out.

The waiter returned with their drinks, setting a glass of gorgeous golden wine in front of Kris. "This is Autumn Oak," he said. "A Scottish wine."

Kris picked up her glass, sniffed, then sipped and nodded as she smiled. "Perfect."

"From the Cairn O'Mohr Winery," he continued. "In Perthshire, near Errol, which is the center of our best fruit-growing area in the Carse of Gowrie."

"Okay." Kris lifted her glass.

He left with their appetizer orders—duck with raspberry sauce for Kris, seafood salad for Dougal.

The wine was fantastic, the food excellent. After the duck, Kris ordered salmon with Cajun spices—who'd have thought?—lime and sun-roasted tomatoes. Dougal had lamb with mint-roasted potatoes, rosemary, and port.

Kris made a face when he ordered it.

"You don't like port?" he asked.

"I don't like lamb."

"But they're so cute," he deadpanned.

"Exactly."

"I've worked with sheep," he said. "I prefer them on my plate. But veal—" Now Dougal made a face. "Baby cows with big brown eyes. How could you?"

"I don't," Kris said. "Believe me."

She ate every last bite of her dinner and drank two glasses of wine. When the waiter suggested dessert, she puffed out her cheeks, but Dougal insisted she try the Pavlova, which was light, or the sorbet and berries, even lighter. With the promise of coffee as an accompaniment, Kris succumbed.

Out on the loch, something moved.

"Did you see that?" Kris stared at what appeared to be three humps bumping along halfway between this shore and the next.

Dougal narrowed his eyes. "It's a wake."

"From what?" Kris didn't see a boat in either direction.

Dougal lifted his chin, indicating the towering mountains. "Those actually continue into the loch and form a basin. When something makes waves, those waves come out." He spread his hands, then stopped them dead as if they'd struck something solid. "They hit the rock, then come back again." He brought his palms toward each other in a rippling movement. "Because Loch Ness is so big and deep, sometimes the boat, or whatever, that made the original wave is long gone before the ripple returns. By then the cause of those ripples has left more wakes, and when the reflected ones hit those coming in the other direction, you get humps." He nodded at the window. "Like that."

Made sense. And Dougal's matter-of-fact tone had Kris feeling foolish. Of course she'd seen a wake. What else could it have been?

The waiter arrived with their desserts and coffee. As soon as the man finished, Dougal spoke softly: "Greater skeptics than you have been fooled by the loch."

"How did you know what I was thinking?"

He shrugged. "Your face doesn't lie."

Great. Not only was she unable to lie with her mouth, but her face gave her away, too. She shouldn't be disappointed—after all, didn't she loathe liars?—but she was.

"Out there," Dougal continued, "everything is deceptive. A wake, a tree, the reflection of a black-throated diver at dawn, or a red deer at dusk."

Kris let her lips curve as he listed some of the things people had seen and thought to be Nessie. How could any intelligent person believe in a fairy tale?

She was nearly done with her sorbet, which she'd preferred to the small taste she'd had of Dougal's Pavlova, when she again had the bizarre sense of being watched. She was used to the feeling—she was on television—so why did the sensation suddenly bother her?

Dougal stared at the loch, scowling at what appeared to be a heavy log with a thick protruding branch that could easily have been mistaken for the head of a sea serpent, if you were inclined to mistake such things. If you were also inclined to paranoia, the log seemed to stare back.

Kris peered around the room. Several people nursed drinks at the bar, but they all peered at the glittering bottles on the wall, no doubt deciding what they might have next.

The other diners were occupied with their own fine meals. Not that one or two of them couldn't have been staring at Kris a minute ago, then stopped. However, she still had that tickle at the base of her neck.

She glanced over her shoulder just as a man left the dining room. There was something about him that made Kris get to her feet, mutter, "Ladies' room," and follow.

She lost him.

How, she wasn't quite sure. Kris had hustled across the restaurant as fast as her long skirt and clunky shoes would let her, and when she reached the place she'd last seen him the man was gone without a trace.

There'd been something really familiar about the guy.

Which made no sense. She was in Scotland. The only males she knew were Dougal, who'd been sitting with her; Liam, who was both shorter and more lithe than the figure she'd observed, and had black hair instead of light brown with streaks of gold; and Alan Mac, who was far too large to be mistaken for anyone but himself.

She supposed she could include both Edward Mandenauer and Rob Cameron on her list, but both of them were much older than the guy she'd seen.

So why did she feel as if she knew him?

Might he be the man asking for her in Drumnadrochit? If so, he appeared to have found her.

But then why would he leave?

Kris was more than a little creeped out. She should have asked Dougal to come with her. He'd spoken with the guy. He'd know if it were him.

"Damn," Kris muttered as she returned to the table. Cloak-and-dagger still not her thing.

Dougal was in the process of paying the bill. Kris insisted on Dutch treat. Dougal protested.

"We're friends," Kris pointed out. "And friends don't let other friends pay the whole bill."

"My friends do," Dougal muttered.

Kris laughed and put down a few of the pounds sterling she had exchanged before getting on the plane. She'd have to find a bank tomorrow and do the same with the money Edward had given her. She hoped it wasn't counterfeit.

"The sun's falling fast." Dougal winked. "We should hurry to the loch before we miss her."

As they left the restaurant, then the building, Kris glanced around for any trace of the man she'd seen earlier. No luck.

"This guy who was asking for me," she began as they crossed the road and headed down the grassy bank. "What did he look like? Height? Weight? Hair?"

Dougal frowned. "Shorter than me. Solid. But not fat. Muscles. Brown hair."

"Light brown? Highlights?"

Dougal's frown deepened. "Highlights?"

"Streaks." She waggled her fingers at the top of her head. "From the sun." Or a bottle.

"Ah." He nodded, then stopped and tilted his head, thinking. "I don't recall."

Kris rubbed between her eyes. "Eye color?"

"I didn't see."

Dougal would never make it as a cop. Luckily, he didn't have to.

"You know him?"

They'd reached the shore of the loch and taken a seat on a conveniently placed bench.

Kris wasn't sure what to say. Dougal's description was worthless. It both matched and did not the guy she'd seen at The Clansman. Someone she thought she might know, and then again she might not.

"I'm not sure. If he comes by again, ask his name."

"I should have before. Sorry."

"It's probably nothing." And it probably was. Still, the whole thing made her squirrelly.

Kris rested her video camera in her lap. They sat side by side, watching the loch, waiting for something that wasn't going to come. Usually she was no good at waiting; she'd forever been impatient. Always on the go to anywhere but here, always searching for the next story or more information about this one.

Which reminded her . . .

"In your museum, you have an unfinished section."

Dougal nodded, still staring at the loch. " 'Supernatural Myths of Scotland.' I've studied a lot of legends from all over the world, but they're my favorite."

"But you don't believe in the supernatural."

"Doesn't matter what I believe. It matters what I can sell to those who do."

His cynical attitude should be grating; however, considering it mirrored her own, Kris couldn't throw stones. Besides, his being a skeptic didn't keep him from being the best-informed source of legendary info on Scotland— now that Edward was gone. Dougal was using the public's gullibility to make a buck; he wouldn't mind Kris picking his brain for the same reason.

"Why don't you sell me?" Kris murmured.

His lips quirked—he knew she couldn't be sold; still, he humored her. "One of the most interesting tales I've found is the wulver—a Scottish werewolf."

Kris straightened. Nearly everything she'd read about Mandenauer involved werewolves.

"Body of a man covered in brown hair, head of a wolf."

Kris resisted the urge to say *Ew!*, because really, it went without saying.

"How do you kill it?" she asked.

"Kill it?" Dougal repeated, expression mystified. "Why? The wulver is benign."

"The wulver isn't real," Kris pointed out. "But if it were, I doubt any werewolf is benign."

Dougal shrugged. "In the legends, wulvers kept to themselves. Except when they were leaving fish on the windowsills of the poor."

A Robin Hood werewolf? *Right.*

"What else you got?" Kris wanted to hear about the Scottish legends that might have led to the tale of Nessie. She'd discovered that hoaxers often followed local legends. Perhaps to more easily convince the residents that the hoax was the truth or perhaps because they had no imaginations of their own.

"The Ceirean. Sea monster so large it ate seven whales."

That had possibilities.

"The Fear Liath," he continued. "An unseen presence that causes feelings of unease."

Kris glanced over her shoulder, suddenly doused with an increasingly familiar sense of unease.

Dougal laughed. "Not real, remember? Besides, the Fear Liath haunts the mountains, not the seas."

"What are those?" Kris indicated the towering hills.

"Good point. I'd considered leaving that one out of the display, but maybe I won't. One of the main sections will be myths and legends that could actually be Nessie."

Bingo! Kris thought, and leaned in.

"The kelpie has always been a front-runner," Dougal continued, warming to his subject. "Here they call it Each-Uisge, a supernatural water horse. Transforms into a human and walks upon the earth. Lures the unsuspecting into the water, where they drown."

"Nessie's not a horse." Although there had been several reports of the monster with a mane.

"Neither is a water horse. They're massive. With tails that resemble the tail of a snake instead of horse and much shorter legs."

"What about a *guivre*?"

Dougal considered this, brow furrowing. "A *guivre* is a French myth. Dragon-like creature that prowled medieval France. I've seen drawings. It resembles Nessie, except for the wings and breathing fire." He sat up straighter, too. "They have horns, which a lot of Nessie sightings describe."

"And which most experts have pointed out resemble the autumn horns of a red deer."

"Aye," Dougal said absently, Foghorn Leghorn resemblance firmly in place. "But they inhabit bodies of water and Scotland is a short trip from France."

"Especially if you have wings," Kris pointed out.

Dougal glanced at her, amusement brimming in his lovely gray eyes. It felt so good to be able to say what she thought instead of prevaricating so she wouldn't have to lie.

"*Guivres* are said to be very aggressive," he continued. "They attack humans."

"And if they were real," Kris said, "I'd be worried."

His amusement deepened. "I just meant that I wasn't sure if I should add the *guivre* to my display on possible legends that created Nessie. She isn't violent." His gaze returned to the loch, where the water remained as smooth as glass.

"See anything?"

When Dougal didn't answer, Kris turned to look at him and he kissed her.

As kisses went, it wasn't half-bad. His lips were firm but soft. His goatee tickled just a bit. Kris didn't pull away, curious if perhaps the air in Scotland, or the water, would make her react to any kiss the way she'd reacted to Liam Grant's.

No such luck. While the kiss was pleasant, it left her uninterested in anything more. She certainly wasn't possessed by the urge to get naked with Dougal right here and now.

Should she be glad about that or sad?

A huge splash erupted, as if something had been dropped into the water. Like a piano.

Or a very large tail.

Kris and Dougal broke apart, Kris reaching for her camera as both of them glanced toward the loch.

But nothing was there.

CHAPTER 9

"Sorry about that," Dougal said again as he dropped off Kris in front of her cottage. "It was just the . . ." He waved his hand toward the loch, where the moon reflected brilliant silver across a gently rolling surface.

"Don't worry about it." Kris got out of the car, lifting her hand when Dougal would have followed. "As kisses go, it was nice."

He winced. "Nice isn't exactly what a guy's hoping for."

"Better than disgusting."

Dougal laughed, and she felt better. She'd been afraid his kissing her, and her letting him, had ruined the friendship. And she wanted this friendship. She needed someone else in this Nessie-nuts town whom she could talk to.

"No harm, no foul," Kris continued. "Thanks for taking me to The Clansman, and thanks for the fantastic meal."

"You paid for your own."

"But I wouldn't have known about the place if not for you. Too bad we didn't see Nessie."

Dougal snorted, waved, then pulled away.

His car negotiated the bend and disappeared. Strange,

but the rumble of the motor seemed to disappear, too. Sounds behaved differently here. Must have something to do with the mountains, the water, the atmosphere. Who knew?

Kris found her gaze drawn to the loch. It *was* too bad they hadn't seen Nessie. If Kris was going to figure out this hoax, she needed to get a glimpse of the monster—or whatever was being used to depict the monster. How could she ever uncover the truth unless she saw with her own eyes the lie?

The night was still except for the lap of the loch and some small animal–type rustles from the distant trees. Up on the hill, a pebble rolled slowly downward. Nothing to be alarmed about.

So why was she suddenly alarmed?

Because that feeling was back—the one where she just knew she was being watched.

But the trees, the road, the loch, the cottage continued to loom empty and dark. All was silent; there was only a hint of a breeze.

Kris began to turn, and pain exploded, right before the entire world faded to black.

Kris swam toward consciousness. The closer she got, the more her head hurt. The *swoosh* of the waves made her nauseous. And there was something about those waves she needed to remember. Something disturbing.

It came to her in a burst of clarity so bright she winced as if lightning had flashed directly in front of her wide-open eyes. She'd been conked on the head, and now she was being carried.

To the water.

Kris struggled. Whoever was carrying her stopped walking; the arms that held her tightened, and everything twirled sickeningly. Her eyes popped open, and she stared directly into the face of Liam Grant.

"How's yer head?" he asked.

Kris turned to the right and saw her cottage. She glanced over his shoulder and saw the loch. Had he been carrying her *to* the house all along? She was too dizzy to be sure.

"What happened?" she asked.

"I was out for a walk, and I saw someone draggin' ye to the water."

"Someone?"

He gave her a strange look. "Aye. Did ye think it might be some*thing*?"

She shook her head, then had to concentrate on not puking when the pain shrieked for her to do just that. "Hush," she murmured.

"I didnae say anything," Liam whispered, and began to move again.

She laid her cheek against his shoulder and closed her eyes. He smelled like freshwater and moonlight. Or maybe that was just the freshwater and moonlight.

"Your hair is wet," she said.

"Yers, too."

Kris reached up. So it was.

"Ye were very near the water." He kept his voice low and the rumble in his chest combined with the chill of the night and the dampness on her skin made Kris shiver. He pulled her closer, but still she couldn't get warm. "Ye fought when I picked ye up. I cannae say that I blame ye."

They reached the cottage, and Liam set Kris on her feet, though he kept his arm around her waist. Kris was grateful for the support. Her hands were twitching like a meth addict's. He had to lay his on top of hers so that she could unlock the door.

She was cold, but he was colder. Once inside, Kris tried to walk to the bedroom and retrieve blankets, but she only made it as far as the couch before she had to sit down.

Liam moved fast, yanking the quilt off the bed and covering her with it.

"Th-th-there are more in the closet." Her chattering teeth barely missed clipping off her tongue.

"I'm all right," he said.

And while Liam's skin had been chilled, it wasn't covered in goose bumps, like hers. He wasn't shivering. Which was amazing considering he didn't have a jacket and his arms were bared by his smoke-colored T-shirt.

"Your h-h-hands are l-like ice."

He glanced at them, then shoved them behind his back. "Family curse." He shrugged. "I've had my share of women tell me I'm a cold-blooded bastard."

Kris frowned. He didn't seem cold-blooded at all. He'd just saved her life.

"C-c-cold hands, warm h-heart," she said.

"I believe one or two have mentioned that I dinnae have a heart."

Kris wasn't sure how to respond. He seemed determined to paint himself in a bad light, even though he'd just risked his health, if not his life, rescuing her from—

Who?

"Tea," Liam blurted, heading for the kitchenette.

"I don't—," Kris began.

"Ye do," he interrupted. "And so do I."

They remained silent while Liam put on the kettle, then searched out the tea and cups. Had she ever seen a man half as beautiful? Why was he hiding in Drumnadrochit? He could earn hundreds with that face alone.

Her gaze wandered over the taut pecs, honed biceps, and flat belly. The body would net him thousands.

Then again, was making a living with your appearance all it was cracked up to be? Constant diets, facials, workouts, highlights. Being told what to do, what to wear, what to eat, and what not to.

Kris was small potatoes in the TV arena, but sometimes she became heartily sick of it all. Maybe Liam had the right idea. At least he was happy here.

Or maybe not. His shoulders slumped; his head, too. His expression was as far from happy as she'd yet to see. She had to wonder what lay in his past that haunted him.

He approached with two mugs of steaming tea and handed her one. Kris took it, immediately grateful he'd insisted as the heat from the cup thawed her aching fingers and the steam from the tea did the same for her stinging cheeks.

"Drink." Liam urged the mug to her lips. "'Twill stop the shivers."

She drank, and in a few moments he was proved right. When she looked at him again, he stared out the window at the loch, a frown marring his perfect face.

"Did you see who hit me?" she asked.

His sapphire blue eyes cut back to hers. "I couldnae say."

"Couldnae? Or wouldnae?"

"Ye think I'm protecting a murderer?"

"I'm not dead," she pointed out.

"Ye would have been."

"You're sure?"

"Aye," he said, and glanced out the window again.

"You didn't recognize him?"

"I didnae see him." He growled low with annoyance. "Hell, with the dark and the mist, it could have been a her."

"What mist?" Kris asked.

He flipped his fingers toward the loch. "It comes and it goes."

She'd seen that already for herself.

"Ye'll have t' report this to the authorities," he said.

"Right." Kris began to get up.

"Not now."

"But—"

"Whoever attacked ye is gone. Won't do any good fer Alan Mac to be out here in the dark. Time enough to tell him tomorrow."

Since she wanted nothing less than to leave her house and walk into the village—she wasn't even sure she could—Kris decided Liam's advice was sound. Even though it wasn't.

"What about evidence?" she asked, but her eyes were so heavy she could barely keep them open.

"Shyte!" he muttered, the Scottish twist to the curse making her smile. "Well, there's naught to be done. Ye cannae walk all that way, and I cannae carry ye. Ye don't have a phone?" She shook her head, then groaned at the return of the pain. "How about some medicine? Fer yer head," he clarified when she frowned, confused.

"Aspirin. In the bathroom."

He returned with the pills and a glass of water. As soon as she took them, he held out his hand. She put the empty glass into it, and his lips twitched. He set the glass on the coffee table, then caught her hand. "T' bed with ye," he said.

Kris suddenly became aware of the small cottage and the even smaller space between her and Liam Grant.

The space shrunk when he pulled her upright, and she stumbled into him. "Sorry." Her balance had gone to shyte.

He murmured nonsense that was really quite soothing as he helped her into her room.

"Am I *supposed* to go to bed?" She sat on the side, kicked off her shoes. As they hit the ground, dried mud broke off, crackling against the floor like sleet on a roof.

"Mo chridhe," he murmured, putting a hand to her shoulder and pushing her onto the mattress. "Ye were made for bed."

Kris blinked. God, he was so sexy. Every word he spoke rippled along her skin like a caress; every caress shot through her like a . . . shot.

She laughed, and he straightened, pulling away. He'd probably never had that reaction in the bedroom before.

Kris cleared her throat. "I meant, if I have a concussion I might . . ." She paused, trying to remember what she'd been about to say. He was so close; he smelled so good. And he was so damn pretty.

"You might . . . ?" he encouraged.

"Fall down and I can't get up."

Leaning over, he kissed her brow. "I won't let ye fall."

Despite the chill of his hands, his lips were warm, and she wanted them to stay right where they were. Or perhaps move about a bit.

The giggle threatened again. She *must* have a concussion. Kris did *not* giggle. Not only was it unprofessional, but she'd rarely found anything in this world worth giggling about.

"I might fall asleep," she clarified, "and never wake up."

She was falling asleep now; she couldn't seem to stop.

Right before everything fell away, he kissed her lips like that infernal prince in every fairy tale and whispered, "I'll kiss ye awake every few hours, aye?"

"Aye," she breathed, and wondered—

When she woke up would she no longer be a frog?

* * *

Liam watched Kris slip into sleep. Her hair, splashed by her struggles, had begun to dry in tangled hanks, and the freckles on her nose that had so captivated him shone stark against the unnatural paleness of her skin. A smudge of mud slashed her cheek like a wound.

Fury sparked, and he had to clench his hands to keep from breaking something.

How dare anyone touch her. She is mine!

Although perhaps that was why.

Liam left the room, shutting the door only partway in case she should need him. He'd stay here all night. He'd wake her as he'd promised. He wouldn't leave until he had to.

He was the protector of the loch. By day and by night, Liam watched over it. Those who had gone into the water and not come out . . . they were on his head. That Kris had nearly been one of them—

He could not bear it.

Was it coincidence that the first woman he'd touched in ages had nearly died tonight? He didn't think so.

Someone was drowning people. He didn't know who any more than Alan Mac did. But it wasn't Nessie.

Liam gave a short, sharp laugh.

That was the only thing he was certain of.

Kris awoke as the gray light of approaching dawn filtered into her room. Her first thought was that she was happy. Then she stretched, winced, and remembered.

She'd been attacked last night, and if Liam were to be believed, she would have been drowned.

Liam.

Kris smiled, understanding the reason for the wash of happiness, even though she should be anything but.

He'd stayed all night. He'd woken her every few hours with a kiss—just as he'd promised.

Of course they'd been chaste kisses on her brow, her cheek, once on her hand. But when she opened her eyes and saw that face . . .

What a way to wake up.

Kris lifted herself, bracing for the pain she expected to shoot through her head. Nothing happened—in her head.

Her back, shoulders, neck, legs, and arms were another story. She felt like she'd been beaten with a bat. Getting conked on the noggin and falling to the ground like a box of rocks must have that effect.

"Shower," she muttered, levering herself to her feet—which also hurt, by the way. "Then coffee. *Mucho* coffee."

Hoping Liam had started a pot, she sniffed the air, but all she smelled was herself—lake water, fear-sweat, a little mud, and . . . was that mold?

"Shower," she repeated more firmly, then as she opened the door to her bedroom, "Liam, could you—?"

Kris stood in the doorway, staring at the empty living area, then glanced at the bathroom, but the door was open and no one was there, either.

Had Liam ever been here at all?

Kris laughed, but the sound was brittle and she stopped right away because she was scaring herself. Just because no one had seen Liam but her, no one seemed to know him but her, didn't mean—

"What?" That she was the only one who *could* see him?

She rubbed her forehead, then reached up and gingerly touched the knot on her temple. Someone had hit her. They'd dragged her to the loch with intent to drown her. Then Liam Grant had saved her. Unless—

"I fell, hit my head, wandered around, tripped into the loch, crawled back here, and hallucinated everything?" She took a deep breath, let it out slowly. "Yeah, sounds like BS to me, too."

Then she spied two cups on the counter and nearly hooted in relief. Until she realized . . .

In her delusion, she could easily have made two cups of tea—one for herself and one for her imaginary friend.

"There has to be something." She peered around the room. Something that would prove to her, and anyone else who asked, that Liam Grant was a real-live boy.

She found nothing.

Determined, Kris opened the door and stepped outside, searching for footprints. Unfortunately, the area around her cottage was too dry. She'd just have to check down by the—

Kris lifted her head and froze just as a tour bus pulled up and belched tourists all over the place. If there'd been any footprints near the loch, any signs of a body being dragged or a struggle, they were soon gone.

A ripple went through the crowd. "Look!" someone shouted; then they were all crowding at the edge, snapping pictures of the same thing. Kris hoped to hell it wasn't another body.

When she at last crossed the road—there was a lot of traffic for so early in the morning—the tourists had lost interest and wandered down the shore. Kris didn't see anything that might have caused so much excitement.

She was headed for the house when a sharp splash drew her around. A small, dark *something* now protruded from the water about a hundred feet away. It seemed like a head-shaped rock, with a hollow well where the eye would be. The sun struck that well just so, making it glitter and appear to move.

When Kris sidestepped right, the shiny "eye" followed. She hustled left and left it went.

"No wonder everyone around here believes in Nessie," she muttered. The loch was so damned weird.

Kris returned to the cottage and discovered her backpack, which she must have dropped in the struggle last night, sitting next to the front door. She peered inside; her camera was still there and apparently unharmed. By the time she glanced again at the loch, the rock was as gone as Liam.

Hell, maybe it hadn't been there, either.

CHAPTER 10

After a long, hot shower that eased the worst of her aches, Kris quickly checked her e-mail and discovered among the usual advertisements to either enlarge a penis she didn't have or buy drugs she didn't want a message from Lola.

NO ONE'S CALLED. NO ONE'S BEEN BY.

Kris wasn't sure if she should be glad about that or not. She'd like an explanation. Then again, having someone ask for her in Chicago, then show up here . . .

Pretty damn creepy.

Most likely the questions around the village had been innocent. Probably a closet writer who wanted to discover how to get published and figured that Kris knew the secret handshake. She heard that happened all the time.

Although after the attack last night, she shouldn't take any chances.

Kris walked toward Drumnadrochit. She would tell her story to Alan Mac, then let the constable deal with it. She would also go to the bank and swap Mandenauer's Franklins for some QE2s.

First she'd stop at Jamaica's. Kris had too many cob-webs on the brain to discuss currency exchanges, myste-rious attacks, and potential drownings without coffee, and this morning she wasn't up to making it herself.

Besides, it was still early. She doubted Alan Mac would be at the station yet and the bank definitely wasn't open, but Jamaica's place had lights in the windows and Kris could smell delicious on the air as soon as she stepped foot on the street.

Inside, the owner once again stood behind the counter. As a businesswoman, Kris understood that often the only way to make a profit was to do everything yourself.

"De usual?" Jamaica asked, tilting a cup back and forth like she was shaking dice.

Kris nodded, liking that she already had a "usual." "I'm a coffee-holic," Kris said. "Comes from a lot of very early mornings at the computer."

"You an early riser?" Jamaica asked as she filled the cup.

"Yeah. I like to get ahead before I even go in to work. My favorite time is before the sun's up."

Kris accepted the coffee, paying for it with her last few pounds. "Can you point me at the closest bank?"

"One block up and another to de left. Can't miss it."

"Thanks. Did you wanna join me?" Kris lifted her cup.

Jamaica glanced around. Locals occupied over half the tables, along with tourists and a few Kris couldn't place in either camp.

"I'd best not. De help shouldn't be seen just sittin' around."

"You're not exactly the help."

"I've always thought 'Do as I say and not as I do' is baloney."

"I'd have to agree."

Jamaica smiled, the tentative friendship they'd begun the first time they'd met deepening.

Then Kris remembered that their last meeting had ended abruptly when she'd questioned Jamaica about Liam. The woman had behaved strangely, although around here everyone did. Kris wouldn't hold it against her.

"I went to The Clansman for dinner last night," Kris said, hoping to keep the conversation alive.

"With dat nice young man who be lookin' for you?"

Kris jerked and slopped hot coffee over the edge of her cup. Hissing, she put it down, then mopped her fingers with the napkins Jamaica tossed her way.

The woman came around the countertop, snatching Kris's hand, peering close. "Come on," she said, and tugged Kris into the back room. "I have some ointment."

The area was a tumble of files and invoices covering a desk with an open laptop. Several bags of coffee lay scattered around in various stages of being packed into boxes.

"I started a Web site," Jamaica explained. "Now I can ship my coffee anywhere in de world."

She really was quite the businesswoman. Kris was impressed.

Jamaica shoved her into a chair. Kris landed on a bag, and the plastic went *oof*. Coffee beans spilled onto the floor.

Both she and Jamaica exclaimed, "Shyte!" at the exact same time; then together they laughed.

"It's a good word," Kris said.

"I like it." Jamaica smoothed a light green gel onto Kris's thumb and the meaty part of her hand just below it. The slight sting immediately disappeared.

"You should sell *that* on the Internet," Kris said. "What is it?"

"Magic," Jamaica intoned, then waggled her fingers over Kris's hand. "Oooga-booga. All better now."

Kris snorted. "Really, what is it?" She lifted her hand and sniffed. The gel had no scent.

"Secret recipe from my great-grandmamma in Kingston."

Kris lifted a brow.

"If I told you what it was, I'd have t' kill you."

Kris almost said that she'd need to get in line. But Kris really didn't want to have that conversation. However, there was one she did want to have.

"What nice young man?"

Jamaica peered into Kris's face, then at her burn, then into her eyes again. "You don't know him?"

Kris spread her hands. "Hard to say since I have no idea who 'him' is."

"American. 'Bout . . ." Jamaica lifted her hand to indicate a height near six feet. "Not heavy, not thin. Brown hair."

"Streaked?"

"He wore a cap." Jamaica narrowed her eyes as if looking into the past. "Boston Red Sox."

"Dougal did say this guy was from the East Coast."

Jamaica started. "Dougal? Dougal Scott?" Kris nodded. "How you know dat man?"

"I went to his museum, and . . . out for drinks and dinner at The Clansman."

"You dating him?" Jamaica did not appear to approve.

"Just friends." Kris had a bad feeling. "Why? Are you dating him?"

Jamaica laughed. "Dat would not happen."

"You don't think he's attractive? Those light eyes and the dark hair. He's got great hands, and his legs aren't so bad, either."

"If he's so wonderful, why you don't want him?"

Why indeed? Kris didn't plan to elaborate on that.

Instead, she prevaricated. She was getting pretty good at it. "I won't be here long enough to get involved. I'm not going to start something I can't finish."

Jamaica's lips curved. "I bet he finish pretty quick."

This surprised a laugh out of Kris. "You don't like him?"

The other woman shrugged and didn't comment.

There was something else going on here, and Kris really wanted to know what. She liked Dougal. She planned to spend more time with him. Unless there was a good reason she shouldn't.

She kept her gaze steady on Jamaica, waiting, and eventually Jamaica gave in.

"He's new to Drumnadrochit, but he t'inks he should be accepted just like he been here since de Kingdom of de Picts. People in Drumnadrochit dey take a little time to warm up to outsiders. Dey like de tourists fine, but to really be from here you must be here more dan a minute."

"I thought his family lived in the village."

"His grandpapa." She waved a hand as if shooing a lazy fly. "Don't mean nothin'. You must be accepted on your own for who you are and not who you came from."

"Okay," Kris said. Sounded like a good policy to her.

"He just pushy. T'inks he's special. He don't like it dat I'm accepted and he's not. Gets a little angry 'bout it. Me, I t'ink he should just chill."

Kris's lips twitched at the hip comment uttered in an accent as old as these hills, but her amusement died at the idea of Dougal being angry over something so silly. She'd known people who got worked up over things they couldn't control, over imagined slights and foolish desires. They were usually prime candidates for "snapping" and doing something violent.

Uh-oh, she thought, remembering that last night someone had.

But last night she'd been *with* Dougal, watched him drive away toward Drumnadrochit; then very soon after she'd been attacked. He wouldn't have been able to double back that fast, would he? And why bother when he could have killed her anywhere on the road to The Clansman and tossed her into the loch?

"I do not like dis." Concern tightened Jamica's lips and creased her brow.

"I won't go out with him again."

"Dat's not what I mean. Dougal is harmless. What I do not like is a stranger asking for you by name. Here, dere." She lifted both arms and tossed her hands outward. "Apparently everywhere."

Kris had to say she wasn't a fan of that news, either.

"Did you tell him where I lived?"

"He did not ask."

"What *did* he ask?"

Unease filtered over Jamica's face, and Kris felt cold all over again. "If you were happy."

Why did Kris find that more sinister than if he'd asked for directions to her front porch?

Kris hung around, finishing one cup of coffee and then another while she assured Jamica that she'd be careful out there.

"You tell Alan Mac about dis weird happy-man or I will," Jamica insisted.

"All right," Kris agreed, but what would she say? Some guy, whose name she didn't know, who was of average weight and maybe six feet tall, with brown hair and a Bo-Sox cap, was asking about her.

Big whoop.

Since Alan Mac already thought she'd invented one imaginary man, she didn't relish him thinking she'd

dreamed up another. Sure, she could have him talk to Jamaica, and Dougal for that matter, but what had the guy
done? Asked if she was happy. Sure it was freaky, but it
wasn't a crime.

Kris decided to keep the info to herself. She needed
the constable to take last night's attack seriously. It could
very well be a lead to whoever had killed that poor girl
Kris had found near the loch and the other one, too.

Stopping at the bank, Kris exchanged Mandenauer's
money for currency she could use, then moved on to the
police station. Alan Mac stood out front. She might not
have recognized him dressed in street clothes—a jacket,
slacks, and white shirt—if not for the orange hair.

Must be his day off. If chief constables had such things.

Kris would have hurried over, except he was already
talking to someone.

"She was walking home from work last night," the
woman said, her shrill, frightened voice carrying. "From
Drumnadrochit to our place is not so far. She's walked it
a hundred times. And now she's gone. I ken ye found another strange girl, drowned just like the first one."

"Shh." Alan Mac glanced around, saw Kris, who waved,
and winced. "That's not to be bandied aboot, Janet. Ye
know that."

"I don't care about the damn tourists. I want my daughter. So do the McCoys." She tilted her head, her silver-
flecked dark hair sliding across the shoulder of her Fair
Isle sweater. "The Brodies maybe no. That Kelsie of theirs
was a real handful. But I'm sure they'd be happy to know
where she got to. Even if it is dragged to the bottom of the
loch."

"She wasnae dragged to the bottom of the loch," Alan
said.

"And how do you know that, Alan Mac?" The woman

set her fists on her ample hips. "We have five girls missing."

An icy finger traced Kris's neck. This was the first she'd heard of anyone gone missing. Of course Alan Mac appeared to operate on the less-is-less theory of police work. Less information for everyone meant less trouble for him.

"I want that loch searched." Janet put a finger in Alan's face. She had to reach up quite a bit to do it, since Alan Mac towered over her by at least a foot. She didn't seem to care. She'd probably known him since he ran "aboot" in diapers.

"Ye know we cannae," he said.

"Willnae," she corrected.

"She's too big and too deep."

"So ye'll just wait for the bodies to appear?"

"Ye know as well as I, Janet, that the loch never gives up its dead."

"The loch?" she asked. "Or the monster?"

Then she put her nose in the air and walked away with more dignity than Kris would have been able to muster if *her* daughter were missing.

Kris quickly took the space Janet had vacated. "Why does the loch never give up its dead?"

Alan Mac sighed. He seemed tired already, and it wasn't even 9:00 A.M.

"The cold and the peat make everything sink like a stone. The water temperature means the bodies don't bloat and come back up." He shook his head. "If anyone was ever to get a camera down there it'd be a regular boneyard."

The disturbing image of dozens of skeletons dancing in an underwater ballroom filled Kris's head. Where the hell had that come from?

"If the loch never gives up her dead, how do you explain the body I stumbled over yesterday?"

" 'Never' might be a wee bit of an exaggeration," Alan Mac allowed. "Sometimes the bodies get caught on logs or rocks. They might be held close enough to the surface, then they'd drift in. Or someone could find them and not want to be involved. So they leave them on the shore for wandering writer women to trip over."

Kris lifted her brows at the last, but he did have a point. Weird things happened, and around here they seemed to happen a lot.

"You never told me girls were missing."

"Why would I? Did ye take them?"

Kris didn't bother to answer. "I found a body. A *second* body," she clarified, in case he'd forgotten. "And now I hear there are five girls missing. Shouldn't you call—" Kris was going to say *the FBI,* then remembered where she was. "Scotland Yard?"

"We've got no proof any of those didn't just leave on their own. No proof, either, that the dead girls were killed. People drown in Loch Ness all the time."

"All the time?" Kris repeated. "Seriously?"

"Aye. The world is composed of fools."

She couldn't argue with him there.

"They fall either out of a boat," he continued, "or into the drink. Within minutes, at that temperature, the whole body shuts down. Yer done for."

"I have a hard time believing that all these women fell out of boats, or tripped off a cliff and into the loch."

"Stranger things have happened," Alan Mac muttered.

"And what might those be?"

He shook his head as if shaking off memories of those stranger things, then rubbed a hand over his face. "Is there something I can help ye with?"

Kris stared at him for several seconds, but his stoic cop mode was back; the tired man she'd glimpsed, the one who might have told her something worth hearing, was gone.

"I was attacked last night."

"When ye say 'attacked'—," he began.

"Knocked over the head and dragged to the loch." Skepticism filtered into the constable's expression, and Kris lifted her hair away from her temple. "See?"

His gaze narrowed on the goose egg, then shifted back to hers. "Ye better come inside and give me a statement."

"Ye saw no one?" Alan Mac frowned at the sheet of paper on which he'd been taking notes as he asked and she answered questions. "Heard nothing?"

"Until I came to and Liam Grant was there."

The constable looked up, and his frown deepened. "Who?"

Kris decided not to mention that Liam was her imaginary friend. There was only so much she could take, and she'd taken it.

"He said his name was Liam Grant." He just hadn't said it last night.

"I dinnae know a Liam among the Grants of Drumnadrochit. Although . . ." His gaze drifted past her shoulder and upward. "There are some with that name in Dores."

Dougal had said the same thing. Perhaps Kris needed to take a trip to Dores. If she could discover Liam Grant living in an apartment, working a job, doing something normal, out in the world where people, other than her, could see him, she'd feel a helluva lot better.

"What time was this?"

Kris considered. She and Dougal had gone to dinner: then they'd watched the sun set near the loch, talked awhile, and driven back.

"A little after nine o' clock."

"That fits," Alan Mac murmured.

"What fits?"

He glanced at her as if he'd forgotten she was there, and his lips pursed in annoyance. At himself or her Kris wasn't sure and didn't really care.

"Carrie went missing shortly afterward," he said.

"You think whoever conked me and was interrupted trotted down the road and found her?"

He spread his big, hard hands. "As I said, it fits."

Guilt flickered, but Kris shoved it resolutely away. She wasn't at fault here. Whoever was snatching women and drowning them was. *That* person should feel guilty, although he or she wouldn't. Because people who did such things didn't feel.

"The two you've found dead," Kris began, and Alan Mac cast her a quick glance. "Do you know who they were?"

He lowered his gaze to his notes. "Not yet."

"Not local then."

"No."

"What's your next step?" Kris asked.

Alan Mac had removed his jacket and sat at his desk in his shirtsleeves. Understandable. In sharp contrast to the nip in the air outside, inside was stuffy and hot. He leaned forward, placing his elbows on the desk and his head in his hands. "I don't know."

The sleeve on his left arm pulled up. A black line encircled his biceps. It appeared to begin, or perhaps end, much thicker than it ended, or perhaps began, and did not resemble any of the tattoos she'd seen encircling biceps in the states. Those usually had thorns, stars, feathers—his was just a line.

Of course she wasn't in the states and Alan Mac wasn't

an American. She had no idea what was common in Scotland. Perhaps such a line indicated membership in whatever military service they had here.

She very nearly asked, but Alan Mac straightened and his shirt slid back into place. "We'll search," he said. "We *have* searched after every disappearance."

"But you haven't found."

He shook his head. "You've seen the terrain around the loch?"

"Some," Kris agreed. She really needed to see more. But not right now. There were going to be constables all over the place.

"Mountains. Forests. Villages. Roads. It's a searchers' worst nightmare."

"With five potential bodies," Kris began, then paused.

"What?" Alan Mac asked.

"Five have been reported. I'm thinking, since you know about them, that they're local?" Alan Mac nodded. "But you weren't looking for the dead girls, because you didn't know."

"I'm not following."

"You have five locals missing and two dead strangers. What about tourists? Students? Hikers? It could take weeks for people to figure out they've gone missing and where. What if your victims were missing, but you just didn't know it yet?"

Alan Mac groaned. "Yer just a ray of sunshine, aren't ye now?"

Kris shrugged. Truth was truth, and she couldn't help but say it.

"On the bright side," she continued, "I can't see how that many bodies could be hidden regardless of the terrain."

"I doubt anyone's been hidin' anything," he muttered.

"You think they're all in the loch, don't you?"

Alan Mac's eyes met hers, and he nodded.

After that, there wasn't much left to do. Alan Mac said he'd be in touch. Kris said he knew where to find her. He strode off barking names, and officers scurried toward him as if a five-star general—or whatever the equivalent rank in the Highlands—had summoned them.

"Definitely military," Kris muttered. The underlings practically saluted him.

Alan Mac seemed capable. So why then were there so many missing? Why did he seem not to have a clue as to a culprit? And how many more would disappear before this was through?

Kris made one more stop before she returned to Loch Side Cottage. Unfortunately, Dougal wasn't in.

"He's off to . . ." The young girl left in charge of the front door scowled mightily as she tried to remember. "Belgium?"

"Why would he go to Belgium?"

"Maybe it was Bordeaux." She cocked her red head. "Bolivia? Somewhere that starts with a *B*."

Terrific.

"Again I ask 'why?' "

"Ach." The girl waved her hand. "He travels all over the world."

"Because . . . ?"

"I thought ye said ye knew him." The girl put her hands atop the plaid that draped her hips.

"I do."

"Well, if that's the case, then ye'd know he goes on these trips a few times a year. Gotta buy bric-a-brac and the like for the gift shop."

"Isn't the gift shop full of Scottish gifts?"

"Not all of them are made in Scotland, ye ken?" Kris shook her head, and the girl leaned over, lowering her voice. "China."

"The gifts are made in China?"

"Most of the plastic and the toys. Ye think anyone in this country would make inflatable Nessies for a competitive price?"

Probably not.

"He also likes to offer wines of the world in the restaurant," she continued. "He'd never serve anything he hadnae tried first himself."

"When will he be back?" Kris asked.

"Before the weekend. We're too busy for him not to be here then."

"Okay. Thanks."

Kris found it odd that Dougal hadn't told her he was leaving for Belgium.

Or Bordeaux.

Maybe Bolivia.

Then again, they were friends. The kiss and their shared lack of belief in the unbelievable aside, they had barely gotten past the acquaintance stage. Why should he?

She returned to Loch Side Cottage. Several law enforcement officers stared dispiritedly at the tramped-down mud and grass near the loch.

"Good luck with that," Kris muttered, and headed inside.

Had her attacker known there would be a bus arriving with the dawn, the footprints of the tourists obliterating any and all evidence? Seemed far-fetched, but what didn't these days?

Once in the front door, Kris paused. Something wasn't right.

She scanned the room. Everything appeared to be where she thought she'd left it.

Maybe.

This wasn't her house. Had that lamp been so near the edge of that table? Had she neglected to close the cabinet over the sink? Or was it one of those that popped open by itself?

The doors to both her bedroom and the bath were flung wide. No one in there that she could see. Of course why would she see them? Anyone in her cottage when she wasn't would not want to be seen.

Kris slid toward the outer door. She'd fling it open, call the police. They'd come running and take care of everything. If there was anything to take care of.

And if there wasn't?

The idea of those officers looking at her with the same expression that had been on Alan Mac's face when he believed she'd imagined the man in Urquhart Castle had her rethinking her plan. Death or embarrassment? Maybe she could compromise.

Kris opened the outer door, just in case she wasn't crazy and she did need to shout for help; then she marched to her room, peered in the closet and under the bed, with a side trip to the bathroom, where she peeked behind the shower curtain.

She felt very foolish when she found nothing. Although not half as foolish as she'd have felt if she'd had the constables in here doing the same thing.

Kris shut the door, then sat on the couch. She had to admit, she was spooked.

But maybe that was okay. Better to be overcautious than floating at the bottom of the loch.

Kris glanced at the computer.

Then she clapped her hands over her mouth to keep from shrieking.

CHAPTER 11

"What have you discovered?" Edward Mandenauer asked.

Kris scrambled over the back of the couch. "How did you get in there?"

"Irrelevant." He waved the question away as if it were a pesky fly, the movement of his monkey's paw hand causing Kris's head to shift back and forth as though she were watching a tennis match. Right now, she really wished she *were* watching a tennis match.

In Prague.

"No, really," she said. "How are you doing that?"

He could have hacked her Skype. But the old man's image wasn't in a Skype window. He filled the entire screen like wallpaper. Not to mention that up here Skype didn't work.

Mandenauer squinted at her from wherever the hell he was. Where she stood, it looked like an abandoned bunker.

"I told you before. The *Jäger-Suchers* are well funded," Mandenauer answered. "We can get 'in' wherever we like."

Kris felt a trickle of unease. An all-knowing, all-seeing, all-powerful agency? Usually meant trouble.

"I have connections," the old man continued. "The tools necessary to do all sorts of things are made available to me and my people first. We try them in the field. If we live, we get to keep them."

Kris frowned. If they *lived*?

"Now." He brushed his hands together. "Your turn."

She told him about the missing girls.

"Strange," Edward murmured, his frown causing his already-creased face to crease further.

"How so?"

"You do not think it's strange there are nearly half a dozen women missing from such a small area?"

"Freaky, yes. Strange? Sadly no. Once a killer gets a taste, they keep on tasting."

"Exactly. Monsters by their very nature are evil. They like to kill, and they do not stop until we make them."

Kris opened her mouth to mention yet again that there was *no monster,* then decided *why?*

"*How* do we make them?"

"By discovering what type of monster it is. Once we know that, we will know how to kill the beast. I must check a few books, ask a few questions. I will get back to you. In the meantime, be careful. If he, or she . . ." He paused. "Well, for the sake of expediency we will use 'he.' If he discovers you are on to him, he will—"

Kris straightened, her fingers going to the knot on her temple concealed by her hair. "Bonk me over the head and try to drown me?"

"Yes." Mandenauer's lips tightened as Kris continued to rub her head. "Let me guess. He already did?"

She'd figured the local killer had been behind the attack last night. What she *hadn't* figured was that she was anything more than a random target, and thus the culprit probably wouldn't be back, since she was now on the alert. However, if he'd been after her to begin with that put a whole new twist on things.

"Shyte," she muttered. "I'm gonna need a gun."

"There's a drawer in that table."

Kris tilted her head, narrowing her gaze before opening the drawer. She wasn't surprised to see just what she'd asked for—a bright and shiny new gun.

"I suppose this was beamed from there to here with some sort of *Star Trek* technology." She couldn't take her eyes off the thing. "Or maybe there's a wormhole." She snapped her fingers. "A hologram?"

"Are you through?" Edward asked.

"How'd it get here?"

"I put it there," he said.

"Time travel," she muttered.

He peered down his nose at her. "Now you are just being silly."

Kris reached for the gun.

"It is loaded with silver."

She pulled back as if burned. "Are you serious?"

"When discussing silver, always."

"Why silver?" she asked, even though she just knew the answer would reignite her headache.

"When in doubt," Mandenauer murmured, "silver wins out."

"Put it on a T-shirt, old man. Why is this gun loaded with silver bullets?"

"Because any other type would be the same as none at all."

Yep, her headache came roaring back.

Mandenauer must have seen she'd reached the end of

what had been, until she'd met him, a much longer rope. "Silver works on most shape-shifters."

"Shape . . . ," Kris began, and then: "What?"

"Do you have a better idea?"

"Than shape-shifter? Damn straight. Se-ri-al kill-er," she said, enunciating every syllable.

"You say serial killer. I say shape-shifter. Tomato. Tomahto," he replied.

"You're crazy."

"You won't be saying that when you shoot your attacker with silver and flames burst from the wound."

Kris blinked. Then she blinked again. Then she glanced at the gun in the drawer and back at Mandenauer. "Seriously?"

"When am I ever *not* serious?"

Kris shut the drawer. The gun slid across the bottom and smacked against the rear. She winced, hoping it wouldn't go off and kill her. A silver bullet was still a bullet and, she assumed, worked pretty much the same way as lead.

"I've never used a gun," she admitted. "I'm not sure I can."

"What is so hard?" Mandenauer lifted one bony shoulder. "You point the long end at what you want to shoot and pull the trigger."

Something she'd already thought for herself. But that had been before she'd actually *had* a gun. Now that she'd held the weapon in her hand she wasn't sure it was all that easy.

Mandenauer must have seen the indecision on her face, because he continued. "Usually these things get very close, and when there are teeth, and claws, and death snapping at you, you will shoot."

Maybe she would, but— "I can't carry a gun everywhere."

"I do."

"How do you get away with that?" she asked. "The whole world isn't Texas."

"More's the pity," Edward murmured. "But I have—"

"Connections," she finished.

"If you are uncomfortable with the gun, there is a silver knife, too." Edward pointed downward at the drawer.

Kris jerked on the handle again. The gun slid forward. So did a knife.

She scowled at Mandenauer. "That was *not* there before."

"Listen to what you are saying."

She did, and she had to agree. She'd hopped the express train to Crazyville. Where they loaded their guns with silver bullets and went hunting for serial-killing shape-shifters.

Was that redundant? Kris shut the drawer.

"Start with the village," Mandenauer said. "A monster could not exist undetected this long without someone, or several someones, protecting it."

"You think Nessie is the killer?" Kris couldn't believe those words had actually left her mouth.

"So far we have two deaths by drowning in a loch where the most famous lake monster in the world lives. What is it that you youngsters like to say?" He put a finger to his temple, then flicked it away. "Ah, yes. You do the math."

"I don't believe Nessie exists. Which really screws up your equation."

"Here is the truth: Either Nessie is killing people or someone wants us to think that she is and then kill her."

"Why?"

"Discover that and you will discover all you need to know."

Mandenaeur was probably right. Just because Kris didn't think the culprit in this case was an ancient water-logged dinosaur didn't mean there wasn't something— *someone*—else out there behaving like a monster and laying the blame on the shores of Loch Ness. If she discovered who was behind the new hoax, she'd have either the perpetrator of the whole hoax or someone who could possibly lead Kris to him.

"Why would Nessie suddenly start to kill people?" Kris asked.

Mandenauer's lips twitched. "I thought you did not believe in Nessie."

"I don't. But won't those who do believe, like you, wonder what the hell?"

"My dear," he murmured, "I always wonder 'what the hell?' "

"It just makes no sense for a lake monster that has, up until now, never hurt anyone—"

"That is not true."

Kris tensed. "What do you mean?"

"The first sighting of the Loch Ness Monster was by Saint Columba, who came along the river Ness and spied a funeral. He was told that the man being buried had been mauled by the water beast. The good Irish priest then sent one of his underlings into the water, where he was promptly attacked by said beast."

"Nice guy."

"He proved his point."

"Which was?"

"God is great. Columba called upon God to banish the beast, and the beast was banished."

"You believe a mere man could call off a monster?"

"He was not a mere man but a saint."

"Not then."

"Men, and women, become saints because of what they do when they are not saints."

"Is there a point in this?" Kris asked.

"The point is that Nessie *has* attacked before."

"Fifteen hundred years ago!"

"Perhaps being seen that one time was enough to make her more careful in the future."

"And perhaps this is all hooey," Kris muttered.

"Perhaps," Mandenauer agreed.

"If she's been drowning people for centuries without anyone the wiser, why is everything falling apart now?"

"Yes, why?"

Kris's eye began to throb, and she lifted her hand to rub at the ache. "Just tell me what you think."

"Either someone's been protecting her—"

Kris dropped her arm. "While she murders people?"

"You would not believe what some will do because of a tradition, a vow, or for money."

Actually, she would.

"Perhaps she has killed someone recently," Mandenauer continued, "or done something else, that has made someone very angry. And while he, or she, cannot throw Nessie to the wolves—*us*—outright for reasons we do not know yet, this person plans to make sure she is blamed for whatever is rotten in Loch Ness."

"She," Kris repeated. "When we talk about Nessie, we automatically use the feminine pronoun. But when we're talking about the killer, we slip into 'he.'"

"And?"

"Are we looking for a woman or a man?"

"Traditionally serial killers are men."

"Middle-aged white men who are the best damn neighbors in the whole world," Kris muttered, and caught the twitch of Mandenauer's mouth once more before he controlled it.

"In the realm of the supernatural most beings kill without compunction. Male. Female. Something in between."

"In between?" Kris's lip curled.

"We are talking monsters, beasts, things that go bump in the night and the day. Many are not bound by gender. Some have none; some have both."

"I don't know what that means."

"Shape-shifters shift shape." Mandenauer spread his hands. "They could be anything."

"Fabulous," Kris muttered. "How is it that you've been coming here for years and you still haven't caught the culprit?"

"It is not a 'culprit.'" Mandenauer's voice had gone soft, but his gaze bored into hers. "The word hints at choice, and a monster has none. It kills. Period. If the beast we are searching for is not in the loch, it is wandering these hills or those streets. You will need to end it before it ends you."

"This is crazy." Kris's voice wavered. "I can't just shoot someone because I *think* they're a supernatural serial killer."

Mandenauer shrugged. "So prove they are, *then* shoot them."

"And how do I do that?"

"If silver will kill them, it will also burn them."

"I should prick anyone I suspect with a knife just to see if they fry?" Kris shoved her hair out of her face. "I am *so* gonna wind up behind bars."

"Not if you touch them with the Celtic cross instead of a knife."

"Celtic cross?" she repeated.

"Since it is basically a type of crucifix, the Celtic cross will work on vampires, too."

Kris let her head fall between her shoulders. "Go away," she murmured. "Just . . . go away."

When she looked up, the computer screen was blue. Kris glanced at the clock. Nearly noon. Though it had felt like a few minutes, over an hour had passed while she talked to him. Not that she had anywhere to go, but she hadn't done much work since she'd arrived and she really needed to.

While earlier she had decided to stay out of the forest and hills surrounding the loch while the constables searched for Carrie, maybe now *would* be the perfect time to go into them. At least she wouldn't be alone.

Kris retrieved her video camera, but as she headed for the door she glanced at the coffee table. Should she really go anywhere without the gun? Although taking a gun around a lot of cops . . . probably a bad idea.

"Ya think?" she muttered. "The knife isn't the best choice, either."

However, she might be able to talk her way out of jail if she was found in the woods with a knife. She could be using it to take samples of . . .

"Trees. Leaves. Branches." Wow. She was lying like a pro these days.

Kris crossed the short distance and opened the drawer. Then she just stared at the items that slid into view.

A gun. A knife.

And a silver Celtic cross on a chain.

Liam watched Kris leave the cottage and head down the road at a brisk pace. She carried a small backpack and appeared like a woman on a mission.

He slid out of sight and made his way to where Alan Mac awaited.

The eastern shore saw far fewer people than the western. The terrain was rougher, the trees thicker, and therefore the loch not as easily seen or reached. It discouraged all but the most competent outdoorsmen.

"We've got trouble, ye ken?"

Liam didn't answer what hadn't really been a question. He knew they had trouble. What he didn't know was what they were going to do about it.

"There are women disappearing all over the damn loch," Alan Mac muttered. "We might have been able to keep this quiet a bit longer. But then that writer woman found a body."

Liam thought that if it hadn't been her, it would only have been someone else.

"Ye should stay away from her."

Alan Mac was beginning to repeat himself.

"She might be a *Jäger-Sucher*." Liam snorted, and the constable's gaze flicked to his. "She's up to something. And she's too nosy by half."

Liam lifted his head; Alan Mac lifted his palm as if to halt any comment. "I know. She was attacked, has a big knot on the head, nearly wound up in the loch with—" Alan Mac's gaze flicked to Liam's, and he sighed. "If she were one of Mandenauer's people, she'd be fine and whoever is doing this would be in pieces."

Liam nodded thoughtfully. Alan Mac was right.

The man scrubbed at his fiery hair in frustration. "There's just . . . something about her."

Liam had to agree. He wished he knew what it was.

Suddenly Alan Mac cursed. Liam followed his gaze to where Kris Daniels had appeared, video camera in hand and trained on the water.

Both Alan and Liam slipped out of sight.

* * *

Kris had tossed the chain that held the Celtic cross over her neck, concealing the icon beneath her sweater. She wasn't sure how much good it would do. Didn't amulets and the like need a wearer's belief in them to actually work?

Kris blew a derisive breath between her lips. Right. An amulet would keep her safe. *Sure. Uh-huh.*

She picked up the knife. She definitely knew *this* would work.

Kris headed south, past Urquhart Castle, following the path of A82, which skirted the loch on one side and brushed against trees on the other. She didn't run into any of Alan Mac's men. When she pulled out her binoculars and peered across the loch, she saw why.

They were all over there.

Well, if anyone had anything to hide, that's where they'd hide it. In the wild, craggy, heavily wooded, mountainous expanse to the east.

However, Kris didn't think they were going to find anything.

She turned her gaze to the murky, swirling waters of Loch Ness. Why leave a body over there when you could simply toss it in here? Some might wash up, but the majority did not.

Kris lifted her camera, filmed a bit of the far shore. It would make good background for the show. Much more foreboding than this side, which was full of tourists and restaurants and castles with cafés.

Something shimmied at the corner of her viewfinder, and Kris shifted the camera a bit. Then she lowered the thing just enough so she could see over the top.

Shadows capered at the edge of the forest and across the surface of the water, chasing one another to and fro. She glanced up. Clouds were moving in. She should probably head back before both she and her video camera got wet. Except—

Her gaze caught on an overlook. If she climbed up there, she could take better footage of the opposite shore.

Minutes later, Kris scrambled to the top of a pretty steep trail and onto a finger of land that jutted out farther and higher than any other in the area. As she had suspected, the view was spectacular.

Kris panned the shore, the water, the trees. At the bottom of the viewfinder, something big and dark slid leisurely from right to left in the water.

Bump-bum.

Had that been her heart? Or the theme from *Jaws*? Was her heart thumping the theme from *Jaws*?

"Stop that," she ordered as she continued to film the large, whale-like shadow gliding just beneath the murky surface.

It disappeared of course. She got no more than ten seconds on film.

Kris again contemplated the sky. Those clouds that had been approaching were here, hovering above the loch, easily reflected in it. She was certain that when she examined the film more closely all she would see would be—

"Big clouds. Bump-bum. Bump-bum." She started to laugh, then saw the flicker in the woods.

Her camera was up and filming again before she even realized what she was doing. Kris adjusted the focus, zoomed in.

Was that a person?

Excitement made Kris's hands want to shake, but she refused to let them. This was it! She was going to have film of whoever had been hoaxing the hell out of people. If she was lucky she'd be able to enhance the water footage and reveal just what they'd done to make it look like there was a big black blob of a monster swimming down there.

Excited, Kris leaned forward, still filming, and suddenly—

She was airborne.

CHAPTER 12

Kris woke on the shore. Cold. Aching. Scared.

But alive.

She wasn't on just any shore, either, but the expanse directly in front of Loch Side Cottage. There was no way she'd gotten here on her own.

The sun had set. The clouds blocked any prayer of a moon.

A car swished by but didn't stop. No one could see her lying on the bank like a dead fish. She didn't want them to.

A twig snapped to her right. Kris jerked in that direction, and every muscle in her shoulders shrieked. Her eyes strained against the night, but she could see nothing beyond the looming curve of the trees.

A sharp, heavy splash had Kris scrambling several feet up the bank before collapsing. She forced herself to glance over her shoulder. The loch gleamed like a sheet of black onyx—smooth and impenetrable—all the way to the distant shore. Kris was as alone as she'd thought she'd been on that overhang. Before someone had pushed her in.

Hadn't they?

"Yes," she whispered, scaring herself with how scared she sounded.

She had not leaned over that far. She had not been *that* close to the edge. She'd been off balance, distracted, then one little shove and down, down, down, until she plunged beneath the surface.

She'd come up once, and she could have sworn she'd seen someone watching her struggle and flail and eventually go under.

Or had that been a hallucination produced by her terrified, dying mind? Right now, she couldn't remember if she'd seen the person on the eastern shore or the western. In the trees or up on the cliff.

And if she couldn't remember *where* she'd seen him, or her, she certainly wasn't going to remember what he, or she, looked like.

Kris needed to get inside. Not only because she was wet and cold and had begun to shake, but also because even though she couldn't *see* anything sneaking up on her, she *knew* that it was.

She risked another glance behind her. A mist had begun to skate across the onyx surface of the loch, swallowing everything in its path.

Forcing herself to stand, Kris gritted her teeth and made her weaving way up the bank. Once she was on her feet, she felt better. Until she glimpsed the smoky fingers of mist curling around her ankles.

With a gasp, she twisted and met a wall of swirling white. From deep inside came another splash.

Then Kris was lurching across the road, into her yard, and up to the door. She had an irrational fear that if the mist caught her she'd drown in it like she hadn't drowned in Loch Ness. She reached for the knob, moving forward eagerly as she did.

And bashed her nose into the wood when the knob refused to turn and the door refused to open.

Locked.

Kris spun about. The fog was cat-footing across the road.

She slapped her hand to the pocket of her jeans, then remembered. The key was sharing space with her video camera.

Out there. Where whatever had splashed was still splashing.

She was going to have to walk into the village and get another key from Effy. Just not—

"Now," Kris muttered, and let her chin sag nearly to her chest. She wanted to let her body slide to the ground, but if she did that she didn't think she'd get back up.

Maybe if she just rested for a minute, she could—

Thunk. Thunk. Thunk.

Footsteps on pavement. Steady. Sure. They knew where they were going. Too bad Kris couldn't figure out where they were coming from.

The utter darkness combined with the mist made it seem as if she existed in a strange otherworld. Sounds were not only magnified but also distorted, impossible to detect from which direction they came.

Sure, the splash earlier had seemed as though it had erupted from the loch. But was that because she'd equated splash with water—go figure—or because it had actually happened there?

Right now she couldn't tell if those footsteps were coming from the highway, the hills behind the cottage, a trail at Urquhart Castle, or her very own sidewalk.

Thump-thump. Thump-thump.

Louder. Closer. Faster.

Kris's gaze flicked right, left. Her flight instinct kicked

into full gear. She no longer felt exhausted and lethargic but twitchy and hyperalert. Still, she fought that urge to flee, because she knew she wouldn't get far.

Number one: No matter how jazzed she felt, she *was* exhausted.

Number two: In the thick fog, she'd probably run right into whomever she was trying to avoid.

Number three: If she didn't run into them, they'd just chase her. That's what predators did.

Then they ate you. Or tossed you in the loch.

"Been there," Kris whispered. "Done that."

The steps now seemed to burst from the right, the left, the ground, the air, bombarding her with sound. At least she no longer heard any splashes from the loch.

She shouldn't run. She really tried to stop. But her legs bunched, and she came away from the door, turning toward Drumnadrochit as she took her first, fleeing step.

Hands descended on her shoulders, and Kris began to scream.

Liam let her go.

Kris didn't stop screaming.

He couldn't say he blamed her. He'd no doubt loomed out of the mist like a monster. After last night, he was lucky she hadn't taken a swing at him.

"Kris," he murmured. "'Tis me. Liam."

Why that would make her stop screaming he had no idea. But it did.

Kris collapsed against him, her arms going around his waist, cheek pressed to his chest. "Liam," she gasped, then more quietly in a voice that made something shift and tumble in his stomach, "Liam."

She was soaked and trembling. He needed to get her inside before she went into shock.

Liam started to back Kris toward the door, reaching for the knob as he did so.

"It's locked," she said. "I lost the key when I fell into the water." She lifted her head, her eyes wide and dark, her face far too pale. "Someone *pushed* me in."

Liam frowned. He'd watched her go into the water. His alarm at the sight of her tumbling from the great height, then crashing into the icy cold loch had kept him from looking anywhere but at her. He hadn't seen her get pushed. But that didn't mean it hadn't happened.

Around here, lately, a lot had been happening that he hadn't seen, couldn't explain, and did not like.

"Then they followed me here." She pulled away, though she kept her hands on his hips, as if she needed the connection, or perhaps just the warmth. "I heard their steps." Her eyes flicked back and forth, back and forth, as she tried to see into the ever-thickening mist.

"'Twas me, lass. Me ye heard. My steps." Liam couldn't help it. He brushed his palm over her still-wet hair.

He didn't mention that he'd seen her fall. If he did, she'd want to know why he hadn't helped and then what would he say?

"There was splashing, too," she said. "Behind me." She pointed at the loch. "Out there."

"And why wouldn't there be? 'Tis a loch. Everything in it goes splash."

"Nothing that big."

"The mist magnifies," he said. "What are ye afraid of? Nessie?"

She jerked in his arms, surprising and confusing him. Though she had come to write about the monster, he'd gotten the impression she did not believe. But if not, then why was she afraid of what might lurk out there in the dark?

"She wouldnae hurt ye." He pushed a stray frizzy lock behind her ear. "I promise."

She tilted her head, and the hair he'd just tucked back swung free. She seemed about to question that statement, and he cursed himself for making it.

"Let's get ye inside." He reached past her and shoved at the door. It gave way with a thick *clunk*.

Kris stared at the broken door. "How did you do that?"

"This place has been rotting in the damp for decades. I dinnae know why Effy doesnae get it fixed." He lifted one shoulder. "Now she'll have to."

Liam urged Kris inside. Since he'd broken the lock, he'd have to stay all night again to make certain she was safe. Not that he hadn't planned to anyway.

Women were being killed, and whoever was doing it appeared to be very interested in having Kris become one of them. Why? She was a writer, come to write a children's book about Nessie. What possible threat could she pose?

Liam had no idea, but he was going to find out.

"Hot shower," he ordered, and urged her toward the bathroom. "I'll make ye some tea."

"Coffee," she muttered, but she went. Seconds later the water beat against the shower curtain, and Liam began to imagine things he had no business imagining.

The steamy heat curling her golden hair about her face, the droplets sliding across the freckles on her nose. He would sip them one by one as they trembled on the edge of that nose or perhaps beaded on the cusp of one breast. Would her freckles taste of their cinnamon shade? Would her nipples be the same?

Liam groaned. How was it that the very thought of her made his hands tremble, even as the rest of him hardened to the point of pain?

Yes, he was a man. He'd spent a lifetime in seduction. But this time she was seducing him.

He shouldn't be surprised. Years of lips whispering lies against sweetly scented skin, his palms skimming waists, thighs, breasts, his mouth tasting ambrosia, then nothing. In truth, the slightest brush of a hand on his shoulder should have made him spurt like a youth.

Liam finished with the coffee, shoving the carafe beneath the brew basket with a little too much force. He had to grab the machine with his free hand before it tumbled backward. He needed to *get a grip* as they said in the states. Sadly, all he wanted to grip was her.

An odd noise made Liam lift his head, the hairs on his neck and arms ruffling as a second muffled sound drifted from the bathroom.

He took the few steps to the door and shoved it open with such force—he'd expected it to be locked—that it slammed into the opposite wall, bouncing back and nearly smacking him in the face as he came through, fists clenched.

Kris, warm and wet, leaped into his arms.

"What is it?" she cried, at the same time he demanded, "Who's here?"

His gaze swept the small area—empty but for them and the steam—then he reached out and yanked back the shower curtain. Nothing was behind it but the still-pounding pulse of the water.

"I heard ye cry out." Liam tried to hold her close, but she kept sliding through his grasp like the loch through his fingertips.

Her lips rounded, a perfect, peach *o*. He wanted to taste her so badly his mouth watered.

"I—" She shoved the tumbling mass of curls from her face.

His gaze was caught by the silver Celtic cross around her neck. Had she always worn it, or was the addition recent? Perhaps a gift from Edward. If so, the old man was betting on shape-shifter.

Liam brushed his fingertips against the cool, bright metal. He'd never known Edward to be wrong.

At Liam's touch, her breath caught. The sharp movement dragged the now-taut buds of her breasts—more rose than cinnamon but perfect nevertheless—across his pecs and his own nipples hardened.

"I slipped," she whispered, her voice hoarse from the chill of the loch, or perhaps the heat of the room, the heat of them. Wherever their skin met—his hands on her arms, his chest to her breasts, his hips bumping hers as she shifted, restless—he burned.

Then he was kissing her, tasting her, touching her in ways he hadn't kissed, tasted, or touched in years.

Kris wasn't sure what got into her. She wasn't the type to kiss a stranger. She definitely wasn't the type to tear at his shirt, yanking it over his head and tossing it to the floor so that she could spread her palms across that smoothly muscled chest.

But Liam wasn't really a stranger, now, was he?

She'd kissed him before, and she was going to do a whole lot more than kiss him now. Then he wouldn't be a stranger ever again.

His tongue explored her mouth; his hands explored her body. She should have been shy to have a man burst in when she was climbing out of the shower stark naked. Instead she'd been thrilled.

She'd thought someone was coming to hurt her, and she'd known that Liam would stop them. Her first response to the sight of him had not been to run, to hide, but to throw herself into his arms. She was so glad that she had.

He skimmed his palms up her ribs, then filled them with her breasts, stroking a thumb over each swollen nipple.

His mouth left hers, trailing over her chin to her neck. His hair, soft and dark, brushed her collarbone and she shivered.

Without lifting his head or pausing one second in what he was doing, Liam slammed the door shut. With the water still running, soon they were as surrounded by steam as they'd been by mist.

But the steam was warm and it welcomed, a sharp contrast to the chilling isolation of that creeping mist.

"Ye taste like spice cake," he whispered against the curve of her shoulder.

"You smell like rain," she murmured into his hair.

His jeans scraped her hips and belly. She tugged at the button, which popped, but the zipper strained tight against his erection. Since she didn't want to injure anything she might need later, she stepped back and let him take the lead.

Besides, she wanted to watch.

The sleek muscles that flexed and flowed beneath his skin made him ripple and pulse in all the right places. His hips were slim, his thighs hard, his shoulders broad but not bulky.

She ran her hand over one, tracing a thumb down the curve of his arm, then skating a palm across his chest. "Do you swim?"

His head came up. The steam cast in front of his face, obscuring his expression. "Why d' ye say that?"

"Shoulders," she mused, and then became fascinated with touching them.

His skin was slick from the heat. Her hair curled

wildly. She'd never be able to tame it now. Beads of water dotted his like the dew at dawn. One such bead ran down his neck and, leaning forward, she licked it away.

He growled, the vibration enticing, exciting, erotic against her mouth, her breasts, then filled his palms with the ample flesh where thighs became ass and lifted her onto the countertop.

She gasped, shocked. Even more so when he slid his hands down the backs of her legs, using his nails just a little, then slowly opened those legs, stepping between them, holding her gaze all the while.

His eyes were sapphire; they seemed brighter tonight. Maybe that was because his blue-black hair was loose and billowing about his face. Or because the heat of the room had caused his cheeks to flush, although his hands still felt so cool.

"Yer eyes," he murmured, "are the shade of the earth as the sun slips away." He leaned forward, kissing the corner of each one. Strange how one man's mud was another man's earth as the sun slipped away.

"And yer hair is the summer moon, gold and shining in a sea of black."

"Poetry?" she asked.

He stroked his thumb over her center, and she jumped. Captured by his gaze, seduced by his words, she'd forgotten that she sat on the edge of a countertop, legs spread, Liam poised between them.

"Truth," he answered, then slowly, achingly, gloriously pushed inside.

She shifted, not uncomfortable but not quite right, and he murmured something in Gaelic that could have been a curse or a prayer, maybe both, before skating his hands beneath her thighs and tilting her so that *not quite right* disappeared.

He drank her gasp with his lips as he looped her knees at his waist. She figured out how to cross her ankles at his back and hold him close all on her own.

His long, clever fingers stroked where her thighs veed, the tender, rarely touched flesh trembling even as she did.

She was open to him in a way she'd never been open to anyone else. He'd seen her fear; he'd kissed away her terror. He'd protected her, saved her, and now he would make her forget everything but this moment and him.

His thrusts quickened. He lifted her knees higher and wider, and they became deeper. She was making desperate, begging sounds, her head thrown back, his mouth at her neck, her collarbone, the swell of her breasts.

"I cannae reach." His teeth grazed her skin.

"Harder," she gasped, surprising herself. "More."

"Aye," he said. "Lift them, *mo bhilis*. Bring them to my mouth, and I'll give ye all that ye ask."

His hips thrust, once, then stilled.

She wiggled, tightened her legs, the muscles of her thighs flexing against the bones of his hips, drawing him closer, but he would not move; he would not give her what she wanted, what she must have.

"Open yer eyes."

If possible his had gone even bluer. They shone like neon in the night.

His tongue shot out, and he licked the swell of her right breast and then the left. "I cannae reach," he repeated, sliding his arms along her back to support her. "Lift them."

She understood what he wanted, and heat shot through her at the image of what she must do. Their gazes locked; she lifted her breasts and watched as he took a nipple into his mouth and suckled, first gently, his tongue slipping over and back like warm water in a bath, then faster and rougher, pressing her against the roof of his mouth, squeezing and taunting, even as his hips began to move.

She cupped her breasts in her palms, relishing the movement of his jaw against her fingers as he worked her above, the slide of his hips against her straining thighs as he did the same down below. Cradled in his embrace, with him cradled in hers, they rose, then fell together, gasping, thrusting, coming.

They stayed that way until the tremors died; then he lifted his head, kissed her brow, disentangled himself, and went to the shower, his hair spreading across his shoulders like an ebony curtain.

Kris sat there, the lovely languor dying as she waited for him to either turn it off and leave or get in, wash up.

Then leave.

Instead, he checked the temperature, turned, and stretched out his hand.

CHAPTER 13

"Le do thoil," Liam murmured. "Kill me."

Kris slept at his side, so warm and soft, so willing. But then how could she *not* be willing? He was seduction in human form. She'd had little choice once he'd kissed her.

He'd had her again after the shower, this time in the bed, and the sex had been as good as he remembered sex being.

No. That wasn't true. The sex was much *better* than he ever remembered sex being.

She'd tasted of the sun on the water and smelled like the moon in the rain. He'd wanted to stay inside of her forever, to hear her sweet cries for the rest of his life, to feel her breath on his face and her skin pressed to his as the years alone melted away.

Kris dreamed of Nessie.

Long and gray and sleek, she slid beneath the water as Kris watched, and filmed, from above.

In her sleep Kris shifted, murmured, and was soothed by cool hands on her fevered skin, gentle lips on a furrowed brow. She settled back into the dream.

Where she fell and fell, then kept on falling. What would she find at the bottom?

Water, and a lot of it. Kris slammed through the surface and shot into the deep. She couldn't see; she couldn't breathe. Her chin hurt; she tasted blood, and in the gloom something slithered.

She jerked toward it, but the murky mill of the loch prevented her from seeing just what it was. She was bumped in the back. She tried to swim away, to kick upward toward air. Instead, a whirlwind surrounded her, throwing her every which way, then pulling her back. Right before she passed out, she saw eyes shining from the face of a snake.

Kris came awake gasping, choking, swimming, or trying to. But she wasn't in water; she was in bed, and her legs were tangled in the sheets. She wasn't drowning; she was breathing—great, greedy gulps of blessed air.

She also wasn't any more alone now than she'd been then.

"A thaisgidh," Liam murmured. "Yer safe. Yer safe here with me. I willnae let anything bring ye harm."

She clung to him, letting him pull her against his chest, murmuring words that flowed like a song.

She did feel safe. She wasn't quite sure why.

"What did ye dream, lass?"

Kris, who'd been slowly relaxing in the warm, sweet cocoon that they'd made, stiffened. Liam ran a palm down her back and whispered, "Shhh."

Why did the soft burr of his voice in her hair make her want to *shhh*? She'd never been one for cuddling or comfort. Perhaps because she'd hadn't had either one in a very long time.

"Ye don't have t' tell me if ye dinnae want to."

"I—" She took a breath, thrilled when it didn't catch in the middle and make her feel again like a child. "I do."

Perhaps it would help.

"I was in the loch," she said. "But I wasn't alone. I think I saw . . ." She paused, unwilling to admit it but unable to stop. "Nessie."

"Understandable," he said, still petting her.

Kris looked into his face, but the night was so dark she could see nothing but the shimmer of his eyes. They reminded her of the shimmer of eyes she'd seen in the depths of the loch, and she didn't like it.

"Why is that understandable?" she demanded.

"Ye are here for her, are ye not?"

"How do you know that?"

"Lass." He ran a hand over her hair. "Everyone in Drumnadrochit knows that."

She sighed. He was right.

"Go on," he said.

"I couldn't breathe. I couldn't find the surface. She came, and she whirled around me, and I think . . ." She paused, searching her mind for the dream, or had it been a memory? "I think she saved me."

"Did she now?"

Kris sat up, and Liam let her go, keeping one hand on her back and rubbing. "She pushed me, and I fought because I thought she pushed me down, but really she pushed me up. Without her, I would have flailed around in the water, thinking up was down and down was up until I drowned. But why would she do that?"

"'Twas just a dream," he said. "Do ye truly think the Loch Ness Monster saved ye from drowning?"

Kris stared into the darkness and admitted the truth: "Something did."

"I thought ye didnae believe in Nessie."

Kris tilted her head. "You're the one who said you'd never seen her."

"I havenae."

"And strangely, no one around here has ever seen you but me."

He laughed. "That's not true."

"No matter who I ask, they haven't heard of you. There are no Grants in Drumnadrochit named Liam. Although perhaps you might be one of the Grants in Dores."

"Is that so?" he murmured.

Question with a question. He was definitely hiding something. But then, wasn't she?

"What's your secret?" she asked.

"No secret. Ye've merely been asking the wrong questions."

"I'm pretty good with questions."

"I suppose being a writer, ye'd have to be."

Kris narrowed her eyes, but she still couldn't see his face, so she could not tell if he was mocking her. Had he gone searching for *her* secret and found the truth? Why would he? Unless he had something even bigger to hide?

Kris turned the lamp on the bedside table to low. "I need to know who you are, Liam."

His eyes appeared almost black in the half-light. "Ye do."

He tangled his fingers with hers, and her stomach turned over with . . . what? Like? Lust? It certainly wasn't love. Not now. Not him. Not yet.

"Ye know more of me than anyone else has in a very long time."

"Ditto," she murmured.

Liam tilted his head, and his sleek, smooth dark hair slid over his equally sleek, smooth shoulder. She was struck by the memory of holding on to those shoulders as he rose above her, his image but a shadow against the night.

"Ye truly think someone pushed ye into the loch?" he asked.

She hadn't been sure until she'd had the dream. But in contrast to everything she'd ever known about dreams, the more time that passed since she'd had it the more real the dream became.

"Yes," she answered.

He ran a hand over her no doubt frizzy, billowing hair. "Do ye think it was me?"

She jerked back. "Why would I think that?"

"Ye said yerself, ye don't know who I am."

"That doesn't mean I think you're trying to kill me."

"Who *would* try to kill ye?" he wondered. "Ye just got here."

"In other words, I haven't been here long enough for anyone to want to kill me yet?"

His lips curved. "Something like that."

"I doubt whoever killed those girls knew them very well, either."

His brow creased. "Have ye noticed anyone following ye about?"

"No," she said automatically, then— "Wait."

He stiffened, the muscles in his arms and chest and stomach rippling, distracting, seducing. "Ye have?"

She shook the foggy *give me* thoughts from her brain and told him about the American who had been asking after her.

"I dinnae like that at all," he said.

"I'm not wild about it, either."

"Ye think he pushed ye in?"

"Since I don't know who he is, maybe."

"Have ye had any trouble like this before? I hear writers have stalkers. The man who shot John Lennon was also obsessed with Stephen King."

"I'm not Stephen King," Kris said dryly. And she never would be.

"Still, ye never know what kind of madmen are out there until they . . ." He paused.

Kris filled in the blank. "Kill you?"

He glanced at the window where the curtain had been turned back to reveal just a sliver of night. "Maybe ye should leave. Go on home to . . . wherever home is."

"Chicago," Kris said, then frowned. Why had she told him that? Hell. Why not just tell him everything?

"I'm not a writer," she said. "I'm a journalist. I do a show . . ." She paused and corrected herself, "*Did* a show called *Hoax Hunters* for public TV."

Confusion flickered over his face. "I dinnae understand."

"I expose hoaxes. Like Nessie."

"Nessie isnae a hoax."

"You said you'd never seen her."

"Seeing and believing are two different things."

"You think she's there?"

"I do."

"Want to help me prove it?" Kris hadn't known she was going to say that until it popped right out of her mouth.

"Prove Nessie exists?"

"Yes." It would be a bigger story than proving she didn't.

"Ye know that's been tried before?"

Kris smiled. "It hasn't been tried by me."

She could do this. She felt more confident proving there *was* a Nessie than proving there wasn't. What was it that Edward had said?

You do realize it is impossible to prove something does not exist? You can merely prove it has not yet been found.

She suddenly understood what he'd meant.

"How will ye find her?" Liam asked.

Kris shrugged. "I'm gonna look."

They slept again, and when they awoke, the sky had begun to lighten. Kris trailed her hand up Liam's thigh.

"I have to go." He brought her palm to his lips and pressed a kiss to the center.

"Go?" she repeated, unable to think when he did stuff like that.

"I'll see ye tonight."

Kris pulled her hand free. "You're leaving?"

He was already out of bed, ducking into the bathroom to retrieve his clothes, coming back out again buttoning his jeans, his shirt hanging from his hand. "I have work."

"What kind of work?"

He glanced up at the suspicion in her voice. "Don't ye trust me?"

"Yes. . . ."

"Yer mouth says, 'Yes,' while yer face says, *But . . .*"

"You don't tell me anything."

"Then why would ye trust me?"

Why did she? *Simple.* "If you don't tell me anything, at least you aren't lying."

A shadow crossed his face, and her stomach clenched. He *was* lying. His name probably wasn't even Liam Grant. No wonder no one knew who he was.

He crossed the room and sat next to her. "Who lied to you so well and so often that ye dinnae trust anymore?"

"Who didn't?" she muttered.

Liam brushed his fingertips over her cheek. "So many?" he whispered. "I'm sorry."

She wanted to rest her head on his bare chest and press her lips to his skin, pull him back into bed, and forget about talking at all. What was it about him that made her not only trust when she shouldn't but also lust at a time when most wouldn't?

Liam glanced at the window again where the darkness had begun to become light. Then he stood and covered all that luscious skin with a shirt. "Meet me tonight at Mac-Leod's?"

"When?"

"After the sun goes down."

"What kind of time is that?"

"The best time. I like the night."

"Why?"

"Because I dinnae have to work."

"What do you do?"

He hesitated, and for an instant she just knew he was going to lie. When he spoke she wasn't all that certain he had not.

"I protect the loch."

"Like a park ranger?"

"A bit. I walk about, do what needs doing. Pick up the garbage. Clip the trees that hang too far down. Make sure the roads are nae full of potholes. Help the wee animals and such."

"You patrol Loch Ness, yet you've never seen the monster."

"Do ye ken how big the loch is?" he asked, then continued before she could answer. "Twenty-four miles long, over a mile wide in places. The deepest part," he jerked a thumb over his shoulder, "near Urquhart Castle is more than twice the mean depth of the North Sea."

Kris wasn't sure what a mean depth was, but she got what he meant. The loch was damn deep.

"The surface sits fifty-two feet above sea level, but the tallest point around it is over twelve hundred feet higher than that. It's bordered by mountains and rock face and forest. There are parts ye can barely get to on foot. Professional divers speak of a terrifying blackness that surrounds them at an easy depth of fifty feet. The shock isnae that I *havenae* seen Nessie but that anyone has at all."

He sounded like a tour guide. Or maybe a park ranger.

"I didn't mean—"

"It's all right. I know ye've been lied to again and again, and I'm sorry for it."

"You aren't the one—" Or ones. "Who made me so mistrustful."

Liam ran a hand through his hair, then changed the subject: "Ye'll meet me tonight, and I'll prove to ye that I'm no ghost."

Said out loud, that sounded as foolish as it had in her head.

"I don't think that," Kris blurted. "How could I? I've exposed several ghosts as fakes."

"There *are* ghosts, lass." His voice had gone soft and a bit sad. "Around here, there are a lot of them."

"*Those* you've seen?"

"Aye," he said, gaze gone distant. "That I have."

"Why?"

He blinked, and his eyes returned to hers. "Why what?"

"Why have you seen ghosts? Have you gone looking for them?"

"No." He leaned over, placing a quick kiss on her lips before he headed for the door. "The ghosts come looking for me."

CHAPTER 14

Had Liam been teasing about the ghosts? Kris didn't think so. His face, his voice, had reflected a sadness she recognized.

He'd lost people, and he felt guilty about it.

Kris's mother had fought. She'd tried. She just hadn't been able to win. However, Kris hadn't been able to forgive her for promising a desperate teenager what she had no right to promise. She should have been honest. She should have prepared Kris and her brother better instead of lying right to the end about her chances of survival.

The denials were what Kris had been unable to forgive. Certainly the lies and her reaction to them had fueled her career, but they'd also fueled her guilt. Kris harbored a deep anger at her mother for them still, and that she did kept her up a lot of nights. Kris was surprised *she* hadn't started seeing ghosts.

Or at least *ghost*.

Of course she didn't believe in visits from the great beyond. But she hadn't believed in Nessie, either. If she proved to the world that the Loch Ness Monster was real, would she also start seeing the spirit of her mother around every dark corner?

Kris wasn't sure she was ready for that.

Despite her strange and disturbing thoughts, Kris fell asleep, waking late and stretching luxuriously. The clock read: 11:00 A.M. She couldn't remember the last time she'd stayed in bed so late. Then again, it wasn't every night you nearly drowned, had your life saved by a lake monster, followed by mind-blowing sex with a hot Scottish park ranger.

Kris went into the bathroom. One glance in the mirror revealed she was grinning wider than she'd grinned in a long, long time. Probably since the last time she'd had mind-blowing sex.

Whenever that was.

Sure, she'd had sex, but she hadn't had this. She hadn't had Liam. She couldn't wait to have him again.

A trickle of laughter escaped as she picked up her sodden clothes and started the shower. It appeared that she'd at last found something in the world worth giggling about.

But the laughter died as she hung her clothes on the towel rack. Someone had tried to kill her. Again. She was going to have to tell Alan Mac.

"Because he's been *so* useful thus far," Kris muttered as she stepped beneath the stream.

However, beggars couldn't be choosers and Alan Mac was the officer in charge. Besides, she should probably report her missing camera. Just in case it washed up somewhere and was turned in to the authorities.

Although what would she do with the thing? It wasn't as if the camera would still work or her film would be—

Kris froze in the middle of rinsing shampoo out of her hair. Could that be why someone had given her a free ride to the depths of Loch Ness? Because she'd been filming Nessie?

She continued to scrub at her scalp, lifting the thick, curling mass of hair and letting the water wash away all the suds as she considered. Every bit of film taken of Nessie was . . .

"Crap," she murmured.

The lack of decent photos—still or cine—was a bullet point of interest on the "Reasons Nessie Doesn't Exist" list. If the monster were real, there would be a physical record of it—especially during modern times when every third person had a camera and knew exactly how to use it.

Underwater attempts understandably produced junk. The damn peat content made seeing your hand in front of your face a fricking miracle. Kris had firsthand knowledge of that.

The motion pictures that had been shot were hazy, spotty, dark, and wavering. Half of them had been ruined or lost.

The still photography wasn't much better. Certainly getting close enough to the loch with the right light, appropriate lenses, and film speed at a time when the monster just happened to appear was a neat trick. But someone in the past decade, when cameras had become damn good, should have been able to manage it.

Yet they hadn't.

Kris shut off the water. Or perhaps they had. Perhaps anyone who'd filmed Nessie without trembling hands or garbage equipment had found themselves at the bottom of the lake.

Like her.

She blew a derisive puff of air through her lips as she snatched a towel. How could that happen? It wasn't as if the loch had someone who watched over it 24-7 like a—

The towel dropped from Kris's suddenly limp fingers. "Park ranger?"

Hell!

Maybe Liam *had* tossed her in.

By the time Kris got dressed, microwaved some of the coffee that Liam had made last night but they'd never gotten around to drinking, then drank it before heading for Drumnadrochit at a brisk pace, she was calmer.

Kris was nothing if not a logical woman. And logic dictated that if Liam wanted her dead, he'd had plenty of chances to kill her.

Of course there was also the little voice that whispered: *He doesn't need to kill you now that your film is swimming with the fishes. At least until you do something else that threatens—*

"What?" Kris muttered. "What did I threaten?"

Proving Nessie existed would be good for business. Why would anyone want to stop that?

As far as Kris could tell, everyone in Drumnadrochit worshiped the creature. But maybe whoever wanted to destroy the legend of Nessie wasn't from here. Or maybe they just wanted the mystery to remain a mystery.

Kris paused for a second. That actually made sense. If the monster was proved to exist beyond a shadow of a doubt, there'd be biologists and naturalists and all sorts of -ists who weren't *tour*ists. And then the government would get involved. . . .

Kris wasn't sure how the British authorities worked, but she was quite familiar with the United States. They'd capture Nessie and put her in . . .

"Sea World," Kris whispered. Or that big, echoing warehouse where they kept the Ark of the Covenant.

So, she could see why someone might want to protect the monster from detection. It *did* make sense.

Until you added murder.

Wasn't killing someone to prevent them from discovering the truth called overkill? *Ha-ha*. Then again, murders had been committed for less than that.

Kris began to walk again, faster than before. Thinking about murder made her twitchy. She wanted to get to the village, where there were other people, a few cops, eyewitnesses, and she wanted to get there fast.

As she continued at power walk speed, Kris eyed the trees that bordered the loch. The sun shone, and everything should appear cheery and safe. Except in those trees shadows reigned and damn near anyone could hide.

Her gaze went to the water, where several boats bobbed, but the surface remained as impenetrable as interrogation room glass. The loch and the forest had a lot in common.

She glanced toward the distant hills. Those, too, were as mysterious as midnight. She was going to need Liam's help to figure this out. Unless he'd tried to kill her.

Then he was fired.

A bubble of hysterical laughter escaped as Kris reached the outskirts of Drumnadrochit. She really needed to stop thinking so much. Her mind was twirling in circles, and she was beginning to get seasick.

Or maybe it was just the reheated coffee. Her gaze went to Jamaica's place. Kris *hated* reheated coffee. It rolled around in her stomach like standing water in a freeway pothole—complete with the top layer of oil.

"Glurk," Kris muttered, gaze still on the coffee shop; then she shook her head.

Not yet.

First Alan Mac, then Effy Cameron—Kris needed to tell her landlady that the door to the cottage was broken—*then* fresh coffee.

She strode to the station. This time the constable wasn't standing out front. He wasn't even working inside.

"He was called to Dochgarroch," the woman at the desk informed her. "Something was stuck in the lock."

"I don't remember there being a Dochgarroch Lake."

"Not a lake loch, lass." The receptionist grinned. "And would ye like to say that five times fast?"

Since she appeared to be waiting for Kris to answer, Kris shook her head, and the woman continued. "A lock on the canal. Helps with the boats and such."

"And this is Alan Mac's problem, why?"

"We won't know until he returns."

Kris thanked her and left. She had a bad feeling she knew what was stuck in Dochgarroch Lock.

Another body.

Strolling back through the village, Kris heard someone call her name. She glanced toward the coffee shop. A hand reached out the door, beckoning her with a go-cup. She could have sworn she saw *Kris* written in the steam that trailed upward.

Kris hesitated. She hadn't actually *talked* to Alan Mac, but she'd tried. That should be enough for at least one cup of the good stuff in reward.

She looked both ways—waiting for a tour bus, followed by a few bikers, to trundle by—then crossed the street, taking the cup from the outstretched hand and her first blessed sip as she stepped inside.

The place was empty.

"What's going on?" she asked.

Jamaica, who was dressed in an eye-shockingly bright yellow skirt that reached to her ankles and an equally bright orange peasant blouse, raised her sculpted brows. "What you mean?"

Kris lifted her chin toward the bare tables even as she slurped coffee like she'd been denied for weeks instead of hours.

"Oh, dat." Jamaica waved her hand dismissively. "Such a nice day. Everyone take dere coffee to go. We'll get busy again once de sun go down."

"How much do I owe you?" Kris asked.

"On de house. You seemed to need it." She narrowed her hazel eyes. "Why you walkin' down de street like a zombie?"

"I . . . uh—" Kris took a swig of coffee. Should she tell Jamaica about being tossed into the lake? Since Kris had no proof that she *had* been tossed, probably not.

"You searchin' for Alan Mac?"

Kris frowned. Why was Jamaica watching her? Then again—Kris let her gaze wander over the empty shop—what else did Jamaica have to do?

"I was wondering how the case was progressing."

True enough, although that wasn't why Kris had gone looking for him.

"He find de man who be askin' all over for you?"

"No." Since she hadn't told him about it, it would be a little hard for Alan Mac to find the guy.

Could the mystery man have been the one who pushed her off the ledge? Sure. Although his question—was she happy?—made her wonder why, if he cared about her happiness, he would then try to kill her. Of course his question was creepy, and so was he. For all she knew, he'd been wandering around other places, asking if other women were happy.

Then killing them.

She really did need to tell Alan Mac about her strange stalker. And wasn't that the most redundant description ever?

"So de case is not progressing?"

Jamaica's voice brought Kris back to the coffee shop, and for an instant she wondered why Jamaica would automatically assume that the case Kris was asking about was the happy-man freak and not the missing and murdered women.

Then she remembered. Alan Mac was trying to keep the whole dead-people thing on the down low. Kris wasn't sure that was a good idea, but then again, she wasn't a cop. She had a feeling that if women continued to disappear and a few more of them washed up around the loch, he wasn't going to be able to keep anything quiet anymore.

"No progress," Kris said. "I think that guy, whoever he was, is gone."

Jamaica's expressive brows shot downward. "Not yet he isn't."

Kris froze with the go-cup a mere breath from her seeking lips; then she lowered it. "Why would you say that?"

"I saw him walkin' down de street bright and early dis morning."

Kris glanced outside. "That's the first time you've seen him since he asked about me?"

"Yes. Although he could have come in and asked someone else. Or asked in any other shop or restaurant in Drumnadrochit. By now, I'm sure he found someone to tell him exactly where you be livin'."

Kris winced. She was sure he had, too.

"Maybe you should stay wid me," Jamaica murmured.

Kris actually considered it, which showed how spooked she was. Sure, she liked Jamaica. But the quickest way to ruin a friendship—especially one so new—was to take advantage.

"Thanks. But I'll be okay."

"You sure?"

She wasn't. Not really. But if she took Jamaica up on her offer of an extra room or maybe just an extra bed, even the couch, there'd be no more getting naked with Liam. Was the sex worth risking her life for?

Yes.

No.

Maybe.

Hell.

"I'm sure," she said.

Jamaica pursed her lips and held Kris's gaze for several beats. She must have seen something there that convinced her Kris was all right, because she nodded once and let it go.

"I'd best put dis place to rights," Jamaica said. "I usually get a rush round four."

"Thanks for the coffee."

"Anytime." Jamaica turned, and her skirt spun with the movement, the bright material flipping upward and drawing Kris's eye to the tattoo just above her ankle.

"What's that?" Kris blurted.

Jamaica turned, expression curious, and Kris pointed downward.

Something flashed in Jamaica's eyes—it really looked like guilt—but what was there about a tattoo that could cause such a reaction?

Jamaica stared at her feet, clad in ugly, but hopefully comfortable, tree hugger sandals. "What?"

"You know what," Kris said softly. "Was that a snake?"

Jamaica jumped, her gaze darting around the floor. "Where?"

"Tattooed on your ankle."

"Oh, dat." Jamaica flapped her hand.

"Yeah, that. The percentage of tattoos in one small Scottish village seems to be freakishly high."

Jamaica lifted her head. "What you talkin' about?"

"Alan Mac has one on his biceps."

"A snake?"

"No." Kris thought back. "Well, I don't think so. I'm not sure what it was, but Effy's definitely wasn't a snake."

"Effy Cameron?" Jamaica laughed. "Dat old woman never get a tattoo."

"It was on her—" Kris waved vaguely in the area of her breasts.

"And how would you be seein' dose?"

"I didn't. I mean, well, I didn't want to."

"I bet not."

"Her dress gaped. Happens to the best of us."

"Mmm," Jamaica said. "Probably a bruise."

Kris considered that. What she'd seen had been bluish and roundish, kind of humped. It could have been a bruise.

"Does her husband—?"

"Effy never married."

"But Rob—"

"He be her brother. They been livin' in dat house all dere lives. Dey might argue like dey want to kill each other, but he would not dare touch her. She'd eat his liver for lunch."

Kris's lips curved. *Good.*

"Most likely she fell."

"That's what they all say."

"Sometimes dey actually fall."

True.

"Alan Mac was in de Queen's Own Highlanders," Jamaica continued. "Military regiment. Dey have a tattoo. I don't know of what."

"And you?" Kris asked. "Were you in the Jamaican branch of the snake charmer's brigade?"

"No," she said.

"That *is* a snake?"

Jamaica lifted her skirt a bit to reveal a diamond-shaped head and long, curving neck trailing upward.

"You don't get comments on it around here?" Kris asked.

Jamaica let go the yellow material. The snake tattoo disappeared from view. "Why would I?"

"Didn't Saint Somebody drive the snakes out of Scotland?" Although if that was true, why had Jamaica practically jumped onto a chair to avoid the one she thought Kris had been pointing at?

"Dat was Ireland and Saint Patrick. Scotland has snakes. Just not very many."

"And Jamaica?"

"Not a lot. Most islands have none."

"Isn't Ireland an island?" At Jamaica's lifted brows, Kris continued. "How did Saint Pat drive out snakes that weren't there?"

Jamaica's lips curved. "De snakes were a metaphor for evil."

"Ah," Kris said. "So he drove evil out of Ireland, and distributed happiness and Catholicism to all."

"Dat would be right." Jamaica shuddered. "I hate snakes."

"Then why do you have one tattooed on your ankle?"

"I don't."

"But—"

"It isn't a snake."

"But you said . . ." Kris paused. Actually Jamaica *hadn't* said it was a snake. She'd merely drawn up her skirt and shown Kris the tattoo when she'd asked. "What is it?"

Jamaica's gaze went distant. "You're de first person to see dat in—" She shook her head, and her dreads flew. "I don't know how long. De tattoo is . . ." She took a deep breath. "Embarrassing."

"It's not the prettiest one I've ever seen, but it's not that bad," Kris offered.

"I'm not embarrassed by de tattoo itself but by what it represents."

"Which is?"

"Evil."

"An evil snake," Kris said.

"Not truly a snake. The image symbolizes Obi, a West African god."

"I'm gonna need more than that."

"In Jamaica dere is an old religion called Obeah. It originated with de slaves."

"Like voodoo?"

Jamaica shrugged. "Obeah is more about magic dan worship. More about evil dan balance. Obi," she pointed to her ankle, "is de mark of a witch."

Kris opened her mouth, shut it again. She met Jamaica's gaze, and the woman spread her hands.

"You're a witch?" Kris asked.

"I was."

CHAPTER 15

"Is that something you can give up? Kris asked. "Maybe for Lent?"

Jamaica gave a weak, burbly laugh. "No. You're right. I *am* a witch. I just don't . . . do dat anymore."

"What?"

"Kill t'ings."

Uh-oh.

Kris took one slow step backward; then she took another.

Jamaica's head went up. She saw Kris's face, and she reached out a hand. "It's not what you t'ink."

"What is it?"

Jamaica rubbed her eyes. "I was young and stupid."

"Redundant."

"Yes. But me more dan most. I got involved in de Obeah cult. I became an Obeah woman. I sacrificed t'ings to get de power I needed."

Kris didn't like the sound of that.

"Sacrificed what? Sleep? Money? Snickers bars?"

"Animals."

"*Not* cool."

"Better dan what you were t'inkin."

True. Kris *had* been thinking people.

"You really believe that sacrificing bunnies brought you power?"

Jamaica's brilliant eyes met hers. "It did."

Kris snorted. Her disbelief in Nessie might have waned, but her skepticism of every other hoax on the planet had not. Witchcraft? "I don't think so."

"T'ink what you like. I know de truth."

"If you were truly able to practice magic, why would you give it up?"

"Black magic." Jamaica wrapped her arms around herself and held on tight. "In Obeah, all de princes of hell are personified, Satan most of all."

"Hell and Satan are Christian boogies."

"Obeah, like voodoo, combines de religions of Africa with Christianity. They use de Sixth and Seventh Books of Moses as guides."

"Wait a second." Kris ticked off a finger with each word. "Genesis. Exodus. Leviticus. Numbers. Deuteronomy. That's five."

"Moses was considered de greatest magician in all of Egypt. A snake charmer. He parted de Red Sea."

"With a little help from his friend."

"Or his books of magic."

"Seriously?" Kris had never heard this, and she'd heard a helluva lot.

"De Sixth and Seventh Books of Moses were left out of de Pentateuch, but dey exist and contain all de magic of Egypt. Did you know de Egyptian word for snake is *ob*?"

"Like 'Obi.' "

"Life's a circle," Jamaica said.

In Kris's opinion, life was a straight line, as long as you stayed on track, but she wasn't going to derail the conversation by arguing the point. "Go back to how Moses wrote books of black magic."

"Not black," Jamaica corrected. "Not den. De black came later. When darkness fell."

"What darkness?"

"Slavery."

"Okay." Kris could buy that. But not much more.

"De magic turned dark when evil ruled. De only way to fight such evil is with more evil."

"Two wrongs do *not* make a right," Kris said.

"Spend a few lifetimes in chains and see how right you feel."

"*You* weren't in chains."

"De ones who blackened de magic were. I was just . . ." Her voice trailed off as she searched for a word.

Kris had no problem helping her. "A dumbass."

Jamaica inclined her head. "I had been hurt. I felt powerless. I went searching for a way to change dat." Her eyes sparked. "I found it."

"What did you do?" Kris asked.

The woman lifted her chin. "T'ings I will never, ever say."

"You left the cult?"

"I left Jamaica." She looked away. "I had little choice."

"Because?"

"Obeah is still illegal dere."

"Illegal? How can they do that?"

"Jamaica is not America," she pointed out. "To practice witchcraft is to beg for trouble."

Kris had done some stories on witchcraft, but only that practiced in the United States, where such things, while not commonplace, were tolerated. She could understand how, in certain countries with certain backgrounds, that tolerance would be nil.

"So you left Jamaica," Kris said, "and you came here."

"Eventually."

There was a story there, too, but Kris had interviewed enough people to know that you had to stick to one mystery at a time if you wanted to discover anything at all.

"Why here?"

Jamaica shrugged and stared out the window. "Dey say one of my ancestors was from Scotland. Long time back."

"Ancestor," Kris repeated. "Buccaneer? Plantation owner?" Basically some white guy who came and took what he wanted. History was full of them.

"Yes," Jamaica answered, still staring outside. "I always wanted to see dis place. Once I did, I never wanted to leave."

"You don't practice Obeah anymore?"

"No." Now Jamaica's gaze met hers. "I swear."

"I believe you," Kris said. But did she?

Something strange was going on at Loch Ness. Kris doubted it had anything to do with witchcraft. Because real magic was hooey. Problems cropped up when people believed in it.

Jamaica appeared to believe.

The door opened, and a flood of college-age tourists flowed in, chattering about the loch, the village, where they would stay that night, and what they would order right now.

Kris backed out of the way, lifting her nearly empty cup to indicate she'd been waited on. Right behind the kids, a family complete with Mom, Dad, the requisite boy and girl got in line. Jamaica would be busy for a while.

Which was fine. Kris wanted to find out more about Obeah and about Jamaica herself.

Sure, Jamaica had said she no longer "did dat"; she

claimed she'd only sacrificed animals. However, there were a lot of missing women in Drumnadrochit, some of them were dead. What if—?

Nah. There was no way Jamaica was sacrificing people. Because if she was, she certainly wouldn't have told Kris about her witchy-woman past.

Unless . . .

She planned to kill Kris, too.

Kris rubbed between her eyes. Now she was being foolish, paranoid. Although, after being bonked on the head and tossed off a cliff, she did have good reason to be. Still—

Innocent until proven guilty.

She needed to get to her computer.

Kris hurried back to the cottage. Though it was broad daylight, she still got a little spooked when she lost sight of the village and the village lost sight of her as she trotted across the deserted fields.

She felt again the same way she'd felt on the way into Drumnadrochit—as if she were being watched.

Kris glanced to the rear. No one.

She faced front. Nothing.

A quick peek at the hills made her shrug. Anyone could be up there, doing just about anything, and she wouldn't see them.

Just like in the trees. Thick, numerous, even in the bright sunlight, the shadows reigned, dancing between the trunks and making her think all sorts of strange things.

Then there was the loch. Boats of all kinds floated there. Someone could be watching her from one of the decks with binoculars. Would *that* make her skin prickle as if a thousand ants marched across it?

Maybe. But what she really didn't like was the large gray rock in the water. The one that shone like monster skin, appearing and disappearing beneath the turbulent waves.

Kris shook her head. Even if the rock wasn't a rock, it didn't have eyes. At least not where she could see.

"You're losing it, Kristin."

What was wrong with her? Wondering if Liam had thrown her in the loch. Thinking Jamaica could be a human-sacrificing witch. Believing that whenever she walked to and from the village someone was following her. It was probably lucky she didn't have a gun.

Except she did. Tucked into a drawer at the cottage.

However, she didn't think she should walk around Drumnadrochit packing. But she could carry the—

"Damn," Kris muttered. The silver knife resided in her backpack up on the bluff from which she'd taken a nose-dive. Should she run up there and retrieve it or shouldn't she?

"Shouldn't," Kris decided. The last time she'd been there she'd nearly died. Revisiting the scene of the crime would be a good way to experience a repeat performance. Although . . .

She *could* take the gun.

Kris let out a derisive breath of air at the circular nature of her thoughts. She wasn't going to shoot anyone with a silver bullet any more than she'd have been able to stab them with a silver knife.

Kris glanced again at the loch, but the dark gray hump was gone. She watched for a few minutes, waiting for the water to draw back and show it again, but it didn't.

Could the tide have changed the level of the loch that quickly? Did a lake even *have* a tide?

The cottage came into view, and Kris had the sudden urge to run into the house, slamming, then locking the door behind her. Or perhaps falling onto the green grass and kissing it as if it were a long-lost friend.

She did neither. If someone was watching her, she didn't

want them to know that she knew it. She didn't want them to think she was afraid.

Kris had been on her own a long time. She'd worked in television. And if there was one thing she'd learned, it was this: If you ran, you got chased. If you were afraid . . . they chased you faster.

So she strolled up the walk, reached into her pocket for the key to unlock the door, then remembered she had no key, the door was broken, and she'd completely forgotten to tell Effy about it.

"Fan-damn-tastic," Kris muttered.

She shouldn't even go inside. If the loch, the trees, the damned empty fields scared her, a house she'd left unlocked for over an hour was really going to be fun.

She *should* walk back to Drumnadrochit and insist that Rob come out here and fix the thing immediately.

Kris glanced over her shoulder, her gaze drawn to the loch, the trees, the still-empty road. The breeze that was actually quite warm gave her a nasty chill.

"Maybe later," she said, and reached for the door. She paused, frowning, with her hand on the knob.

The door had already been fixed.

Kris stilled, then stared at the door for a very long time, before stepping back and staring some more. Liam wanted to join her, both on the porch and inside.

He peered at the bright sunlight, and he wished it would go away. While it blazed, he was stuck at the loch, unable to do anything but his cursed duty. It seemed like he'd been doing it for eternity.

Of course he hadn't been doing a very good job this morning. Instead of trolling north and south, then patrolling either shore, he'd watched Kris's house until she'd come out and then he'd watched her.

From the way she kept gazing at the trees, the loch, the hills, she knew he was there. He should be ashamed of himself, but he wasn't.

Someone was killing women. They had tried to kill her. They planned to blame it on Nessie.

Liam couldn't allow that to happen.

"Hello?" Kris stepped inside.

No one answered. Had she really thought they would?

Her gaze swept the living area and kitchen; she peered into the shadowy bedroom and bath. From where she stood, she couldn't see any mad killers lying in wait.

But that was the thing about mad killers. They never let you see them until it was too late.

Kris let out a shaky laugh. The last time she'd checked, mad killers didn't fix broken doors.

A shiny new key lay on the counter. But no note had been left identifying the culprit.

The sole explanation was Liam. He'd broken the door; he was the only one who knew about it besides her. He'd either fixed it or told Rob Cameron to do so.

She was still going to explore the bedroom and bathroom.

"And I'm taking my gun with me," she announced, yanking open the drawer of the coffee table, relieved to find the weapon still in residence.

Taking it along as she'd promised, Kris strode to the bathroom and slammed the open door against the wall as hard as she could. No one yelped. Or shot her. She did the same to the bedroom door, with similar results.

A cavity search—shower, closets, darkness beneath the bed—revealed no bodies, live or dead, unless you counted the bugs.

She had to say, having the gun in her hand made her

feel better. Of course if anyone had leaped out, they could have grabbed the thing easily from her hand. If she didn't drop it first and shoot off a toe.

That accomplished, Kris pocketed the key, locked the front door, put the gun back where she'd found it, and turned on her computer.

She tried to raise Mandenauer. It was like raising the dead. Impossible unless you knew how.

Kris rubbed her eyes again. What was wrong with her? There was no "knowing how" to raise the dead. All that talking with Jamaica about magic and sacrifice and ancient religions was screwing with her brain.

She almost wished she would hear Mandenauer calling her name from the computer. She bet he knew all there was to know about Obeah.

But the computer remained just a computer, so Kris cracked her knuckles and began to surf.

Most of what she discovered Jamaica had already told her. There seemed to be a dearth of info on Obeah, which was most likely a result of the respect—i.e., fear—in which it was held. Considering that many in Jamaica considered Obeah to be a dangerous form of sorcery and refused to even speak the word out loud, it followed that those who knew the most about it—Jamaicans—were not being interviewed for scholarly books, Web sites, or seminars.

She did find one thing when she tried a search on sacrifice, witches, and power. She didn't much like it.

"The more you give, the more you shall receive," she read. "The greater the sacrifice, the greater the gift of power."

At first she considered that meant sacrifice an elephant, you were in damn good shape. Unless the poacher patrol found you. Then you were fucked. As you should be.

But the more she uncovered, the more she read about just what a sacrifice meant, the more Kris figured they were talking about something other than size, and it scared her.

"Intelligence," Kris muttered. "Ferocity. Cunning. If they're easy to kill, what kind of a sacrifice is that?"

Therefore, the harder the life was to end, the greater the gift to the god.

So a lion netted more oomph than a lamb. A gorilla more juice than a mouse.

"And a person . . ." Kris lifted her eyes to the window, through which she could see the distant drift of the dirt-shaded loch. "That's gotta light you right up."

She was letting her imagination run away with her. Something she'd never been accused of until she came here. Kris dealt in facts. Facts never lied.

She tapped the screen of her laptop. These were not facts. You could sacrifice a whole baseball team to Obi and still not have enough juice to fuel your Magic 8-Ball. Because—

"Magic isn't real," Kris said.

Of course whoever was killing people might not know that.

CHAPTER 16

Did she truly believe that Jamaica was sacrificing women to the snake god she had tattooed on her ankle?

Not really. If Jamaica had anything to hide, she wouldn't have told Kris about her past at all. And she'd have covered the damn ankle.

Kris Googled *Jamaica Blue* anyway. All she found were coffee sites, one of them Jamaica's own. Kris hadn't expected anything else.

She could ask Alan Mac what he knew about the woman, but he already thought Kris was paranoid, with a side order of nuts. What would he think if she started talking about witchcraft, human sacrifices, and snake gods? Nothing good.

Kris spent the rest of the day answering e-mail. It took the rest of the day because the Internet had decided to flicker on and off at will. Frustrating, but nothing she could do about it beyond curse impotently. During "off" times, she made notes about what she'd learned thus far. She even took a nap, the lock on the door and the knife on her night table allowing her to fall asleep.

Unfortunately, the stray thought that whoever had

fixed the door might have kept a key for themselves woke her up. She needed to find out who had done that. If it was Rob or Liam, she was all right.

"Or not," she said as she readied herself for the return to Drumnadrochit. Where was it written that old men and hot guys couldn't be murderers?

Nowhere that she'd ever seen.

Kris headed to the village long before the sun went down. She didn't plan to be out alone in the dark, even though she hadn't been any less wigged about it in the daylight. She told herself she needed the extra time to stop at Effy's.

A short while later Kris entered Drumnadrochit for the second time that day. She passed by the coffee shop and was surprised to discover a *Closed* sign perched in the window. She could have sworn the place stayed open later.

Kris continued on to Effy's. She wasn't there, and neither was Rob. Turning away, Kris looked up and down the still-bustling street. Where was everybody?

She hung around, figuring one or both of them had to come back sooner or later, but as it got to be later and the sun dipped below the western horizon, casting the loch and Drumnadrochit into shadow, Kris gave up and left for MacLeod's.

She turned the corner just as a slim, dark, familiar figure approached the pub. Kris opened her mouth to call, *Liam!* but before she could, he slipped inside.

The scuff of a shoe on pavement had her glancing over her shoulder. Just past dusk, and the streetlights had not come on, but a golden glow spilled from the windows of several shops. Instead of being inviting, the contrast of flickering light and encroaching darkness made the shadows dance like demons around the bonfires of hell.

Kris hurriedly crossed the street and went in.

At MacLeod's the lights were on and everyone was home. Except Liam. She didn't see him anywhere.

Kris frowned. She'd watched him walk in only a few moments ago. Could he have strode right through the bar and out the back door?

Why? Unless he'd ducked around the corner to watch her from the shadows, scuffling his shoe just enough to make her paranoid.

Kris sighed. No one had to *make* her paranoid. She was already there. She glanced around again, certain she'd just missed him in the crush.

However, though Liam wasn't tall, he was distinctive. Gorgeous shone like sun through the clouds. Right now all she saw was a storm.

Effy and Rob sat at the same table in the corner, drinking as they'd been the last time she'd seen them, and they appeared to be having the same argument, if the sloshing of Effy's ale out of her glass and onto the table was any indication. Since Kris had been searching for them, too, she put aside the issue of Liam Grant and crossed to the Camerons.

Though people moved when she said, "Excuse me," no one greeted her or even smiled. She felt a little out of place, perhaps because she was an American in a local Scottish bar. No one would ask her, or any other foreigner with money, to leave. But that didn't mean they had to welcome her into *their* place.

As she approached the Camerons' table, Effy gave her brother an evil eye that seemed so out of place on her cherubic face Kris stifled a laugh.

"No fool like an old fool," Effy snapped.

Rob took another swig of his ale and said nothing.

"Aaah!" Effy picked up her own glass, tilting her arm

with the obvious intent of tossing the contents into her brother's face.

Rob set his down with a click, pointed a finger at his sister, and said, "Dinnae," in a voice as calm as the loch on a windless night beneath the moon.

Effy's glare became even more evil, but she *didnae*.

Rob's movement pulled up the long sleeve of his shirt, revealing the tattoo of a flipper on his wrist.

"Hi," Kris said.

The two turned their heads at the exact same time, with the exact same tilt. However, Effy's face welcomed Kris even before she saw who it was, while Rob's held no expression at all.

Kris pointed at Rob's wrist. "Can I see?"

Rob glanced down, then yanked the cuff of his shirt over the tattoo.

"It—uh—looks like a duck," she said.

"If it looks like a duck, and it quacks like a duck," he took a hearty draw on his ale, "then it must be a duck."

Did that mean it was a duck?

"There are a lot of tattoos in Drumnadrochit," Kris observed.

"Is that so?" Effy asked. "Who else?"

Kris's gaze lowered to Effy's breast, but when she lifted her eyes Effy still appeared only mildly curious. Kris didn't have the guts to ask about hers. Perhaps it *had* been a bruise.

"Jamaica has a snake on her ankle," Kris blurted. "And Alan Mac has a . . ." She paused. *Line* wasn't very descriptive.

"Never mind," Kris said. What difference did it make if everyone in Drumnadrochit had a tattoo? It didn't mean anything except the village had a high tolerance for body art.

"Join us!" Effy cooed.

Rob continued to drink.

"Actually, I'm . . . meeting someone," Kris said. "I just wanted to ask—"

"Ye've got a man friend already?" Effy clapped her hands over her apple cheeks. "How lovely."

"Mebe she's got a woman friend," Rob muttered.

Effy let one hand fall back to her pint, where she caressed the glass thoughtfully, and glared. Rob continued to drink. He didn't appear worried. Nevertheless, Kris jumped in to smooth things out: "I wanted to ask if you'd fixed the door to the cottage?"

Effy's face crinkled in confusion, and Kris's heart took a quick, concerned thud. Then Rob murmured, "Ye think there's a mad handyman strollin' through the Highlands, repairin' whatever he finds broke as he goes?"

Both Effy and Kris glanced at him. Rob took a slow sip of his ale before continuing. "Of course I fixed it."

"What was wrong with the door?" Effy asked.

"What wasnae?" Rob returned.

"How did you know it was broken?" Kris asked.

"Had a note on me own door this morning." Now he frowned. "That wasnae from you?"

Kris shook her head. Maybe it had been from—

A mere brush of his fingertips across her arm, and she knew it was him.

Kris turned, half-expecting to find no one there. A ghost of a touch from a ghost.

But Liam *was* there, and she reached out to touch him, too, releasing a relieved little *huff* when her hand encountered solid, male flesh beneath the usual dark shirt.

His hair was tied back, revealing the fine bones of his face, and his eyes blazed bright blue. He took her hand, and her foolish heart stuttered.

"There ye are. I was afraid ye hadnae come."

Kris felt like she was in junior high and the coolest guy in school had asked her to dance.

She needed to watch herself. What if she fell in love with Liam and then discovered—

What? That he wasn't real?

Liam was right here. She was touching him. She could see him, and so could—

Kris faced the Camerons, concerned they'd be staring at her with pity as she mooned over empty space.

But they were staring at Liam, their expressions hard to read, especially as those expressions disappeared faster than a bunny down a hole as soon as Kris saw them. She could have sworn they were shocked, but why would that be?

"You know Liam?" Kris asked.

"Liam?" Effy repeated. Rob just snorted.

"Of course they know me," Liam said. "Isnae that right, Effy?"

When Liam said her name, she started. "Right! I've known him all of me life."

"Don't ye mean ye've known me all *my* life?" Liam asked quietly.

"Yes. Of course. Since ye were a wee, sweet lad."

"Rob would let me trail around after him while he worked," Liam continued. "Learned at his knee just how to use a hammer."

"Mmm," Rob said, and lifted his nearly empty pint.

"Let me get ye another." Liam snatched it from the man's hand, sweeping Effy's up, too. "Would ye like one, Kris?"

Kris nodded, unable to stop her gaze from flicking back and forth between Liam and the Camerons, searching in vain for a reason their conversation seemed so weird.

Liam left. Effy and Rob contemplated their empty hands.

"Liam grew up here?" Kris asked.

The Camerons glanced at each other, then back at their hands.

"Aye," Effy agreed.

"In Drumnadrochit?" she clarified.

"Aye," Rob said.

Kris looked over in time to see Johnnie lean across the bar so he could hear what Liam had to say. The man straightened, glancing in Kris's direction, then nodded.

"Strange," Kris murmured, and turned away.

Effy lifted her wide, startled gaze. "Why?"

Kris didn't answer immediately, thinking back on whom she'd questioned about Liam and what they'd said. It had all been pretty much the same.

"I asked several people in the village about Liam Grant, and no one had ever heard of him."

"That's because most people in Drumnadrochit call me—"

Effy took a quick, sharp, audible breath that had all of them turning toward her. But she put her hand over her mouth as if she'd hiccoughed and said, "'Scuse me."

Liam set three pints on the table. "Billy," he finished.

"Most people call you Billy?" Kris laughed. He looked *nothing* at all like a Billy.

"'Liam' is short for 'William,'" he said. "And when I was young . . ." He handed her a pint.

"Billy," she finished, lifting her brows at the Camerons.

Rob shrugged and picked up his fresh drink, but Effy nodded, fluffy white hair bobbing. "Aye. Billy he was." She frowned. "Is?"

"I prefer 'Liam' these days," Liam said.

"I bet ye do," Rob murmured.

Effy gave her brother a sharp glance and reached for his pint. He slapped her hand.

"Dinnae," he said, and she sniffed. But she took her hand back, and she didn't try to touch his ale again.

"Liam!" a voice called.

Johnnie held up another glass, smiling widely. Liam crossed over and took it, then reached for his back pocket. The owner appeared horrified and waved away the offer of payment.

"I'm glad you two are keeping company," Effy murmured.

Were they? Kris supposed that was as good a term as any. Or at least one she was willing to acknowledge.

"Why's that?" she asked.

"He's been too long alone. It isnae right."

Rob muttered something that sounded a lot like: "Is, too."

But when she would have asked him to repeat it, Effy continued, "He's had a sad and lonely time. When he sees you, he smiles." Effy glanced past Kris. "Everyone should have a reason to smile."

Liam joined them, and he did smile, which made Kris smile, too.

"You don't have to pay?" she asked.

Rob snorted again. This time Liam cast him a quick glance. The old man tugged his ale closer and crooked an elbow around it as if he were in a prison cafeteria protecting his last piece of meat.

Liam returned his gaze to Kris. "I help out when they need it. Johnnie wouldnae charge me for a few pints."

A slow, easy melody replaced the faint trill of bagpipes, and a few couples drifted onto a portable plank dance floor in one corner of the pub.

"Dance Wednesday," Liam explained. "They try to get folks in for the middle of the week." He set down his pint, then reached for hers. "Would ye?"

"Dance?" Kris let him take the glass. She wasn't much for dancing. Hell, she wasn't much for bars or gatherings or even men.

Liam took her hand again, and she was lost. What was it about him that made her do things she normally wouldn't?

The other couples shifted to the side when Liam and Kris stepped onto the floor, though the movement seemed more deferential than polite. She tried to catch someone's eye, to smile, to fit in, but they were all too involved with each other to notice. An instant later, so was she.

She went into his arms, and he pulled her close, until her cheek rested against his shoulder just right. He had a natural grace, and where he led it was very easy to follow. Where he led she wanted to follow.

Kris lifted her head, disturbed by the thought. She was not the type to follow anyone, let alone a man she'd just met, in a country she was only visiting. She couldn't let great sex fry her brain, although she could see now, when she'd never been able to before, how that might happen.

"Thug mi gaol," he whispered. "Thug mi gaol."

As he slowly twirled her about the floor, she found herself lost in the beautiful lilt of that voice. She wanted to press her cheek back to his shoulder and listen. So she did.

"Thug mi gaol don fhear bhan." His chest vibrated as he sang. She rubbed her skin against his shirt, and the scent of him surrounded her.

"Wicked," she murmured, and he kissed her hair. How was she ever going to leave him?

The song continued, and so did they, around and

around, captured in each other's arms. Kris wished the music would last forever.

She had found few occasions to dance, and she wasn't very good at it. But Liam was an exquisite dancer, and with him she became one, too. They never brushed another couple, never bumped butts or tangled heels. They seemed shrouded in a bubble of music and warmth that existed only for them.

"Agus gealladh dhusta, luaidh," Liam murmured.

Kris lifted her head. "What does that mean?"

"'I will never let anyone harm ye while I am here.'"

The music ended, but they stood in the center of the floor, staring into each other's eyes. She wanted to kiss him. But the way her skin felt—buzzing, humming, calling out for his—she didn't think she could stop at a kiss. From the blaze of his eyes, she didn't think he would, either.

She slowly became aware of their surroundings. The pub was quiet, the dance floor empty but for them. She glanced to the right, then the left.

Everyone was staring.

"Liam," she whispered.

"Dinnae worry about them."

"Maybe we should—" She stepped back. His arms, still around her waist, held on, and she stumbled into his chest.

He kissed her, and she forgot that everyone was staring.

He still tasted of sinfully expensive chocolate, of midnight and seduction, with a side of nut-brown ale. His tongue was warm, but his lips were cool, a blessed oasis amid a sudden heat.

She'd been right. A kiss wasn't enough. She had to touch him, bury her fingers in his silky black hair, run a nail down the side of his neck until he shuddered, hardening against her belly, which was pressed tightly to him, shielding him as he'd promised to shield her.

What on earth was going on? Kris had no idea, but she didn't want it to stop.

Of course it did. Nothing good lasts forever. And something that great . . . well, it only lasted a minute, maybe two, before a voice interrupted.

"What the hell are you doing here?"

CHAPTER 17

Dougal Scott barreled toward them, fists clenched. Kris wasn't sure if he was talking to her or to Liam.

Dougal swung. Liam ducked. Kris tried to, but she wasn't as quick as Liam and the fist caught her on the cheek. Everyone gasped.

Light exploded, then the pain. Kris didn't fall, but she staggered. Liam turned, caught, then righted her. She thought he would hold her and she even began to go into his arms, but as soon as she was solid on her feet he was gone.

His arm was a blur, shooting out, popping Dougal on the chin. The blow seemed too fast to pack much punch, but it must have, since Dougal went down like a house of cards in a sudden wind.

No one came forward to help. No one stepped in to stop them, not even Johnnie. Back home, a place like this might keep a shotgun under the bar, or at least a bat. But here, the owner just watched, as did everyone else.

It was weird.

Dougal lay sprawled on the dance floor, the hand that had hit her now rubbing his own chin. His gaze went past Liam to Kris. "I'm sorry," he said.

Kris wasn't sure what to say. It wasn't "all right." Her cheek hurt like a son of a bitch. She was going to have a bruise, if not a black eye. But he did seem sorry, and he hadn't meant to hurt her. But what the hell had gotten into him?

"Here, dearie." Effy appeared at her side with a dish towel of ice. "Press this right there." She showed Kris what to do.

"None for me?" Dougal asked.

Effy sniffed and ignored him.

Dougal got to his feet and shoved past Liam, headed in Kris's direction.

Liam grabbed him. "Ye willnae go near her again."

Dougal drew himself up, towering over Liam, yet Liam was the one who appeared fearsome.

"I'll kill ye if ye hurt her," Liam vowed.

"Whoa," Kris said—ignoring Effy's murmurs of, "Shh, dearie."—"Calm down."

Both men turned, blinking as if they'd forgotten Kris was there. Which they couldn't have considering they'd been talking—no, *arguing*—over her.

"You slept with him, didn't you?" Dougal demanded.

The question was so shockingly inappropriate Kris's mouth fell open. Then her cheeks flamed, giving him the answer he did not deserve.

Dougal made a disgusted sound. "Of course you did. Women can never help themselves around a pretty face, a perfect body. I'm sure he's got a cock the size of Inverness."

Kris winced. *Nice.*

"Dinnae listen to him," Effy said. "Sometimes Dougal can be—"

"Honest?" Dougal interrupted. "Forthright?"

"An ass," Liam muttered.

"Takes one to know one," Dougal returned, and Kris couldn't help it; she giggled.

Dougal's face flushed, and Kris blurted, "Sorry! It's just so school yard. Fighting over a girl and 'takes one to know one.' It struck me—" Dougal turned on his heel and strode out. "Funny," she finished as the door slammed behind him.

The room remained silent for several ticks of the clock, then broke into loud conversation as if nothing had happened.

"What *was* that?" she asked. "He and I— We— Didn't. I mean, we talk. We were friendly. But—"

"Dougal tries so hard to fit in," Effy said softly. "But he cannae. He must have thought, in you, he'd found a kindred spirit at last."

Kris cast her a quick, suspicious glance. Did Effy know she and Dougal were fellow skeptics? How?

"Yer both American," Effy continued. "Newcomers. Interested in Nessie and the like. I'm sure he felt ye were his special friend."

"Not anymore," Kris muttered.

Liam pulled the ice pack away from her throbbing cheek. He grimaced when he saw what lay beneath.

"Mo gradh," he whispered. "Tha me duilich."

When he spoke to her like that she forgot who she was, who he was; she only remembered what they'd been like together.

"What does that mean?" she asked.

Liam shook his head, gently putting the ice pack to her cheek once more and holding it there with his hand atop hers.

"'My love,'" Effy translated, considering gaze on Liam. "'I am sorry.'"

"If I wanted her t' know," Liam growled, "I could have told her myself."

Effy winked at Kris, then returned to her table.

Silence settled between them. This only made the loud conversation, the tinkling of glasses, the music, which had started up again but now played a rousing, modern tune, seem to pulse all around, separating Kris and Liam from everyone else.

"Why didn't you want me to know what you said?" Kris asked.

Liam shrugged and looked away. "We've just met. I shouldnae be callin' you *my love*."

Except Kris didn't want him to stop.

And that was probably her most foolish thought of all in a day that had been full of them.

Couples jiggled on the dance floor. Liam took one glance at their gyrations, made a face, and clasped her hand. "I'll walk ye home," he said.

Considering everything, she'd let him.

As they made their way to the exit, Alan Mac's large form sprouted from the crowd. Perhaps Johnnie had not been as nonchalant about the fight as he'd seemed. Perhaps instead of pulling out his gun or his bat, he'd pulled out his telephone and called the cops.

Several people spoke at once. Alan Mac frowned. When someone jabbed a finger in Liam and Kris's direction, he followed it, and his eyes widened.

Liam sighed as the constable headed toward them. Kris prepared to tell Alan Mac just who was at fault in the altercation. She didn't get a chance.

"What are you doing here?" Alan demanded.

Kris turned to Liam. "Why is that the first question everyone asks you?"

"I dinnae get out much."

Alan Mac choked; then he started to cough. Johnnie appeared at his side with a pint, which the big man chugged like water. When he lowered the empty glass and handed it to the bartender, his face had gone as scarlet as Dougal's.

"What's going on?" Kris handed the now-sopping dish towel to Johnnie as well. "Everyone acts like you're a hermit. If they aren't saying they never heard of you." She narrowed her gaze on Alan Mac. "*You* told me he was a ghost." She filled her palm with Liam's ample biceps. "He doesna feel like a ghost t' me," she mocked.

"Ye were talking about him?" Alan Mac shoved a finger in Liam's face. Liam appeared ready to bite it off.

Kris's head began to ache. "Let me guess. You grew up together. It's hard for you to think of him as anything other than Billy."

"How'd ye know?" Liam murmured, his gaze holding Alan Mac's.

The constable remained silent.

Johnnie brought Alan another pint, and he took it, breaking eye contact with Liam to down this one nearly as fast as the first.

"Should you be slamming those while on duty?" Kris asked.

"Not." Alan Mac wiped his mouth with the back of his hand and shoved the glass at Johnnie. "On duty, that is. I'll have another." He rubbed at his eyes. "I need it."

Liam straightened. "What happened?"

Alan Mac glanced around as if afraid they'd be overheard. Considering they were in the middle of nearly a hundred people, he had a legitimate concern. Except everyone had lost interest in them and returned to their drinking and dancing. Nevertheless, the constable lowered his voice: "Another body. This one caught in the lock at Dochgarroch."

"Woman?" Liam asked, and Alan nodded. "Same as the others?"

Kris cast Liam a sharp look. How did he know so much about it?

"No," Alan Mac said. "Not bopped over the head and drowned. Not this time." He took a breath. "Maybe it's not the same killer."

Liam lifted a brow. "Because two would be better?"

Alan Mac's broad shoulders slumped. He obviously hadn't thought of that.

"If not drowned," Liam continued, "then what?"

"Knife to the chest." Kris stilled. "But that wasnae the strangest part."

"A third dead woman, this one with a knife in her chest, isnae the worst of it?" Liam asked.

"I dinnae know about worst, but strange, aye?" Alan Mac took the pint Johnnie brought and drank it more slowly than he had the others. "The knife was silver." His gaze held Liam's. "And not just silver plated, ye ken? Pure silver, through and through."

Uh-oh, Kris thought. How many pure silver knives could there be in the area?

It didn't matter. She was pretty sure this one was hers.

Silver, Liam thought. Could Edward Mandenauer still be in the area?

Ach, no. If the dead girl had been a shape-shifter, she would be ashes. No body left behind to become stuck in the lock at Dochgarroch. Edward, for all his faults, was very good about not stabbing humans with knives meant specifically for the inhuman.

Still, everyone made mistakes, and Mandenauer *was* getting quite old. Though it would be best not to tell him that and meet the pointy end of another silver knife.

Alan Mac continued to stare at Liam, lifting his brows up and down like a demented Groucho Marx. As if Liam didn't know what silver meant. But if Alan kept it up, Kris soon would. If she didn't already.

Kris wasn't a *Jäger-Sucher,* but that didn't mean she wasn't something else.

Mandenauer had come here off and on for decades, if not centuries—Liam was not all that certain the man wasn't immortal himself—and he'd never discovered their secret. However, Liam wouldn't put it past the wily agent to pay someone like Kris—smart, resourceful, with an agenda of her own that paralleled that of the *Jäger-Suchers*—to keep an eye on things, then call Edward if anything turned up.

Hell, Liam wouldn't put it past Mandenauer to kill a few women, toss them in the loch, blame it on Nessie, then wait for her to show up and—

Pow!

Liam had gone so far into his thoughts, he actually jerked as if he'd been shot. Stabbed. Blown up. Whatever.

Alan Mac frowned. Liam shook his head just once.

Not now, he thought, then shifted only his eyes to the left. *Later.*

Alan Mac's chin dipped in a nearly imperceptible nod.

Liam glanced at Kris, expecting her to be staring at him with lifted brow and a *do you think I'm an idiot?* expression. Instead, she stared at the door with longing. The dark shadow of a bruise already marred the perfection of one cheek.

He'd promised to care for her, and less than a minute later she'd been hit. He'd said he'd see her home, yet he stood in the center of a pub while she became paler and paler.

"Time to go," he murmured.

Her eyes met his, and something shifted in Liam's chest, so sudden and startling, he rubbed at the spot.

What was that? Both pleasure and pain, which left behind a sense of joyful sorrow. He'd never felt anything
like it before.

Outside, the night was cool and dark. Clouds had
moved in, covering the moon and the stars. Liam didn't
mind. Sometimes the moon only reminded him of things
he'd prefer to forget.

Kris slid her arm around his waist, leaning into him.
The warmth of her caressed; the scent of her soothed. He'd
never strolled down the street with a woman before. Never
held her to his side, matched his steps, his very breath, to
hers. When Kris left, he was going to miss her for the rest
of his days.

When she left, the ghosts would come back. They
would torment and haunt him. But it was nothing less
than he deserved.

Liam shook off the sudden melancholy. Kris was here;
so was he. Yes, she'd leave, but that was for the best. If
she stayed—

He stiffened, pausing mid-step as Kris continued on.
They came unstuck, and Liam was suddenly as cold as if
he'd just dived into the loch.

"You all right?" She offered her hand. He stared at it
for several seconds before he took it with a nod.

Once they were away from the village, the night grew
even darker. They said nothing; however, the silence
wasn't awkward. Liam had never been with a woman
who didn't want to talk all the time. Not that he'd been
with so very many, at least not lately, despite what that
ass Dougal Scott had implied.

The man had never liked him, and the feeling, even
before tonight, was mutual. Dougal Scott was just one
of those people who rubbed Liam, and a lot of others, the
wrong way.

Liam glanced at Kris. Should he say something about Dougal's implication that Liam was the village lothario?

Probably.

Before he could, a movement near the loch distracted him. There, in the trees, a shadow slid from one to another and then on to the next. Silent, stealthy, whoever lurked there was very good. But Liam knew the banks of the loch better than anyone, and that shadow could slither all it liked, but that shadow did not belong.

Kris stared straight ahead, oblivious. Why wouldn't she be? She didn't have the training, the experience, the background that he had. It was only through pure luck that she'd survived thus far.

The idea of someone stalking her, perhaps killing her, made his skin prickle and his heart beat ever faster. The mental image of Kris in the loch with Nessie scared him more than anything had in—

Actually, nothing had ever scared him. He did not like that suddenly something could.

Liam considered running into the forest and grabbing the culprit, but if he did, he'd have to leave Kris alone, and he couldn't.

He'd see her safely home. Tucked into bed with the door locked.

The door. The lock. He'd broken it.

"Maybe you should stay at a hotel," Liam murmured.

"Why?"

He could barely see her face; the night was so damn dark. "Your door's broken," he said. "Ye shouldnae stay there until it's fixed."

"It *is* fixed. Rob had a note on his door. I thought that maybe you—?"

"No," Liam murmured. He'd been a little . . . busy all day. He always was.

He didn't care for that note, although why would anyone who wanted to do her harm have Rob fix the door?

They reached the cottage, and Kris used her new key on the new lock. Liam was so glad to see it. If the door had still been broken he would have had to stay here; then he wouldn't have been able to slip out and discover who had followed them.

His luck, it would be Dougal Scott. The ass.

"Dougal," he began. "What he said . . ."

Liam paused. Dougal didn't know about Liam's past—he couldn't—the man had just assumed. Unfortunately, he'd assumed correctly.

Kris walked inside and switched on the light. "Which is it?"

"Which?" Liam repeated.

"Effy said you were too long alone. Dougal implied you have more women than the Pasha of . . ." She spread her hands. "Pashaville."

Liam wanted to smack both Effy and Dougal, or perhaps knock their heads together. Kris had been lied to so often she trusted no one at all. He wished he could say that she should trust him, but he was lying, too, and he wasn't going to stop. But he could clear up *this* misunderstanding.

Liam shut the door, then crossed the room until he stood so close Kris had to crane her neck to see his face.

"Both," he said.

"Both?" She let out a short, sharp laugh and stepped back. He caught her hand before she could turn away, holding on when she tried to pull free.

Though he hated to agree with Dougal on anything, he'd vowed to tell her this truth. "*Once* I had more women than that pasha, 'tis true. But I have also been too long alone."

Aeons, it seemed. Such was the way of loneliness.

Kris peered into his face with a measuring look. "You said the ghosts come to you." He stiffened, and when he would have pulled away *she* held on. "Are they the reason you're alone?"

He sighed. Another truth he could share.

"Yes."

"Your family? He shook his head. "Did you . . . love and lose someone?"

Liam didn't think he'd been capable of love. At least not until that night beneath the moon. Now . . .

He still wasn't sure.

"I understand." She squeezed his hand. "You turned to sex to forget."

At his confused expression, she continued. "You lost someone you loved, and you turned to meaningless sex with an endless string of women."

"They were mistakes," he said. Horrible, terrible, haunting mistakes.

Kris tilted her head, studying him. "Why me?"

Good question. He wished he knew. What was it about her that made him break every vow he'd made since he'd become what he was?

"I don't know," he admitted. "I don't care."

Because, right now, he was going to break every one of them again.

CHAPTER 18

There was something Liam was supposed to do, some-where he was supposed to be. But staring into Kris's eyes, soft and dark and filled with sympathy for him, made the ache in Liam's chest both worse and a little better. When he kissed her, he felt reborn.

"Liam," she whispered, right before his lips met hers and the name—truly his and one he hadn't heard for far too long—had his breath catching as his body hardened.

He'd had women. Scores of them. But they'd been—

Mistakes. Aye. He had not known any better.

He wished he could forget them, but he was cursed to remember. And that was right; that was justice.

Kris had said he'd used sex to forget. But he hadn't.

Until now.

When he touched her, when he loved her, all that he remembered *was* her.

The catch of her breath when he wrapped her in his arms, rubbed her breasts against his chest, and opened her mouth just enough for him to delve.

She tasted of ale, but a hint, the tangy flavor enhancing

what was hers alone. He drank from her, seeking oblivion. Finding it.

His chilled hands crept beneath the hem of her sweater, and she jumped, then nipped at his lip. But when he would have removed his hands, she snatched them back, warming them with her own.

Beneath the confines of her bra, her breasts blazed; his palms tingled from the heat. When he squeezed them she moaned. His name again, the sound of it enflamed him. No one had cried out his name in forever, and he discovered that he needed it.

Her fingers encircled him. How had she gotten her hand down his pants? Not that he was complaining.

His head fell back; his hair had come loose on the dance floor, and the slide of it along his neck made him shiver. The heat of her palm along his shaft nearly made him come.

Though his body barked in protest, he encircled her wrist and removed that clever, clever hand from its home.

"Keep that up and we'll be done before we start," he muttered.

"We wouldn't want that." She ran a thumbnail up his erection. His eyes crossed, and she laughed.

"Maybe I should—" She rolled her thumb over the tip. His jeans did little to alleviate the friction or that eternal, blessed, heat. "Take the edge off."

"Huh?" He couldn't think.

Mission accomplished.

Her smile was all woman as she unbuttoned, then unzipped, his jeans. "Lose them," she ordered.

He did.

"The shirt, too."

Liam drew it over his head and tossed the garment to

the floor with the rest. Then he stood in the glaring light of the lamp and let her stare.

He knew he was lovely to look at. Always had been, always would be. He couldn't help it. He also knew that beauty could be as much of a curse as ugliness. Beauty seduced and it tempted, but beauty had no substance. It was as worthless as the sheen of the moon.

Kris didn't look long. Perhaps, as a thing of beauty herself, she understood how passing frail human beauty was.

When she dropped to her knees and took him into her mouth, he was so shocked he let her. Then he was so captivated he could do nothing but yearn. He'd never had a woman's mouth on him.

The scalding, wicked, wet heat spread through him. Her tongue swirled over him, and she suckled.

Ah, God. Why not?

He cupped her head with his palm as she began to move in the age-old rhythm. *Just a few seconds,* he promised himself. *Just a few—*

His hips thrust, in and out, in and out. The pressure. The heat. That tongue. What was she doing to him?

He was seduction; he had never, yet, been seduced. He wasn't sure that he liked it. He had no restraint. His body spun toward something he wanted, needed, craved.

Liam pulled away. "No," he said. "I'll—"

He bit his lip. He who had had so many women he'd lost count, who had taken them in ways they'd begged for, ways that had surprised but never shocked him, couldn't find the words for a simple, inevitable response of the body.

"You'll come?" She glanced up, lips full and curved and wet. "That was kind of what I was going for."

As she leaned forward, her tongue darted out, swirling around his head. He lost control.

"No," he said again, reaching down and dragging her to her feet. Then he tossed her over his shoulder, stalked into the bedroom, his cock leading the way, where he dropped her onto the bed. "I'll not come until I'm inside of ye."

Her eyes lowered; her gaze brushed over him like a caress, and his penis leaped. "You'd better hurry."

"I never hurry," he promised, then slowly removed every stitch of her clothes, echoing the movements of his hands with the press of his lips, the skim of teeth and tongue. By the time he finished, she was writhing.

"Liam." She lifted her hips—an offering he could not help but take.

His tongue darted out, and those hips jerked. His lips curved as he feasted. This was familiar. This he had done. Some women needed more . . . help.

Not Kris. She began to swell against him; desire rolled toward them, given voice by the ever-increasing beat of their breath.

She grabbed him by the hair. He knew better than to argue. Lifting his head, he met her eyes.

"You said you'd come nowhere but inside of me."

"Aye."

"I don't want to come with you anywhere but there, either." She gave his hair a tug, and he followed that lead, sliding up and then sliding home.

He'd kept his orgasm at bay by pleasing her. Not that the taste of her, the feel of her, didn't arouse. But he'd used his mind, his powers of seduction, and now he let everything go.

The blessed warmth, the friction, the press of her all around. Her hands on his shoulders. Her nails in his skin.

Her mouth, her tongue, the memories of where both had last been.

And still it wasn't enough. Until . . .

"Liam," she said. "Liam."

He came in a rush so strong his sight ebbed, narrowing to all that was her.

Her body answered, tightening, pulsing, welcoming him. "Yes," she said. "Yes." And then . . .

"Liam."

He fell asleep still tangled up in her. Her breath in time with his, her scent and the memory of that husky voice whispering the name he hadn't heard in so long following Liam into a dark and peaceful land.

He awoke tense, almost vibrating with the certainty that something was wrong. When he opened his eyes and saw her cuddled against him, her arm across his belly, her cheek against his chest, he understood.

This was wrong. He'd promised without words something that could never, ever be.

Liam gently disentangled himself from her body and her embrace. She murmured, turning toward him, reaching out, and he couldn't help himself; he brushed her hair from her face and kissed her brow. She settled deeper into sleep, and he watched her, rubbing at the ache that seemed to have taken up residence in his soul.

Did he even have a soul? He'd never been quite sure.

A shadow passed between the moon—when had that come out?—and the house, a flicker against the shade, and Liam glanced up just in time to see a figure slide by.

He was shoving his feet into his pants, his arms into his shirt, even as he raced on silent, bare feet for the door.

This was what he'd forgotten—that shadow in the trees, which appeared to have graduated to Kris's backyard.

Liam yanked open the door, already stepping forward, prepared to run around the house and surprise whoever dared hover in the middle of the night.

Instead, he nearly knocked over the man who stood, head down, deep in thought, directly on the other side.

The guy glanced up, eyes wide and strangely familiar. Liam, whose reflexes were honed to an edge so fine he sometimes amazed himself, reached out, grabbed a handful of dark cotton shirt at the neck, and yanked.

"What are ye doin' creepin' about in the night?" he demanded.

The stranger blinked, then grasped Liam's wrists and attempted to pry them free.

Liam made a derisive sound—*not in this lifetime, brother*—and, spinning, slammed the would-be intruder against the open door. "Did ye dare t' touch her? Did ye dare try and bring her harm?"

His fingers tightened, and the man began to choke. Liam hadn't heard that sound in years. He'd hoped never to hear it again, but right now he quite liked it.

"Who are ye?" He pulled the stranger close, then shoved him back, bouncing his head off the wood with a lovely dull thud. "Who?"

He sputtered, opening and closing his mouth, still pulling on Liam's hands with a surprising amount of strength for one who would soon be dead.

The lights clicked on. Both Liam and the newcomer were left blinking, though neither of them let go of the other.

"You might want to loosen up on his windpipe." Kris, wearing nothing but a T-shirt that came to mid-thigh— and hopefully panties—stood a few feet away. "Just until you can get a name."

Her hair was tousled, her lips swollen from Liam's. The

bruise that had been but a hint when they'd arrived was now the shade of ripe eggplant, puffy and pained. He wanted to drop the intruder to the floor and find her some ice.

Liam must have been blocking her view, because when he shifted, Kris's eyes widened; her face paled, causing the bruise to flare a shiny black, like the skin of the monster beneath the moon.

"Marty?" she whispered.

Liam yanked away his hands. He figured the man would slide down the door and pool at his feet, which would give Liam a chance to find out just who in hell he was and why Kris knew him. Instead, the stranger's eyes narrowed on Kris's face, then his own flushed with fury.

"You bastard!" he announced, and punched Liam in the nose.

Kris cried out, rushing forward as blood spurted everywhere.

However, Liam didn't react like most men who'd just met the business side of another man's fist. Instead of clasping his hands to his gushing nose and howling, he wrapped them again around Marty's throat.

"Liam." Kris put her hand on his arm. "Let him go."

"I think not," Liam muttered.

"I know him. It's all right."

It wasn't. Not really. But she didn't want Liam to kill him, either.

At least not yet.

"Liam," she said again, and at last he sighed, then let Marty go.

"Who the fuck is he?" Liam snarled at the same time Marty shouted, "He hit you?"

Kris lifted a hand to her cheek. Her fingers encountered skin long before she'd thought they would, and she winced.

Her face was swollen, painful, and no doubt ugly as sin; no wonder Marty had gone ballistic.

"He didn't hit me," she said. "And even if he had, what is it to you? You walked out on me a long time ago."

Liam stilled, cocking his head. "Dinnae tell me he is your husband or I may just kill him after all."

Kris might have rolled her eyes at the statement, which would have sounded like it came straight out of an action movie if Liam hadn't appeared to mean it.

Marty drew himself up until he and Liam nearly bumped chests. "You and what army?" Marty asked.

Now Kris did roll her eyes. "Can it," she said. "He'd annihilate you."

"I would," Liam agreed, then reached out and shoved Marty into the door.

Kris jumped between them before they started wrestling like eight-year-olds. She put one hand on Liam's chest, another on Marty's. "Stop," she ordered.

Marty blinked, staring at her as if he'd seen a ghost. Liam growled, but he stopped, at least for now.

"Liam, my brother, Marty. Marty, Liam Grant."

The two men eyed each other warily.

"I ask again," Liam murmured. "What are ye doin' here?"

"I could ask you the same thing." Marty looked Kris up and down. "If it weren't so obvious that what you've been doing is her."

This time Liam popped Marty in the nose. Then they both stood there and bled together. Maybe it would help them bond.

Kris stalked to the kitchenette and yanked open drawers until she found the dish towels, then tossed one to each man. She'd tell Effy to put them on her tab. While she was there, she filled a third with ice and set it against her face.

"Shut the door." She waved with her free hand. "Then we'd better have a seat."

They did as she ordered, though they continued to stare at each other like two dogs with one bone. That she was the bone in question should have been amusing but wasn't.

Both men had headed for the chair, but when she plopped onto the couch they changed direction and sat next to her, one on either side.

The fit was a tad cozy. Kris considered getting up and taking the chair herself but feared that if she did that, they'd only wind up grabbing each other, then falling on the floor, flailing around, and breaking more than their noses.

"Would you sit there, Marty?" Kris pointed at the chair.

Her brother wasn't happy, but he moved.

Kris hadn't seen Marty since she was eighteen, and he'd been only a year older. She'd thought him full grown then, but she'd been wrong. He'd gained a few inches and a few pounds. His hair was also different. She remembered it being light brown, and it was in places. But the blond streaks suggested he'd been either working outside or visiting a salon.

Several puzzle pieces suddenly came together. "You've been asking about me in Drumnadrochit."

Marty lifted one shoulder, then lowered it. He also lowered the bloody dish towel. His nose had stopped bleeding but *had* started swelling. It also listed to the side.

She glanced at Liam, who stared at Marty in speculation. Liam's nose, though flecked with blood, seemed just fine.

"He's the one who's been slinking about asking fer ye?"

"Apparently," Kris murmured. "The question is why?"

"Why do you think, Squirt?" She started at his use of the nickname only Marty had called her, probably because she'd hated it so much. "I was worried about you."

"Squirt," Liam repeated. "I think that might be an insult, aye?"

Kris sighed. It was. But she wasn't going to tell him that.

"American term of endearment," she said shortly, and Marty smirked. "You didn't call. You didn't write." Marty's smirk faded.

Or show up once in the past seven years, goddammit.

Her brother glanced away. "I didn't think you'd want to see me."

Did she? Kris wasn't sure.

"She certainly didnae want to see ye creepin' about outside her bedroom window in the middle of the night," Liam muttered.

Kris straightened. "What?"

"I saw a shadow slip past, so I went to find out who it was, opened the door, and—"

"Grabbed me by the throat," Marty finished.

"What did ye expect, sneakin' around like ye were? A handshake?"

"I was just checking to make sure the door was fixed."

"*You* left the note for Rob?" Kris asked.

Marty shrugged again.

"He's been skulking about a lot longer than tonight," Liam murmured.

Marty ignored Liam and kept his gaze on Kris. "I saw someone following you."

"That appears to be the new national pastime," Kris said.

"If ye saw that someone, then you were followin' us, too," Liam pointed out.

Now Marty glanced at Liam with interest. "You saw them?"

"Or perhaps just you."

Marty opened his mouth to reply, and the trill of a cell phone split the air. His hand went to his pocket. He pulled one out, glanced at the display, hit the mute, and stood. "I have to go."

"It's the middle of the night." Kris stood, too. "Who's calling you?"

But he was already heading for the exit. "I'll be in touch," he said.

Kris laughed, the sound as derisive as a playground bully's.

Marty turned, expression bleak. "You have every right to doubt me. I don't blame you. But I stayed away for your own good, Squirt. I did it to protect you, not to hurt you."

A chill trickled over Kris. "What are you involved in, Marty?"

He shook his head and went out the door.

Kris ran after him, but the mist had come in, swallowing her brother as if he'd never even been.

She stared into the fog, ears straining for the rev of an engine—car, boat, cycle—or the flap of shoes on pavement. All she heard was the distant splash of the loch.

"That was weird." Kris closed the door and turned.

Liam peered out the window, beyond which the mist swirled. "Weirder than ye think, lass."

"Weirder than the brother I haven't seen in seven years showing up in Scotland when hardly anyone knows I'm here?"

Liam's gaze switched to hers. "No, that was the weird I was talking about."

Kris smiled, though the effort wasn't her best.

"What does yer brother do for a living?" Liam asked. Kris spread her hands. "Ye dinnae know?"

"I haven't heard a word from him since I was eighteen."

"Mmm," Liam murmured. "He said he'd stayed away from ye to protect ye. Which makes me wonder what he needs to protect ye from. Considering there's someone out there who's been tryin' to kill ye."

There had been so many things going on, so many things being said, Kris had forgotten about that one. And really, that was the one she should have remembered.

"What did he study in college?"

"Business." Kris frowned. "Psychology? Maybe English."

"I take it ye're not a close family."

"We were." Kris tried to leave it at that, but she couldn't. "Then my mother died."

"Ach." Liam touched her hair in that way he had that almost, but not quite, made everything all right. "It's sorry I am to hear it."

"Water under the bridge," Kris said, though it wasn't. It never truly would be. "After that Marty and my dad couldn't wait to get away from me."

Liam's lips turned down. "Perhaps not you so much as the place where they still saw her even though she was no longer there."

"Whatever," Kris muttered. "They left, and they didn't come back."

"Until now," Liam said. "So ye didnae tell yer brother where ye were?"

"I haven't told my brother anything in years. I wouldn't have known how to get hold of him even if I'd wanted to."

Liam's brows lifted, but he didn't comment. "Who *does* know you're here?"

Edward, but she doubted Marty had talked to him. Or if he had, that the old man would have told him anything.

"Lola," she said. "My roommate."

"To be fair, he could have talked to her."

Kris shook her head as she sat in the chair her brother had vacated. "I asked. No one's called. No one's been by."

"Maybe he called or went by after ye asked. When was the last time ye heard from her?"

Kris thought back. It had been several days, but—

"I asked *her* because there'd been a man in the village asking about *me*. Tall, streaked hair—" She snapped her fingers. "Red Sox cap. I should have known."

"Yer brother likes the Red Sox?"

"Hates 'em," Kris said.

Confusion spread over Liam's features. "Then why would ye have known?"

"You'd have to understand Marty," Kris said. "He's always been rabid about the Red Sox. Hated them like most people hate the Yankees. If he were trying to keep me from figuring out he was here, what better way than to wear a Red Sox cap?"

Liam obviously didn't understand how her brother's mind worked—Kris was surprised she still did—but he let it go. "Why wouldn't he want you to know he was here?"

"Yeah, why?" Kris murmured, staring at the door through which her brother had disappeared.

"Perhaps it wasn't so much you he was hidin' from as . . ." His forehead creased.

"As?" Kris prompted.

"Whoever he wanted to protect ye from. Ye think he could be involved in something illegal?"

"He could be involved in anything."

Liam's scowl deepened. Then he saw her watching and

forced a smile that was no cheerier than the one she'd forced. "At least his asking if ye were happy is less strange now."

"How you figure?"

"He's yer brother. Of course he wants to know if ye're happy."

"Then why not ask me to my face? Why sneak around and ask strangers?"

"Aye." Liam turned to look out the window again. "I see yer point."

The sight of his perfect profile brought up another question. "I think you broke Marty's nose."

"I did," he agreed.

"Yet yours looks just fine."

Liam met her eyes. "Yer brother hits like a girl."

Kris's lips twitched, but she managed not to laugh. "Why do you dislike him? You don't even know him."

His gaze softened, the way it did when he was deep inside her, and her breath caught on the memory. How was she ever going to leave this place, this man, this . . . whatever it was they had between them?

"He hurt ye, *mo chridhe*. I could see it in yer eyes, hear it in yer voice. Anyone who made ye ache like that deserves a broken nose."

"No one's ever . . ." She paused, embarrassed.

He sat on the couch and took her hand. "Ever what?"

Kris had meant to say *stood up for me;* then she remembered. She was a big girl; she didn't need anyone to stand up for her. She didn't need anyone to fight her battles. She could fight her own. Had been doing so for a very long time. But it had felt amazingly good to have someone fight just one.

"No one's ever called me *mo chridhe*," she blurted. "What does it mean?"

Liam glanced away; then his face took on an expression of shock before he jumped to his feet.

Kris did, too, whirling with her fists up, ready to face the next fight. But nothing was there.

"What is it?" she asked.

"Dawn. I have to go."

The window still appeared pitch-black to her, but with the mist it was a little hard to tell.

"I'm going to start thinking you have a wife and five kids the way you rush off at the slightest threat of sun."

"Just like a woman." His lips quirked. " 'T think wife and not vampire."

"I'm funny that way. But—"

He stepped in close and kissed her. She forgot what she'd been about to say.

Then he was gone—out the door and into the mist. She wondered if he'd run into her brother. That could get ugly.

Kris shook her head. Her brother.

What the hell?

CHAPTER 19

Liam thanked God for the mist that shrouded everything. Dawn was still an hour away, and he needed the time.

There was something strange about Marty Daniels. Liam planned to find out what. Or at least talk to someone who could.

That Kris hadn't seen the man in years, had no idea even what he did for a living, was troublesome enough. That he'd shown up at Loch Ness at the same time as a murderer was bloody disturbing.

Not that Liam thought Marty had tried to kill his own sister. What possible reason could he have? But the guy was hiding something—most likely himself—from someone who might.

Liam had been wondering why anyone would want to hurt Kris. Certainly she'd come here to debunk Nessie, the livelihood of hundreds, if not thousands. But Kris wouldn't have been able to, and everyone in Drumnadrochit knew it.

Most likely the culprit was an outsider. Most likely the same culprit who had been snatching and killing young girls. Kris's brother was the first lead they'd had.

As usual, the lights were on at Alan Mac's house. Sometimes Liam thought the chief constable slept less than Liam did himself.

A soft knock on the back door was answered so quickly Alan Mac had obviously been nearby. The steaming cup of tea on the kitchen table proved it.

At the sight of Liam, the big man stilled. "Another body?"

"No."

He stepped back, an invitation to enter that Liam accepted. "What then?"

Alan Mac poured a second cup of tea, pulled bread from a cabinet, set out butter and jam. Whenever Liam wasn't occupied with the loch, he tried to eat as much as he could. Otherwise he just didn't have the time.

Between bites, Liam related all that he knew. In the process, he discovered that Kris had never told the constable she'd been shoved off the cliff.

"Did ye see anyone?" Alan Mac asked.

"No."

"She could have slipped."

"Which is probably why she didnae tell ye." Liam took more bread, loading it with both butter and jam. "Ye never believe what she says."

"That's my job, if ye recall."

"Yer job is to make sure no one knows what *I'm* up to. It isnae to make women who've been attacked believe they're crazy." Liam fixed Alan Mac with a glare. "Dinnae do it again."

Alan Mac swallowed as if he'd just downed a dry biscuit with no tea. "Aye, Uilebheist."

Liam narrowed his eyes.

The constable straightened. "Aye, *sir.*"

"Find out all ye can about Marty Daniels," Liam ordered,

gaze on the window, where the dark had now truly begun to lighten.

"Do ye want me to round up the man? Ask him a few questions at the station?"

Liam shook his head. He doubted Alan Mac would be able to "round up" Marty. The guy hadn't stayed out of sight this long by being bad at it. Besides—

"He willnae tell ye anything. Best to let me ask."

Liam could be quite persuasive when he was of a mind to be.

He remembered Kris's face in the dim light of the cottage. That yearning sadness, the past memories of hurt.

He was definitely of a mind to be.

"Find out where he's been," Liam instructed. "Why is he here? What does he do? Where does he do it? Ye ken?"

"Aye." Alan Mac nodded. "Ye can count on me."

Kris was still trying to get her mind around her brother being in Scotland when her computer screen shimmied. She was reminded of the front window of the starship *Enterprise,* which sometimes shimmied exactly like that right before a transmission came in from a Klingon warship. Instead, a transmission came in from Edward Mandenauer.

The old man appeared as tired as Kris felt. What was going on out there in the world?

Quite a bit, and all the time, from the looks of him.

His gaze paused on her bruised cheek, as everyone's would until the mark healed, but he merely narrowed his eyes momentarily, then spoke in his usual manner—as if he had somewhere else to be and yesterday.

"I've found similarities to other murders."

"In Drumnadrochit?" If that was the case, these people were *really* good at keeping secrets.

"No. There have been a string of deaths throughout the world matching the manner in which a local legendary being might kill."

Kris, who had picked up the yellow legal pad on which she'd first doodled Effy's tattoo and begun to sketch the others, glanced up. "I don't understand."

"In Crete," he continued, "seven victims have been found at the bottom of cliffs, with donkey tracks on the roads above."

Kris rubbed her forehead. "I'm gonna need more than that."

"There is a legend in those mountains of the Anaskelades, a donkey that wanders the hills offering free rides."

"Offering? As in 'Hey, pal, want a ride?'"

"Though I have often been amazed at the stupidity of humans, I do not think that anyone confronted with a talking donkey would decide that accepting a ride was a good idea."

"You never know," Kris muttered. Humans and stupidity did seem to go hand in hand, regardless of race, creed, or international borders.

"Touché," Edward agreed. "However, the Anaskelades is not a talking donkey. It is a shape-shifting donkey."

"Which is so much less weird."

"It does not shape-shift until its victim climbs aboard. Then it grows to the size of the nearest mountain and tosses the unsuspecting traveler into the abyss."

Kris couldn't think of anything to say to that, except: "What else you got?"

"In Australia, over a dozen bodies have been found in remote areas without their heads. Investigation reveals they were followed for many miles by a human with very large feet." Kris lifted her eyebrows, waiting for more. "The locals began to whisper of the Thardid Jimbo, a cannibalistic giant that tracks its favorite food—humans—and partakes of the delicacy of their heads."

"Okay," Kris said. She didn't know what else *to* say.

"In Hudson Bay cairns have been discovered. Beneath them lay the corpses of five whose backs had been splayed and holes drilled through their bodies."

"What kind of monster does something like that?" Kris asked.

Edward answered as if the question had not been rhetorical. "The Ikuutayuuq, an Inuit legend, which translates to 'one who drills.' The Ikuutayuuq hunt down any human in their territory and torture them to death, then build a cairn to mark the kill."

Kris considered what he'd told her. She was still missing something. "Why do you think these incidents are similar? They're all different places, different legends, different modes of death."

"And they are all fake."

"Fake legends?" Kris perked right up.

"Of course not. Haven't you discovered by now that legends are real?"

Had she? Kris remembered plunging into the loch, the cold, the murk—

The monster.

"Maybe," she allowed.

She wasn't ready to tell anyone else what she'd seen while in the loch. She'd been scared, drowning, dying—*not* having a hallucination would have been strange. Certainly Kris was less inclined to dismiss Nessie as fiction, but she wasn't willing to completely accept her as fact, either. Not until Kris saw the creature with her own eyes, in broad daylight or even beneath the moon. However—

"I don't think Nessie is doing this."

Mandenauer's gaze sharpened. "Why not?"

Kris explained how she'd been attacked in her yard and again on the overhang above Loch Ness, finishing with: "The last victim had a silver knife stuck in her chest. Why drown and then suddenly stab? Why stab if you can drown? Besides, Nessie doesn't have the opposable thumbs necessary to—" Kris made a stabbing motion.

"Unless she's a shape-shifter," Mandenauer said. "Then she could take human form, use the weapon, then become . . . whatever the monster is."

"I thought shape-shifters couldn't touch silver."

"Most can't. Some can."

Fabulous, Kris thought

"There's one other problem," she began, and the old man lifted his bushy white brows. "The silver knife that was found in the chest of the latest victim . . ." Kris pressed her lips together, not wanting to say the rest, but she had to. "Was probably mine."

His brows crashed downward. "Whoever is behind the murders is aware you are looking into them."

"I kind of got that as I was flying off the cliff and into the water."

"So you conclude that a human is behind the attacks?"

"The ones on me, definitely." Human hands had bonked her on the head, then attempted to drag her into the loch. Nessie could not have pushed Kris off the cliff when she'd been waiting below to pull her out.

"What about the bodies?"

"If there's a body attached," Kris said firmly, "Nessie isn't involved."

"Continue," Mandenauer murmured in the tone of a professor with a brand-new but very promising student.

"If the monster were killing humans, she'd make certain they remained at the bottom of the loch. Why ask to be hunted any more than she's already been?"

"You think Nessie possesses the intelligence to reason that far?"

"I think to avoid detection this long she's gotta have human-level intelligence."

Edward nodded slowly. "You're right."

"One thing I don't get," Kris continued. "Nessie's legend is of a benign being that slowly trolls the loch and peeks out at the tourists now and again."

"Saint Columba would disagree."

"Considering that there have been no documented cases of monster attacks since, I'm thinking Columba used his tale of the monster to make a play for sainthood."

Edward tilted his head. "It wouldn't be the first time."

"All the cases you mentioned involved a—," Kris made quotes in the air with both hands, "bad monster. But Nessie, according to most reports, isn't bad. So how is this case similar to the others?"

"Nessie isn't really the legend."

"Everyone knows that the Loch Ness Monster is called Nessie."

"Only since the 1930s." Mandenauer frowned, glanced down, rustled some papers, and squinted. "May 1933 to be exact. The *Inverness Courier* followed up on several sightings, and within the year Nessie was born."

"But, according to Columba, Nessie has been here since the sixth century. Probably before."

"The *monster* was here; however, the legend of Nessie was invented by the media. Before 1933, the locals called it the beastie. And they knew what it was."

"What?" Kris asked.

"Of all the local legends the one that most fits is the tale of a supernatural water horse. Each Uisge."

"Kelpie," Kris murmured. "Except if Nessie is a shape-shifter, wouldn't she *have* to be human some of the time?"

"Not necessarily. Monsters do not survive a million millennia without adapting—to time, to place, to climate. If they are very smart, they even encourage the wrong legend to be passed down, thereby ensuring that no one truly knows what they are, where they are, how to find them, or how to kill them. There are also variations within the legends themselves that relate to how they became what they are."

"How?" Kris echoed.

"Some are born; some are cursed; some are engineered. Bitten. Injected. The possibilities are endless, and any one of them can alter that legend. Sometimes I think there are nearly as many *kinds* of werewolves as there *are* werewolves. And even though silver will kill most of them, with others it only pisses them off."

Kris was beginning to understand why Mandenauer walked around armed for Armageddon. He never knew what he might face, where he might face it, or what he might need to kill it.

She began to wonder not only how he'd survived this long but also how he'd done so with his sanity intact. Although a week ago if an old man had told her how to kill werewolves and other assorted shape-shifters she would have been the first to call for psychiatric assistance. Now, though she couldn't say with absolute certainty that she believed *everything* Edward said, she was willing to give him the benefit of the doubt.

"When you first learned about these deaths, you believed they were committed by the creature in question, right?" Mandenauer inclined his head. "Then why didn't you, or one of your agents, go there with plans to blast a monster to smithereens and either do that or snatch the imposter?"

He sent her another of those withering looks that made

Kris feel as if she were too stupid to live. In his world, she probably was. "I sent an agent to each place. By the time he or she arrived, the perpetrator was gone."

"Gone," Kris echoed. "Isn't a cannibalistic giant kind of hard to lose?"

"One would think," Edward said without missing a beat. "Which again makes me favor human and not monster."

"Because?"

"Monsters remain near their lair. Depending on the myth, some *can't* leave. That the killer does says a lot about his humanity."

"Maybe your agents just couldn't find him."

A glare followed this statement. Obviously, if a *Jäger-Sucher* was dispatched and did not find a monster, there was no monster to be found.

"In each incident," he continued, "there were clues that led us to believe someone is mimicking the supernatural rather than truly *being* a supernatural."

"Like what?" Kris asked, fascinated. She loved taking apart a legend, piece by piece, discovering the truth, then proving it a hoax.

"The actual legend of the Ikuutayuuq involves brothers who hunt together, stalking whatever is in their territory and eliminating it. In the cases reported, only one set of tracks was found and the victims were restrained, hand and foot, indicating a single killer."

"Maybe this Ikuutayuuq doesn't have a brother."

"If the inconsistencies existed in one place only, I might agree. However, as I said, there are inconsistencies in every case. For instance, in Crete the donkey tracks were the size of donkey tracks. They did not grow to the size of a mountainous donkey. The same in Australia.

The giant's tracks . . ." He flipped his chicken bone fingers outward.

"Not so gigantic," Kris finished. "So in your opinion we have a traveling serial killer, making use of local supernatural legends to dictate his modus operandi."

The old man nodded, his gaze distant. "At first I considered the likelihood of a superior shape-shifter with the ability to become each one of these legendary beings. But I concluded that was too far-fetched."

"Well, thank God for that," Kris muttered. The idea of a super-duper shape-shifter roaming from country to country, leaving a trail of dead and mutilated bodies in its wake, before parking itself in Drumnadrochit made her very nervous.

"These monsters are rooted in the histories of their cultures," he continued. "It is very rare for a shape-shifter to be able to assume the form of a being with which he does not share an ancestry. Only a Scot could become a kelpie. Only a Cherokee can become a Raven Mocker. Only a Norseman could become a Berserker. Although . . ." He frowned. "In America you have that infernal melting pot."

"So someone could become each one of these shape-shifters if they possess an ancestor from the country of legend."

"Theoretically," Mandenauer agreed. "Regardless, what you need to do now is find the culprit and kill it."

"I'm not so good with the killing."

"Everyone thinks that, until they are faced with the option of death or pulling the trigger." He straightened his stack of papers. "I will e-mail you an inventory of the deaths, their legends and locations."

"I can remember three."

"Those are only the tales I chose to tell. The list is

much longer—Iceland, South Africa, Brazil." He made a "and so forth" motion with one hand. "We are still searching our databases, speaking to agents about unsolved cases. I will no doubt have updates daily."

The idea that the murderer in their midst had killed so many times they needed a catalog, and that more instances could crop up daily, scared Kris more than anything ever had. And it should. She was a reporter dabbling in things she had no business dabbling in.

But was she going to stop?

Hell, no.

This was the story of a lifetime.

CHAPTER 20

Alan Mac found Liam lolling in the sunshine. After the thick, chill mist of dawn, the warmth was too welcome to ignore.

"Aren't ye supposed to be trolling the loch?" the constable asked, then glanced in the direction of Loch Side Cottage. "Ye're going to get fired if ye keep this up."

Liam snorted. He was definitely *not* going to get fired.

Alan Mac lifted the paper in his hand. "The information ye wanted. Yon wee girlie's brother has been quite the busy boy."

Liam's eyes narrowed.

"I traced his passport." Alan Mac peered at the white sheet. "Went from America to France, then Russia, Tasmania, blah-blah, Africa, yada yada, Canada, and Scotland. This is all in the past year. Couldn't find anything on what he does for a living, which would be suspicious even without all that gadding about."

Liam resisted the urge to rush across the loch and station himself in front of her door to prevent Kris's mysterious brother from gaining entrance again.

"I put in a call to Interpol," Alan Mac went on. "But

they have some sort of security hold on his file." He lowered the paper with a frown. "That he *has* a file is not a good thing in my experience. But as soon as they get back to me, I'll let ye know."

Liam, still peering at the cottage, lowered his head in acknowledgment. He hadn't seen Kris come out. He hadn't seen any kind of movement in there at all. For all he knew she wasn't even *in* there but had gone to the village, to Inverness, or even back to America.

The despair that swamped him at the last location was sharp and deep and a little frightening. They didn't have a future. Someday she would return to her life and he would return to his. Such that it was. He'd always known this, yet still he had touched her.

He'd understood that being with her was a mistake, that any relationship would end badly. But he hadn't been able to stop himself.

"I'll leave a copy of the list at your place."

Liam started when Alan Mac spoke. He'd been so intent on the cottage, on Kris, he'd forgotten the man was there.

But the constable was used to Liam's broody silences, especially when he was on duty at the loch. With a lift of the hand that still held the paper, Alan Mac left.

Long after the sound of the constable's car had faded toward Drumnadrochit, Liam remained. The sun caused his eyes to droop, his body to warm and become languid. But the sharp splash to the north jerked him awake. Within seconds he was headed in that direction. He knew that sound.

It was the exact *thump-cush* a body made when it hit the surface of the loch.

As Kris came out of the bedroom, freshly showered and dressed, she noticed the yellow notepad she'd been scribbling on while she and Mandenauer talked sitting on the table. Something about it made her skirt the couch and pick it up.

"Whoa," she said.

She had doodled each tattoo separately. She remembered doing that. Then, with her brain occupied by other legends, her subconscious had put them together and she'd drawn something else.

"What is so disturbing about that?"

The voice made Kris start. Mandenauer was back on the screen, sharp gaze focused on the sketch of Nessie that had formed on Kris's yellow pad.

"Nothing, until you understand that this—" She tapped the monster. "Contains all of these." She tapped each of the four tattoos.

"Explain."

"I saw . . . ," Kris indicated the hump, "tattooed on my landlady's . . ." Now she waved vaguely in the direction of her own breasts. "This—" The flipper. "On her brother's wrist. That," the thick line that had circled Alan Mac's biceps, "was on the chief constable's arm. And here—" Jamaica's ankle tattoo. "We have the head of what I thought was a snake but could, when put together with the rest, become—" Again she pointed at the picture of Nessie.

"Interesting," Edward murmured. "Tattoos have been employed as a . . ." He searched for the word. "Magnet. For instance, some Native American shamans used tattoos to draw their magic from—" He shrugged. "Wherever they drew it from."

"Bullshit land?"

"You don't believe in magic?"

"Not yet," she said. Which was a far cry from last week's answer of *Not in this lifetime.*

"I've also known tattoos to be used as an aid in

shape-shifting." Mandenauer's thin lips pursed. "You saw the marks on four different people?"

"So far." Kris paused, putting two and two together. "You think they're all Nessie?"

"Some say there are a herd of them." Now he paused, doing some addition of his own. "Of course, they could take turns, which would help avoid detection."

"How so?"

"If someone comes too close to identifying one shape-shifter, that shifter merely allows himself or herself to be seen at a time when Nessie—another shifter entirely—is seen as well. And the theory falls apart. I've also known tattoos to be used with guardian cults."

"Say what?" All she needed, on top of everything else, was a cult.

"Imagine living in a hut, or on a hill, eking out an existence. You hunt. You gather. Yet barely you survive. Then a being comes along that is stronger, faster, it has powers that defy logic, and it rarely, if ever, dies. What would you think?"

"God."

Mandenauer inclined his head. "At first, paranormal creatures were worshiped. As time went on, and the demands for human sacrifice became excessive—"

"Wait a second," Kris interrupted, remembering what she'd learned about Obeah. "Could the killings be some sort of sacrifice to a god?"

The old man's eyes narrowed. "I have never heard of the Loch Ness Monster being considered a god." He lifted his thin shoulders, then lowered them. "But who knows? Do you have a suspect?"

Kris hesitated. If she told him about Jamaica, would he send one of his agents to interrogate her? Would they kill her? Should Kris stop them? If Jamaica was sacrificing people to the great god Nessie, something had to be done.

So Kris told Edward what she knew.

"Sacrifices involve blood," he said. "There is power in it. These drownings . . ." He shook his head. "Not very bloody. There is also a ceremony. Tossing bodies into the water or leaving them on the shore with no ring of fire or midnight chant is not sacrificial. Still, you should keep an eye on her."

"All right. What happened when the guardians decided the requests of the god became too demanding?"

"A few humans went searching for methods that would kill the un-killable. Their adventures added to the legends. Stories were told. Information passed down."

"And hunters were born."

"Yes. But there were some places where the god, the creature, bonded with its subjects. Perhaps it began to prey on their enemies instead of them. Perhaps it saved them from another monster."

Kris had a thought, one she didn't like but had to address. "Considering the dark side of human nature, maybe some of them enjoyed the murders; they wanted the mayhem."

"There *are* guardian cults that guard horrible things. In the past I have had to fight my way through humans to reach the monsters." He shoulder-twitched in lieu of a shrug. "Whether the creature be evil or reformed, some did not want their god dead; they did not want it gone and began to guard it from every harm."

Kris lifted her gaze from the computer to the window where the sun had finally come out and burned away the last trace of mist. Had that happened here?

"Many of these guardian cults employ some type of code—like a tattoo—so they know who is with them, who is one of them."

"You think there's a guardian cult for Nessie?"

"Yes," Edward said simply.

"I'll talk to them."

"Unless you wear the mark, no one will tell you a thing. And remember—they may not be protecting the monster; they may *be* the monster. Asking the wrong question of the right person would be a good way to find yourself at the bottom of the loch."

Kris had nearly found herself at the bottom of the loch once already. She didn't relish a repeat performance.

Besides, there was someone else she could talk to. When Liam got done guarding the—

Ah, hell.

"What is the matter?" Edward asked. "You look like you've seen a—"

"Gotta go," Kris said, and shut the computer, ignoring calls of: "Kristin! Come back here this minute!" while she considered where she'd look for Liam. She wasn't going to tell Edward anything until she knew for sure what she had to tell.

Kris headed first for Urquhart Castle, according to all the reading she'd done a favorite haunt of the beastie. Unfortunately for her, but fortunately for the tourist trade, the place was a zoo. She saw no evidence of Liam anywhere.

"This is insane," she muttered. In more ways than one.

That she was even entertaining the idea that the man she'd had sex with, a man she had started to care for, to trust, was secretly a shape-shifting lake monster, or at least the guardian of one, had her mind scrambling so fast for any other explanation, she felt kind of dizzy.

The more logical explanation was that he was a protector, as he'd said. Sure, he'd told her he protected the *loch,* but wasn't that just splitting hairs?

She couldn't believe that she—Kristin Daniels—purveyor of truth, hater of lies, was making excuses for a liar. She should be crossing him off her to-do list and never seeing him again.

"Lied right to my face," she muttered. Except it hadn't *smelled* like a lie, and Kris had become very good at sniffing them out.

"His being so hot probably threw off your radar." Although that had never happened before. She worked in television. She saw hot all over the damn place. What she'd discovered the first week she was on the air was that hot equaled "big fat liar" more than just about anything else.

Beautiful people seemed to believe they were above the rules of decent behavior. Probably because they'd been cut all kinds of slack since "Oh, so cute!" babyhood.

Kris knew she was considered attractive. However, she'd had the truth driven home to her as a teen. She wasn't pretty enough, sweet enough, smart enough—she wasn't anything *enough*—to keep her brother or her father from leaving her. So she'd thrown herself into her job, into a quest for success that would echo across the country, if not the world, and would force those who'd turned their backs on her to notice.

Had they? She didn't think so.

Since searching for Liam at the loch was as pointless as grubbing through the proverbial haystack for that needle, Kris decided to see if anyone in the village knew where he might be. While she was at it, she'd discover if her brother had checked into any of the local hotels.

As Kris strolled into Drumnadrochit, she was, as always, assailed by the heavenly scent wafting from Jamaica

Blue. Not only was she unable to resist coffee, considering she hadn't had any, but she should probably quiz Jamaica about her tattoo. If she could do so without giving away what she was really asking.

Are you a guardian or a human-sacrificing witch? Maybe both.

Wait a second.... Kris paused with her hand poised to open the door of the coffee shop. Shouldn't Liam have a tattoo?

She hadn't seen one. However, she hadn't looked *everywhere.* She'd kissed, she'd touched, but she hadn't searched for anything specific.

Other than the specific thing she'd needed at the time. No sign of a tattoo *there.*

Kris opened the door to Jamaica Blue.

Well, no help for it. She was going to have to explore every inch of Liam's body.

Poor her.

A young man—perhaps sixteen or so, with reddish brown hair and very bad teeth—stood behind the counter today. Kris ordered a cup of Blue Mountain and craned her neck to see around him. "Where's Jamaica?"

"On a buying trip." The kid handed Kris the cup.

"For coffee?"

He nodded. "She likes to do that herself."

"When will she be back?"

"Few days." The boy squinted at Kris's bruised face. "You walk into a door or something?"

"Something," Kris agreed, then paid and left the shop, haunted by a strange sense of déjà vu. It wasn't until she saw the sign for The Myth Motel that she remembered.

Dougal had gone on a sudden buying trip, too.

Kris glanced toward the loch; then she turned and contemplated the motel. Did Dougal have a tattoo as well? Might these "buying trips" coincide with a guardian's duty at—or perhaps *in*—the loch? How was she going to find out?

Well, she hadn't gotten as far as she had in journalism—which wasn't exactly far, but she was still pretty good at it—without knowing how to ask questions.

Kris stepped inside The Myth Motel. Dougal stood behind the counter. His gaze flicked to the mark on her cheek, then quickly away. But he didn't apologize. She wasn't sure if she was relieved not to have to address the incident again or annoyed that he'd decided to ignore it. She decided on the latter.

They weren't married. He had no right to be so angry that she'd slept with Liam. In fact, she wondered *why* Dougal was so angry. His behavior *was* a bit stalkerish.

"What was wrong with you last night?" she asked.

He kept his gaze on the counter and not on her. "I thought we had something."

"Friendship."

His lips tightened. "If you're going to be friendly with him, I don't want you to be friendly with me."

Kris narrowed her eyes. She hadn't planned on being "friendly" with Dougal, so— "That suits me just fine."

He still wouldn't look at her.

"I'd like to check if my brother is staying here."

Dougal glanced up, surprise flashing in what she'd once thought to be intelligent, attractive gray eyes. Now they just looked like eyes. "Your brother's in Scotland?"

"It was news to me, too. Is he here? Marty Daniels."

"I can't give out my guests' names. You could be a stalker."

Pot. Kettle, Kris thought, but she kept it to herself.

"He's my *brother.*"

"Maybe you don't get along. Maybe he doesn't want you to know where he is."

"He came to Scotland to see me."

"Then he should have told you where he was staying, because I'm not going to."

His tone was so *nah-nah-nah-nah-nah,* Kris waited for him to finish the statement by sticking out his tongue. Thankfully he refrained.

She tried to return the conversation to a semblance of civility. "Did you have a nice trip?"

"Trip?" he repeated.

"You went to . . . something with a *B,*" she said. "A buying trip?"

"Oh. Yeah. Great." He turned away. "If that's all, I—"

"Is there a tattoo parlor in the village?"

His gaze flicked to hers. "You want a tattoo?"

"I might. Do you have one?"

"I'm not a biker. Or a soldier. Or," his lip curled, "an NBA basketball player."

She was liking Dougal less and less with every passing minute. She kind of wished Liam had broken *his* nose instead of just popping him on the chin.

Kris focused on the spot. "Why don't *you* have a mark?"

He saw where she was staring and lifted his hand, rubbing his face. "I don't bruise easily. And he barely touched me."

Kris would beg to differ, but Dougal still wouldn't have a bruise. Which just wasn't fair.

"Lots of people have tattoos these days," Kris continued. "Lots of people around here."

"I didn't notice."

Kris had a hard time believing that, but she wasn't going to push it. If Dougal had a tattoo, he wasn't going to show it to her anyway.

"Thanks a lot." Kris headed for the door. She couldn't help it if the sentence came out sounding more sarcastic than thankful. Of course he'd been more asinine than helpful.

"Why him?" Dougal murmured, something in his voice making her turn back, though she didn't want to.

"Why do you hate him so much?"

"I have my reasons." Dougal's expression went from disgusted to sly. "Maybe you should ask yourself: Why do you *like* him so much?"

"What kind of question is that?"

He twitched one shoulder. "You haven't been here more than a week. Are you the kind of woman who falls into bed with a man that fast?"

Kris almost asked, *What kind?* but decided that she didn't want to hear anything else from a man whose opinions of women and sex were slightly outdated. She should count herself lucky that she hadn't felt the overwhelming attraction for Dougal that she'd experienced the first time she'd seen Liam at Urquhart Castle.

When she'd frenched him and she hadn't even known his name.

"Huh," she murmured. That *so* wasn't like her.

"Yeah," Dougal agreed, though he could have no idea what she was thinking.

Kris walked out. She wasn't going to listen to any more of Dougal's crap. However, he had made her wonder what it was about Liam that had caused her to behave contrary to all her usual habits.

Was it because he was beautiful? Because he had an accent? Because he was manly and mysterious? She wasn't the type to fall for that.

So why had she? Kris couldn't answer that for herself any more than she'd been able to answer it for Dougal.

After stopping at the Drumnadrochit version of Walgreens and purchasing heavy foundation and powder to cover her bruise—she'd only brought along the bare basics of makeup to Scotland—as well as a sandwich and chips, Kris headed to the cottage.

She'd just come over a hill, leaving Drumnadrochit behind and a stretch of empty road ahead, when a splash from the loch drew her attention. Believing she'd again see a whole lot of nothing, Kris cast a quick glance toward the water. This time what she saw there made her stumble and nearly fall, before stopping dead and staring.

Because, this time, something stared back.

The head that lifted from the surface could have been that of an eel, a snake, an otter. But the large, humped body that played hide-and-seek with the waves was nothing like any of the three.

Kris glanced around. They were completely alone. No cars on the road. No hikers in the hills. No boats dotted the water anywhere in sight.

"Figures," she muttered. She was not only without a camera but also without witnesses.

The creature just floated there, nearer to the shore than a being of her size should be able to float. Though Kris's feet felt encased in cement shoes, she forced them across the road and down the slight incline to the loch, expecting at any moment for the monster to disappear. But she didn't.

Kris stood at the water's edge. Had Nessie ever revealed herself to anyone like this for long? If she had, no one had ever admitted to it. Which made Kris wonder if anyone who got this close went swimming and never came back.

Kris began to inch up the hill, away from the beastie. Her heart thundered so loudly she thought she might faint.

Her face was hot, her hands like ice. She felt kind of sick to her stomach.

The creature continued to drift, head lifted, glistening eyes the same shade as her gray-black coat fixed on Kris. Then she—was it a she? If not, then why the Nessie?—shifted, a flipper flapped as if shoving something in Kris's direction. Like a ballet, slow and graceful, the monster's body slowly slid the other way, creating a wake that brought a bobbing *something* toward the shore.

Transfixed, Kris forgot about retreating and instead retraced her steps until her shoes slipped in the wet dirt at water's edge.

"Jamaica?" she whispered.

Nessie tilted her head as if she knew that name. Then she sank straight down, disappearing from view, leaving no sign that she'd been there, not even a ripple.

Something bumped against Kris's toe. She glanced down.

Then she began to scream.

CHAPTER 21

An hour later Kris was still on the bank of the loch, but she was no longer alone.

She'd only screamed once, and she was embarrassed she'd done that. If she was going to cry out you'd think she would have done so at the sight of her first dead body, not the second. But when she'd looked down, the dead girl's hand had been resting on her shoe and Kris hadn't been able to help herself.

A passing motorist had heard her and come to the rescue carrying a tire iron. Alan Mac arrived shortly thereafter, giving Kris a glance that was easy to read: *You again?*

She supposed it was odd that she kept finding bodies. Particularly odd that Nessie had brought this one to her. It was almost as if Nessie had been saying, *See? I didn't do it. If I had, why would I bring you the evidence?*

Because monsters reasoned like that all the time.

A hysterical giggle escaped Kris's freezing-cold lips. She was in shock. *Again.* Luckily, the man who'd come running in answer to her screams kept a lovely plaid blanket in the trunk with his tire iron. Kris pulled it more tightly around her shoulders and huddled on a rock.

Local law enforcement had set up their perimeter and begun to process the scene. A crowd had gathered on the road, kept back by several of Alan Mac's men. Kris wasn't sure how long it was, but eventually the wide shadow of the constable blocked the sun.

"Let me guess. Ye were just out walkin' and lo and behold, surprise! Another body."

Kris hesitated. Should she go with that? Or tell him the truth?

That she, who had always valued honesty above all else, was considering a lie to the lead officer in a murder investigation showed how far Kris had come from the woman she'd been.

Kris's gaze went to the arm where she'd seen Alan Mac's tattoo, covered now by a jacket. He was either a guardian or a shape-shifter. If he was the former, she should tell him about Nessie bringing her the dead. He'd want the monster exonerated. If he was the latter . . .

Kris cursed beneath her breath. She should pull out the silver Celtic cross she still wore beneath her clothes and take it for a test drive on Alan Mac's skin. If he fried, probably shape-shifter, and then . . .

Well, she wasn't really sure. If the chief constable transformed into one of many Nessies would he be okay with Kris's knowing that or wouldn't he? Was a shape-shifter test really her best option with all these people around and the possible shape-shifter wearing a gun?

Alan Mac raised one hand and scratched at his arm, right where the tattoo would be, and Kris blurted, "Yep. That's what happened. Walking along, saw what I thought was debris on the shore, came down here, and—" She spread her hands. "You know the rest."

"Mmm," Alan Mac said. He didn't believe her. Hell, *she* didn't believe her. "Did ye touch the body?"

Kris shook her head. Not this time. This time she'd known what dead looked like.

Alan Mac peered out over the loch. "I dinnae know the girl," he said quietly. "She's not local. From her clothes, her hair, I'd say American. Which means . . ." He sighed.

"Shit storm," Kris filled in. When Americans died in foreign countries, Americans went ballistic. Kris kind of liked that about America.

"Aye," Alan Mac agreed. "There'll be no keepin' it quiet now. I have to wonder who hates Drumnadrochit so much."

"Hates the village or hates Nessie?" Kris asked.

"Arenae they one and the same?"

An interesting comment. Did he mean that if Nessie was proved a real monster and tourism died, then Drumnadrochit would die, too? Or was he talking about the tattoos? If everyone in Drumnadrochit had one and everyone who had one was a Nessie, then the village and the monster *were* one and the same.

Kris started to see sparkly white lights at the edge of her vision. Exhaustion? Or was her brain about to explode?

She closed her eyes tightly, and when she opened them the lights had receded, though they had not disappeared. She decided to ignore them. "You think whoever's doing this isn't from here?"

"I'd like to," the constable said. "Really, why crap where ye eat?"

"I'm sorry?"

"Why kill where ye live? Isn't there some kind of rule about that?"

"In the serial killer rule book?"

"Right." Alan Mac's impressive shoulders slumped. "Serial killers dinnae like rules."

"Except for their own. Twisted though they might be."

"That's yer statement then? Ye just happened on another body, and ye touched nothing."

"That's my story, and I'm stickin' to it," Kris murmured.

He sighed. "Ye can go."

Kris wasn't far from the cottage, but she was still kind of surprised, considering the way she stumbled up the hill and zigzagged down the road, that no one offered to take her there. With her shambling gait, no doubt freakishly pale face, the flapping plaid blanket she wore like a cape, and the bag of makeup and food she still clutched in one hand, anyone seeing her might think Kris the local loony. Right now she felt like it.

She reached the cottage, let herself in, and tossed the bag onto the couch. She wasn't hungry. She was cold, and she was tired.

She stood under the heated stream of the shower until the water went cool, then donned her flannel pajama bottoms, a sweatshirt, and heavy socks before going to bed. When she awoke it was dark and someone was pounding on the door.

Groggy, Kris turned on the light, then, blinded by its brilliance, shuffled into the other room. She opened the door without thinking, and Liam rushed in.

"Are ye all right, *mo gradh*?" He took her in his arms and, still desperate for warmth, she let him. "I heard what happened. I would have come sooner but—"

Kris pulled his mouth to hers. The only way she'd ever be warm again was this.

In the middle of speaking, his lips still parted, she drank his breath, inhaled his heat. Her tongue plunged; her hands clenched on his neck.

His hair, which had been captured in a rubber band, she released; the spill across her wrists smelled like rain.

He began to lift his head, no doubt to ask her again if she was all right, and she nipped his lip. No words now, no thoughts, only this.

She slid her arms around his shoulders, tangled her fingers in that hair, and the movement tugged up her shirt, exposing her to his touch.

His palms were cool like the night, but they warmed, as did she. Her blood seemed to bubble, and she imagined it red and hot, flowing like lava, glowing like magma beneath her skin.

Wherever he touched, she burned. Ah, the blessed, blessed heat. She might die of it or perhaps of wanting it, wanting him.

They left a trail of clothes across the floor, flinging a shirt here, a sock there, then tumbled naked onto the bed in a tangle of limbs, reaching for and finding each other.

"Kris," he gasped, and she straddled him, shoving his shoulders flat to the bed and leaning down.

"No," she murmured against his lips, then whispered, "yes," when he framed her breasts with his palms, stroking the nipples in time with the thrusts of his tongue.

He kept silent, fast learner, although when she lifted her hips and lowered herself onto him he did say something like, "Urgh."

At first she kept the movements slow, shallow, just a tease, a bit more seduction. She matched them with her tongue, and he scraped the tips of his nails across her breasts to the rhythm of their bodies' song.

She hissed in a breath, sitting up, liking both the change in the pressure and the view. Liam's deep blue eyes appeared black in the flare of the lamp; his dark hair spread across the stark white pillow like an onyx fan. His skin, tanned from days spent outdoors, gleamed slick and smooth. She had to touch it.

It *was* smooth, but not hot like hers, and that was strange. She felt on fire. He should be, too.

His palms cupped her hips, urged her to keep moving as she roamed, first her fingers across his chest, then her lips, then her tongue. She explored every inch she could reach. She ached to explore those that she could not. Perhaps after she would examine—

Her head had just fallen back, her hips rocking, very close to the end, when she remembered. She'd planned to search every inch of his body for a tattoo.

She stiffened, and the movement rubbed them together just right. His fingers tightened, digging into her hips, and then she was coming. She couldn't stop it, regardless of who he was, perhaps *what* he was, and she didn't want to.

She set her palms over his and rode the tide, rode him, until the last tremor died away.

Before the glow was gone, her mind began to click. Did Liam have a tattoo? How would she find out? She couldn't inspect him like a monkey trolling for fleas, but there were other ways.

Kris, who had collapsed onto his chest, buried her face in his neck not only to keep him from seeing her thoughts but also because having his skin against hers was as seductive as inhaling the scent of him.

Before she could be completely won over, before she gave in to the desire to lie there and sleep, she rolled to the side, then sat next to him on the bed, trailing her fingers over his belly, his hips, following the path with an admiring gaze. His legs were tightly muscled, with a light dusting of hair, just enough to be manly, not so much that the hair obscured skin. She found nothing but Liam from his face to his feet.

"Turn over." She pushed at his shoulder, then traced her hands up his legs, drew her nails over his buttocks, brushed her palm over the smooth, unmarred skin at the small of his back, and swept it up his pristine shoulders.

He was clear of tattoos. But what did that mean?

"I'll nae be able to go again so soon, *mo bheatha*. Ye must give me a bit o' time."

She was swamped by a sudden desire to hold him, just hold him close, and never let him go. "What does *mo bheatha* mean?" she whispered.

He turned his head. Their eyes met, and a strange feeling hit her in the chest so hard she couldn't breathe.

"'My life,'" he translated, and his hair, which had been spread across his upper back like a curtain, slid sideways.

The tattoo wasn't very big. But it *was* very Nessie. From the tip of her snake-like head, past her humps and her flippers, right down to her long, thin tail.

Liam saw Kris's expression and sat up. "What's wrong?"

"The— That— I mean . . . It—"

"Did ye want to talk about what happened today? I'm sorry ye had to find her. Sorry it upset ye so."

"Tattoo," she blurted. Liam stilled. "You have a tattoo."

His eyes became wary. "Aye."

"What does it mean?"

"It means—" He stopped, pursing his lips and looking toward the living room with a frown.

"Don't lie," she said, and her voice broke. She didn't think she could bear it if *he* lied to her, too.

Liam tilted his head, opened his mouth, and someone knocked.

He· was off the bed and reaching for his pants before whoever was there had stopped tapping.

"Wait." Kris got up, too. "I can—"

"No." The sound of his zipper served as emphasis, if his glare hadn't been enough. "Stay here."

He left pulling on his shirt. Kris kept her gaze on the tattoo until it disappeared.

The front door opened. A curse erupted. Kris yanked the quilt off the bed, hastily made a toga, and followed. By the time she got there, her brother and Liam were already bumping chests, or near enough.

Marty's nose was swollen, and he was sporting two black eyes from the last encounter. Since there wasn't a scratch on Liam, she couldn't believe her brother was begging for a second round.

"Go away." He shoved Liam. "I need to talk to my sister."

"I willnae leave her alone." Liam's tone said without words, *Like you did*.

Marty flushed. "I had my reasons."

"What are they?" Liam asked.

"Yeah," Kris interjected. "What are they?"

Both men turned. When they saw what she wore, their faces took on comically similar expressions of disapproval.

"Ach, put on some clothes."

"I have to agree with the limey here," Marty said.

"*Limey* is for the British, ye Yankee bastard."

Marty lifted his brows. "Paddy?"

"That's Irish, ye no-account fool."

"Jock?"

"There ye go."

"*Jock* is an insult?" Kris asked.

"Aye."

"Why?"

"I've no idea. It's what the bloody English say. Something about there being a lot of Scots named John or Jack or some such nonsense."

"That makes no sense," Kris said.

"What does?" Liam asked, still standing too close to Marty, staring at him like a wolf trembling for a fight. "Clothes, lass, if ye please."

"Can you two manage not to strangle each other while I'm gone?"

"Maybe," Marty muttered.

"Doubtful," Liam returned.

"Then I'll just stay right here."

The two sighed and backed away from each other a few paces.

"Go," Liam ordered. "I willnae touch him unless he touches me first."

"Me, either," Marty said, but he was staring at the couch and his face kept getting redder; the bruising beneath his eyes seemed to pulse.

Kris followed his gaze. Her bra lay on the arm, her underwear across the back. She snatched up both as she went into the bedroom, then closed the door.

The murmur of voices from the living room had her throwing on clothes faster than she ever had before. For those two, talking was bad, as evidenced by the steady increase in volume during the short time it took her to don sweatpants and a T-shirt before bursting back out.

"You can leave," Marty was saying.

"I willnae."

"What do you think I'm going to do? She's my sister."

"Ye've hurt her enough already, Yank."

"Why do foreigners," Marty considered, then continued, "and southerners, too, for some reason, think that's an insult? Maybe if you're a Red Sox fan, but I'm not."

"I dinnae ken anything about yer American football."

Marty glanced at Kris. "Are you serious with this guy? He doesn't even know the difference between football and baseball."

"Yeah, that's something I look for in a man."

Liam frowned. "Really?"

"Sarcasm," Marty said. "Try to keep up."

Kris had forgotten just how annoying her brother could be.

"Now get out," Marty continued.

"No."

"Kris, tell him I won't hurt you."

"He won't hurt me," she repeated.

"Dinnae be so sure." Liam pulled a paper from his pocket and handed it to her.

Kris glanced at the sheet, which appeared to be a random list of dates and places. "What's this?"

Liam, still staring at Marty as if he expected her brother to break into song and dance, or perhaps just break his nose, lifted his chin. "Ask him."

Kris handed the list to Marty, who took it, read it, and frowned. "You had me investigated?" Strangely, his voice sounded more impressed than angry.

Liam dipped his chin in assent.

"Why?" Kris asked.

"Ye didnae think it odd he just showed up? After all this time he suddenly wants to bond—in a foreign country no less—with the sister he abandoned."

"I did not—," Marty began.

"Ye did. Ye say ye had yer reasons, and we will get to those, but ye left her, and ye didnae come back, and it pains her. So I wondered what brought ye here, and why now? Now, when we have a wee problem of our own."

Click. Kris could have sworn she actually heard the

puzzle piece slip into place in her mind. "I need that list back."

Marty handed it over.

"What is it?" Liam asked.

"Hold on." Kris booted up her computer, accessed her e-mail, and downloaded what Edward had sent her.

The lists matched.

CHAPTER 22

Kris opened what she now thought of as the gun drawer, picked up the weapon, and pointed it at Marty. "Liam, move away from him."

Kris was shocked that she could point a gun that was no doubt loaded with silver bullets at her brother, who just might be a shape-shifter, and neither her voice nor her hands shook.

Liam came to stand at her side. "Are ye daft?"

"You're the one who investigated him."

"I didnae find a shooting offense."

"I did." She decided to leave Edward out of it. "The places Marty's traveled match a list of places where there have been murders that appear to be the work of a local legend."

Her brother's lips curved. "Loup-garou outside of Paris. Hyena shifter in Ethiopia. Giant in Tasmania."

"Thardid Jimbo," Kris said. "Was it you?"

"No."

Kris lifted a brow. "You think I'll just believe that and put away the gun?"

"Ye have not been much for the truth so far," Liam agreed.

"Did I do a lot of shape-shifting when we were kids?" Marty asked.

"Just because you didn't shift then doesn't mean you aren't doing it now. You could have been . . ." She paused, remembering what Edward had told her. "Injected. Cursed. Bitten."

Dear God, had she really said that?

"Got anything silver?" Marty asked.

Kris glanced into the drawer. A box of bullets, but she didn't want to put the gun down to open it. Instead, she pulled the Celtic cross from beneath her shirt and tossed it.

Marty snatched the icon out of the air with one hand. He didn't catch fire. For an instant Kris was relieved, until she recalled something else the old man had said.

"Not all shifters react to silver. Sometimes it only pisses them off."

"You're right." Marty threw the cross back, and Kris looped the chain over her head. "Now what?"

Kris had no idea.

"Listen, Squirt, I'm not a supernatural."

"Then how do ye know so much about them?" Liam asked.

"I hunt them."

Kris frowned. If Marty was a *Jäger-Sucher*, wouldn't Edward have mentioned that?"

Liam snorted. "Sure ye do. And that's why Interpol had a file on ye."

"Personnel file," Marty said.

"You work for Interpol?" Kris was almost as surprised by that as she'd been by Marty showing up here in the first place.

Marty reached for his pocket, and Kris lifted the gun. "My ID." Slowly he pulled it out and threw it to her.

Sure enough. He was with Interpol. Kris set the gun back in the drawer, but she left the drawer open and her hand lingered nearby.

"Why didn't they just tell us you worked for them?" Liam asked.

"I'm kind of a secret . . ." He rolled his hand as if searching for a word. "Consultant."

"Why secret?" Kris asked.

"Investigating the paranormal." He shrugged. "They don't like to admit it exists."

Neither did Kris.

"How did you end up doing that?"

"Remember all the fairy tales Mom used to read to us?"

"Yeah," Kris said slowly, not sure where he was going or if she wanted to go there.

"I would complain that they were girlie, but you loved them, and, to be honest, so did I. I guess it makes sense that we both ended up in jobs where we chase things that most people believe are fairy tales. You debunking them and me . . ." He paused.

"What do ye do," Liam murmured, "that has caused ye to turn up in all the places where people are dyin'?"

Kris felt a trickle of unease. If Marty had been chasing the legends, most likely studying their origins, finding out all he could about them, then he knew enough to imitate them.

"I've been traveling from kill site to kill site to investigate," Marty answered. "But by the time I get there, the kills have stopped and there's no trace of the creature. At least until I came here."

"Nessie isn't the killer," Kris said.

Liam cast her a quick glance, but she ignored him.

"How you figure?" Marty asked.

"The Loch Ness Monster has avoided detection for centuries. They've brought sonar and radar and all kinds of 'ars, trying to catch a reading, a picture, some film. But they've got bupkes. The only way for her to stay hidden so well is for Nessie to possess human-level intelligence. And if she's that damn smart, she'd keep the bodies as hidden as she is."

Marty appeared intrigued. "If not Nessie, then what?"

"Someone's been trying to pin the killings on her. Get her killed."

Marty frowned. "Who'd kill Nessie?"

"You?"

"I don't kill these things."

"You said 'hunt.' "

"As in 'search for, track, investigate.' " He spread his hands. "All I do is find them."

"And you let them keep on keepin' on, piling up the bodies as they go?"

"Of course not. If the creature is harmful, we out-source the killing."

"Let me guess," Kris said. "You hire the *Jäger-Suchers.*"

Silence fell over the room. Marty broke it first. "I should have known. All those hoaxes. It was cover for being a hunter."

"Me?" Kris laughed. "No."

Marty lifted a brow at Liam.

"I dinnae even know what ye're talkin' about."

Kris glanced at him. There was something more to that; she could hear it in his voice. Was *he* a hunter? He did disappear all the time, wandered around the loch, showed up whenever he was needed. He was either a *Jäger-Sucher* or a superhero. If he wasn't a shape-shifter.

"Are you a serial killer?" Marty asked.

"Are you?" Liam returned.

"All right," Kris interrupted, afraid they'd start shoving each other again. "Why do you think we're dealing with a serial killer and not a super shape-shifter?"

"Maybe we are." Marty shrugged. "In my experience shifter and serial killer are the same damn thing."

Kris kept her gaze on Marty's face. "But you don't think we're dealing with a super shifter, or you'd have contacted Edward the instant you got here and discovered the killings were still in progess."

"Killer creatures don't stop until someone makes them. But these did."

"Because we aren't dealing with killer creatures but a killer human. All the murders on the list might look like they've been committed by a supernatural creature but were in fact committed by an unnatural human."

"How do you know that?" Marty's gaze narrowed. "You weren't there. You didn't see the crime scenes. I'd have been told."

Kris lifted her brows. "You have someone spying on me?"

"Not spying exactly. I've made sure you were safe, happy." He took a deep breath. "At least until you came here."

Kris wasn't sure what to do with that information. Her brother hadn't deserted her. Not completely. She still thought he could have sent her a card at Christmas.

"And how *did* ye end up here?" Liam asked. "Right when she did?"

Marty flicked Liam a quick glance, but when he answered he spoke to Kris: "Did you ever wonder why you were able to prove so many hoaxes?"

"Because they *were* hoaxes."

"Not all of them. There were times I got there first, found

the creature, and had it eliminated before you arrived. With no monster to find, a hoax is pretty easy to prove."

"You were helping me?" she asked. And here she'd thought she was just damn good at her job.

"*You* kind of helped *me*. By keeping track of what you were working on, I had a place to start searching for supernaturals. You excel at sniffing them out."

"Ye say ye were at these other places, yet she never saw ye. Why are we so lucky to be seein' ye now?" Liam asked.

"Because you grabbed me by the throat and yanked me into the light."

"You mean if Liam hadn't caught you, you wouldn't have . . ." Kris's voice drifted off as hurt washed over her once more.

"He wouldnae have even said hello," Liam finished.

"I couldn't. This is dangerous, Kris. If any of them find out you're my sister they will—"

"Knock me over the head and drag me into the loch," she murmured. Had her relationship with Marty been behind the attacks? Did it even matter?

"No one will hurt her while I am here," Liam said. "And I will be here. I wouldnae leave her to face danger alone."

"I'm not leaving." Marty's jaw tightened. "Not until I've cleared this entire place of everything that doesn't belong."

"I'm not a complete incompetent," Kris pointed out. "I am the one with the gun."

"And how is that?" Marty's curious brown gaze flicked around the cottage. "Where's Edward?"

"Lately, he's in here." Kris tapped the computer. "He'll suddenly be on the screen. I'm not sure how he does it. It's not Skype or any kind of conference call that I've ever heard of. It's like he's *in* the computer."

"Edward always has the best toys," Marty muttered. "But if you aren't a *J-S* agent, why are you talking to the old man at all?"

"He paid me to keep him in the loop. Says he's short-handed."

Marty's brow creased. "There've been rumors of a purge. Supernatural creatures banding together and hunting the hunters. Which is how I got pressed into service. The old man's been sticking to the U.S. for the most part letting me and a few others deal with anything outside its borders. Even asking Interpol to handle certain problems." He flicked a finger at the computer. "Like the ones on that list. But he keeps fighting back. Using all his resources." Marty's frown deepened. "And taking advantage of whatever and whoever he can."

"He didn't take advantage of me. I needed the money, and he needed the info."

"You're not a hunter, Kris. You're a reporter. You could have been killed."

"Aye," Liam agreed, and he looked furious.

For an instant Kris wondered if he was furious with her. Be he shifter or guardian, she'd been feeding info to someone he would consider the enemy.

She wanted to ask him about the tattoo, about what he did, who he was. But she wasn't going to do it in front of Marty. She owed Liam that much.

His gaze went to the window, which had begun to lighten, and when he glanced back his expression was torn.

"Liam?" She moved toward him, but he was already headed for the door.

"'Tis nearly dawn." He laid his hand on the knob. "I'm late." And then he was gone.

"There's something strange about him," Marty said.

"There's something strange about *you*," Kris returned, gaze still on the door.

Liam hurried to the loch, for the first time in a long time needing its peace, craving the solitude. If he'd stayed with Kris she'd have asked him things he could not answer.

He should never have let her see the brand, which marked him as it had marked the others—binding them together, proving their loyalty for life.

Why had he touched her? Why had he let her touch him?

Simple. He'd been unable to stop. From the first moment, he'd felt a connection. That he would love, then lose, her was inevitable. Liam supposed he deserved nothing less.

He should disappear. Lurk about. Remain in the darkness. It was what he did best.

However, he wouldn't leave her alone. He'd sworn to protect her as he protected the loch. Nothing would harm her while he was here.

But, for both their sakes, he must never touch her again.

"What else do you want to know?" Marty asked.

Kris hesitated. They had a lot on their plate—serial killers, shifters, *Jäger-Suchers,* Interpol. Her issues with family could wait.

However, when she opened her mouth the questions spilled out. "Why did you leave?" Kris lowered her voice, afraid that if she didn't it might break. "Why didn't you come back?"

"You don't realize how much you're like . . ." Marty took a deep breath. "Mom."

"But . . ." That made no sense. "I don't look like her at all."

And Kris often wished that she did. At least then she'd always see a bit of her mom whenever she looked into the mirror. As it was, sometimes Kris panicked when she tried to remember the exact shape of her mother's face and couldn't.

"Not looks, no, but nearly everything else. Your voice is the same. You move just like her. Your hands. Your walk. It's eerie." He shook his head. "It was too hard for me. Too hard for Dad."

"Too hard," she repeated. "So you just disappeared?"

"I can tell you I'm sorry, and I am, but it isn't enough, and it never will be."

Kris wasn't sure what to do with this information. She'd thought she wasn't "enough" for them to love. She'd worked and strived and pushed herself to become someone. But all the time she'd actually been too much.

Like Mom.

"Dad," she began.

"I tried to get him to watch one of your shows. He broke down, walked out. I don't think he'll ever be able to visit or talk to you on the phone. Maybe a letter, or e-mail."

Kris made a derisive sound. For the first time since her mother had died and her family had left, she didn't mourn their loss. They'd walked out. They'd lost *her*. She wasn't going to feel "less than" anymore. Because she wasn't. She never had been.

"I wouldn't blame you if you never wanted to speak to either one of us again," Marty murmured.

Kris wouldn't blame herself, either.

They'd been a family. They should have been there for each other—when they were needed and even when they weren't. *That* was love. Not running away because something hurt too much.

"I understand," Marty said when she didn't answer.

"But there's one thing you need to know. This Liam—" He jerked his head at the door. "He doesn't exist."

Kris laughed. "Yeah, he's a ghost."

"A ghost? Well, maybe if you're thinking spook . . ." He frowned. "But he's Scottish, so I'm not sure what they call them here."

Kris would have laughed again, except he appeared to be serious. "What the hell, Marty? You saw him. You shoved him. He's solid. He's real."

For an instant Marty stared at her, obviously confused. "Of course he's real."

"Then what are you talking about?"

"There's no record of him. No passport, no license. He's off the grid. When you said 'spook,' I thought, *CIA, yeah that would make sense.* But being Scottish—"

"Hold on. I had the same problem when I got here. His name's actually William. A lot of the locals call him Billy."

"What does he do for a living?"

"He . . . uh . . ." Kris frowned. "Protects the loch." Or the monster. Maybe both.

"Like a park ranger?"

"Sure," Kris agreed.

Marty didn't appear convinced.

"I've been taking care of myself for a long time now, Marty. I travel. I meet people. I make decisions on their characters. I trust Liam."

Strangely, even though she knew Liam was lying, she did trust him. More than she'd ever trusted anyone else. And she didn't know why.

"Okay." Marty glanced at the window, which was still pretty dark. "I should let you rest."

"You're leaving?" Her voice sounded bereft, and she wanted to take the words back. Especially when Marty gently set his hand on her shoulder. She must have sounded pathetic.

"Just to The Clansman. I really can't leave until I find out what's going on here and get it taken care of. Man or monster? It's gotta be one or the other."

"Or both," she murmured.

"Yeah. But until I know what needs killing, I won't know who to call to kill it."

"You won't call Edward regardless?"

"*Jäger-Suchers* only kill monsters. They're very picky about that."

"So if we have a serial killer . . ." And Kris was almost certain they did. "You'll just leave it to the locals?"

"Uh—" Marty glanced toward the door as if he wanted to be anywhere but there. "There are certain cases where I call in someone who eliminates the problem without any need for legal mumbo jumbo."

"I'm not following."

"No long-drawn-out trials. No extradition hang-ups. Bad guy just—" Marty wrapped his hands around his own throat and made a choking sound.

Kris's mouth dropped open. "You hire a contract killer?"

"Problem solver," he corrected, dropping his arms. "One call, that's all."

Kris wasn't sure what to say. Whoever was killing women in Drumnadrochit had probably been killing people in other countries. And if he or she was even caught, the chances of the killer meeting a lethal end were slim with all the countries involved. But was it right to execute someone without a trial?

Before she'd come here, Kris would have answered that question with an unequivocal "no." Now she wasn't so sure.

"First I need ironclad proof," Marty said quietly. "I'll get it. One way or the other."

"Okay." Kris nodded. "Okay."

"If it's your . . . friend, I'll still call."

"Friend?" Kris echoed.

"Lover." Marty's lip curled. "God, I hate thinking that about my little sister, but I guess you're all grown-up."

"You think Liam is a serial killer?"

"He thought I was one."

"You just said he doesn't have a passport. How could he have left here and gone to all those other places?"

"*You* just said I was looking under the wrong name." He glanced at the door through which Liam had disappeared. "I've got a bad feeling. . . ."

Kris did, too, but not about Liam's passport. She didn't believe Liam was a serial killer. However, he *was* up to something. She only hoped it wasn't something that was going to get him killed.

"I spent some time at the Inverness Library," Marty continued.

"Good for you," Kris said, still thinking about Liam. And that tattoo.

"I've been trying to decide what legend the killer is imitating." Kris forgot about the tattoo. "I found an obscure story in a really old book."

His voice became more animated, as did his face. He obviously loved researching fairy tales as much as she'd once enjoyed listening to them.

"Didn't find the account anywhere else," he continued, "which is strange, because usually they get repeated and repeated until they become the basis for a lot of local boogeyman tales. For instance, you'd think that folks along the loch would use the threat of Nessie to warn kids away from the water."

" 'If you go too close, the monster will get you,' " Kris said, and wiggled her fingers in the universal sign for "scary."

"Exactly. But I couldn't find anything like that, and considering the story I uncovered, I should have."

"What's the story?"

He motioned for them to sit and, when they had, continued. "Once upon a time, there was a kelpie." Kris sat up straight, and her brother's eyes widened. "You've heard this?"

"I've heard about kelpies, but nothing specific."

"According to the librarian, every body of water in Scotland and Ireland has a kelpie legend. Which again makes me wonder why they aren't telling one here."

"Because it's all Nessie all the time?"

"Or because they're hiding something."

"For a gazillion years?"

"You'd be surprised. The legend I read equates kelpie with Each Uisge."

"Supernatural water horse."

He nodded. "The beautiful horse would lure the unsuspecting onto its back to swim across the water; then for kicks and giggles it would become a fish, a frog, an eel, the very water around them. In over their heads, and most unable to swim in those days, the victims would drown. But the Loch Ness kelpie was different."

"Different how?"

"It was a gorgeous human that lounged along the banks of the loch, where it seduced unsuspecting victims, then lured them into the water—"

"Where it drowned them for kicks and giggles."

"Pretty much," Marty agreed.

"Man? Woman?"

"Didn't say. But I'm thinking man because of the curse."

"Well, this just gets better and better," Kris muttered.

"The kelpie seduced and killed the daughter of a very powerful witch, who then cursed it to swim the loch as a monster for all eternity."

"You're thinking man because of the curse, but doesn't *Nessie* indicate female?"

"Nessie came from the newspapers, not the legend. In a 1933 London *Times* the monster was referred to as Mac-Ness, which has definite masculine connotations."

"All the recent victims have been women," Kris murmured, then had a nasty thought. "Were they raped?"

"I got a look at the reports. No signs of intercourse—consensual or otherwise—which was a big red flag that we're dealing with the same traveling killer." At Kris's curious expression, he continued, "There's always one thing that doesn't fit the monster profile. And if an actual kelpie seduced its victims, then drowned them . . ."

"There'd be evidence of sex before death."

"Bingo," Marty said.

Silence settled between them. Kris let her mind mull what her brother had said. She'd have kept mulling—he'd said a lot—but then Marty broke the silence.

"There's one more thing."

"What?"

"Know any witches?"

CHAPTER 23

"Why?" Kris asked.

She liked Jamaica. She didn't want to turn her over to Interpol—and from there perhaps the *Jäger-Suchers* or the "one call, that's all" assassin—if she didn't have to.

"The legend said that a descendant of the original witch would remain nearby to make certain the cursed one remained cursed."

"How do you get uncursed?"

"Got me. But I think the ever present descendant was meant to ensure that the kelpie would remain miserable. Something about eternal torment."

"Hell on earth," Kris murmured. ""Nice."

"The thing *did* drown her daughter."

"You get what you pay for. Or at least this beastie did."

"Who's the witch?" Marty pressed.

"You think that the ancestor lurking about the village is also a witch? Isn't that kind of obvious?"

"It's all we got."

Kris took a deep breath, hoping another way would become clear, but it didn't. "Jamaica Blue owns the local coffee shop. She told me she was an Obeah woman."

"Huh?"

"Black magic. From Jamaica. Involves sacrifice for power. I thought that maybe she was killing people as a sacrifice to Nessie, but Edward didn't agree."

"Sacrifice involves blood," Marty murmured.

"And, according to him, a ceremony, which we don't have evidence of here."

"Even if Jamaica isn't sacrificing people to her god, she could still be the watchdog ancestor. Who's to say one of the original witch's children couldn't have emigrated, had kids, and then one of them come back here."

"Anything's possible," Kris agreed, and Jamaica *had* been pretty secretive about her past. Although she had mentioned one of her ancestors was a Scot.

"Let's go see her." Marty stood.

"Okay." Kris headed for the bathroom.

"I meant now."

"I'm not going anywhere without covering up this bruise." Kris pointed at her cheek. "I'm sick of explaining where I got it. You might want to make use of my paints and powders, too."

"I'm a man." He puffed out his chest comically. "No paint. No powder. Besides . . ." He lifted his arm and made a muscle. "You should see the other guy."

"The one without a mark on him?"

Except for that damn tattoo.

Marty just scowled, which should have hurt his nose but apparently didn't.

Five minutes later Kris and her brother headed for Drumnadrochit. Both of them were deep in thought, trying to put together the pieces of two different puzzles.

"Hold on." Kris paused. Marty did, too. "Where's the shape-shifting come in?"

Her brother gave her nothing but a blank stare.

"A kelpie is a shifter," Kris explained. "Usually a horse that becomes a . . . whatever. But you said our kelpie is a handsome man or gorgeous woman who seduces the unsuspecting into giving up their goodies, then drowns them."

"Right."

"Where's the shape-shifting? Horse became whatever. But the human became . . . ?"

"Oh!" Understanding spread over his face. "The legend said *nathair*."

"Which means?"

"Snake."

Kris winced. This was looking worse and worse for Jamaica.

"Except . . ." Marty's brow creased. "The picture in the book wasn't of a snake." He glanced toward the loch. "It was Nessie."

Kris followed his gaze. The water rolled merrily to the opposite shore, broken by nothing but boats, the odd log and beady-eyed stone. "So the gorgeous human transforms into a cold, ugly, snake-headed lake monster."

"You see why this legend caught my attention?"

"Certainly caught mine."

The same kid who had been behind the counter before was there again, and he had the same answer to Kris's request for Jamaica.

"She willnae be back for a few days."

"You said that yesterday," Kris pointed out. "So shouldn't she be back tomorrow?"

The kid only frowned and repeated, "She willnae be back for a few days."

"You're confusing him," Marty said, and after ordering

a cup of coffee for them both urged her out the door. "Now what?"

Kris hadn't wanted to tell him about Jamaica's snake tattoo, which had closely resembled Nessie's head when combined with all the other Nessie parts Kris had seen on other bodies, but she kind of had to. Jamaica was missing. Either something had happened to her or she was the one who'd pushed Kris off the cliff, not to mention conking Kris over the head and burying Kris's knife in the chest of an innocent woman.

And Lord knows what else.

"She's got a tattoo," Kris blurted.

"Who does, and why should I care?"

"Jamaica has a tattoo on her ankle of what I thought was a snake but—" Kris took a deep breath and told him the rest.

Marty's face went from curious to concerned. He pulled out his cell phone and began texting. *He* appeared to have no trouble getting reception near the mountains. "I'm having a check run on this woman. Jamaica Blue can't be her real name."

"I don't think it is."

"That, combined with the tat, her background in witchcraft, and her disappearance, means trouble. We just have to find out what kind."

He hit *send*, then pocketed the phone. "Show me the other tattoos."

The Camerons' place wasn't far away. They'd go there first.

"Problem with the door?" Rob asked as he opened his.

"No. It's—uh—great." Now that she and Marty were here, Kris wasn't sure how to get a gander at Rob's forearm.

Marty elbowed her in the ribs. "Aren't you going to introduce me?"

"Oh yeah. "This is—um—" Was she supposed to say he was her brother? An agent with Interpol? Or the reincarnation of Bonnie Prince Charlie?

Lying? Never her strong suit.

Marty handed his half-full coffee cup to Kris, who'd already finished hers, then stepped forward, arm outstretched. "I'm Marty Daniels. Kris's brother."

He shook Rob's hand heartily; then as if seeing something disturbing, he pulled up Rob's sleeve to reveal . . . the tattoo of a pair of flippers.

And nothing else.

"Sorry." Marty released Rob, who scowled mightily and appeared as if he might just pop Marty in his already much-maligned nose. "I thought I saw a spider, but it was just your tattoo. Interesting choice. What's it mean?"

"I like ducks," Rob said, then slammed the door in their faces.

"Who's next?" Marty asked.

Kris didn't mention Effy. She didn't want to know, or even think, about what Marty might do to get a peek at her landlady's tattoo. Besides, knocking on the door again after Rob had just slammed it . . . probably not the best idea. Instead, Kris handed Marty his coffee, then led the way to the station. Moments later they found Alan Mac in his office.

Pleasantries were exchanged. "Meet my brother." Smile. Nod. "Did ye walk into a door?" Nod. Smile.

Marty attempted to switch his cup from right hand to left so he could shake, and muffed it so badly the coffee went flying into the air . . . landing all over Alan Mac's clean shirt.

Kris contemplated her brother with new respect. He was really very good at this.

She waited to see how Marty would finagle his way into the locker room or the men's room or whatever room Alan Mac would retire to in order to change his shirt.

However, the coffee must still have been hot enough for discomfort, because Alan Mac yanked off the shirt in a great big hurry. With him left in what they called a wifebeater in the states, his tattoo was clearly visible. It looked like a tail.

Just that. A tail, winding around his ample biceps before curling up at the end like the head of a question mark.

"Let me buy you a new shirt," Marty said.

"I've got another right here." Alan Mac reached into a lower desk drawer and pulled out a crisply folded shirt. "Since I get into all sorts of muck, I keep a good supply."

"That's an interesting tattoo."

Alan Mac, who had been shaking out the clean garment, glanced up at Marty, then down at his biceps.

"What is it supposed to be?"

The constable quickly shoved his arms into the sleeves, covering the object in question, then got busy with the buttons as if they were the hardest puzzle he'd solved in years.

"I've never seen one like that," Marty continued.

For an instant Kris thought Alan Mac would ignore Marty until he went away. But the constable finished the last button and lifted his head. "I was in the Queen's Own Highlanders."

"Military." Marty nodded. "And they all have those?"

Alan Mac's eyes narrowed. "Aye."

"What is it?"

"Circle of trust," the constable said.

"All for one, one for all," Marty replied.

Alan Mac tilted his head and said nothing.

The silence became oppressive. Kris began to feel uncomfortable. Alan Mac was obviously lying. They knew it, and he knew that they knew it.

"What exactly are ye doin' in our fair village?" Alan Mac asked.

"Visiting my sister."

"Mmm," Alan Mac said. "Strange place for a family reunion."

"Isn't it?" Marty returned amiably.

The constable was clearly suspicious. Since he'd been the one who'd investigated Marty, he had good reason. Which only gave him grounds to throw her brother into a cell if he was so inclined. Maybe he'd throw Kris in there, too, just for fun. And if Alan Mac was up to something nefarious, no one might ever find them.

Marty's phone chimed an incoming text message. He took a glance at the display and nodded to Alan Mac. "Nice to meet you. Sorry about the shirt. Kris?"

He walked out and kept walking. Kris scrambled to keep up. The constable's gaze followed them all the way out the door.

Her brother scooted around the corner of the building, then leaned against the wall and read whatever was displayed on his phone with a growing frown.

"What is it?" Kris asked. "Is Jamaica wanted for murder in ten other countries?"

"No." His frown deepened as he peered at the screen. "Maybe. I don't know. This." He lifted the phone. "Isn't about her specifically."

"What is it about?"

"When I asked for the check on Jamaica, I also asked about tattoos. What they're used for. Other cases where they've been found. Someone in my division had an interesting case not too long ago that involved body art. Long story short, there was a creature and there were those who watched over it."

"Guardian cult," Kris guessed.

Marty blinked. "How did you know?"

"Edward got there ahead of you."

"If you knew what they were," Marty muttered, "why didn't you tell me?"

"I didn't know. It was just one of many theories. Why do you think that what your colleague encountered was the same as what's going on in Drumnadrochit?"

"Because the guardians all had tattoos."

"A lot of people do. That doesn't mean they're protecting a big squishy monster."

Marty cast her an annoyed glance. "Let me finish, Squirt. The tattoos were the same as they are here."

"Flippers and tails?"

"No, because this creature had fur and fangs and two heads."

"I don't even want to know what that is."

"No," Marty agreed. "You don't. When I said 'the same,' I meant each guardian was tattooed with a different part of the monster. Separately they are nothing, but together they are invincible. Like that monster."

"Interesting," Kris murmured as her mind added two and two, then her heart began to thud fast and loud as it whispered, *Four*. "You'd think that maybe their . . . leader—"

Please let it be their leader.

"—would have the entire monster tattooed somewhere. Kind of like a lieutenant's stripes."

"No. The tattoo of the whole monster . . ." Marty paused to pocket his phone, and Kris had to clench her hands to keep from grabbing him and shaking the rest of the words out. "That's only found on the monster itself."

Kris's thundering heart seemed to stop. *Bam.* She couldn't even breathe.

"You see anything like that?" her brother asked.

Her heart started. Kris tried, and managed, to take a breath. Then she looked her brother right in the eye and said—

"No."

Kris got rid of Marty. Later she wasn't sure exactly how.

It didn't matter, as long as he was gone and she was alone.

Somehow she made it back to the cottage. She was in shock. She knew that. Yet still she couldn't snap out of it.

Only talking to Liam would do that.

Maybe.

More than likely talking to Liam would make her brain explode and then shock would be the least of her worries.

She waited all day and into the night. Dawn was only a short time away when her inertia broke. Obviously he wasn't going to come to her. She'd have to go to him.

Except she had no idea how to find Liam. No idea where he lived or if he even had a place.

Beyond the loch.

"Fine." She pulled on a sweater and boots. "I'll just walk around and around and around the damn thing until he shows up."

Or someone else tossed her in.

Hand on the door, Kris paused, remembering that day, the huge, black beastie with the oddly familiar eyes. Certainly they'd been gray instead of blue, but a mere change in color could not take away the soul inside.

If a shape-shifting, cursed kelpie even had a soul.

Kris yanked open the door and stepped into the night. She couldn't believe she was accepting this . . .

"Insanity," she muttered, tromping across the road, then down to the loch.

But was it insanity?

She was going to find out.

Kris scanned the shore—nothing, not even a body— before turning her gaze to the loch.

In this darkest hour when the moon had fallen and the sun was not even a hint upon the horizon, the water skated like black ice to the opposite shore. Waves sloshed, but she couldn't see them or anything else. Not a boat. Not a log. Not a rock. Not a—

"Nessie!" she shouted, then picked up a stone and threw it with all her might into the darkness. "I know you're out there. I know who you are."

The stone hit. *Kerplunk*. The silence that followed seemed to roar in her ears. Kris began to speed walk down the shore. He couldn't hide from her. Not forever.

"Liam!" she shouted. "Liam Grant!"

She reached a thick grove of trees. Beneath them the night loomed ever darker. *Fuck it!* she thought, and plunged inside.

"William! Billy! Whatever the hell your name is. Come out, come out, wherever you are!"

She felt like a fool, but she didn't stop. She *wouldn't* stop. Not until he faced her and told her the truth.

She reached Urquhart Castle. This time no one stood at the top. The wind wailed through the ruins like a banshee.

"Hey!" she shouted. "Are you deaf? Or maybe you've just got water in your ears. If you have ears."

Kris paused, listened, heard nothing but the wind and the water. Still, she could have sworn—

She tilted her head, caught that wicked scent. He was here. Somewhere. The back of her neck even prickled.

Her gaze scraped the castle, the ruins, the loch, and the trees. Then suddenly she knew.

"You're right behind me, aren't you?"

CHAPTER 24

"I do have ears, *mo chridhe*."

Kris spun. Liam couldn't see her expression, but he heard the pain in her voice, even before it broke on the final word. "You don't get to call me *mo* whatever."

"My heart," he whispered, and his chest ached.

Her chin came up. "You don't have a heart."

"I do, and it is yours. Forever."

"I hear forever for you is really forever."

He lowered his head. What could he say?

"What are you?" she asked.

He kept his gaze down, trying to breathe, hoping to die, knowing he couldn't. When he didn't answer, she muttered something vile, then reached into her pocket.

Curious, he followed the movement of her hand as it came toward him. She pressed the silver Celtic cross to his forearm, then snatched it back as if expecting flames.

But there were none.

"What—?" she began, and then stopped. Doubt lightened the word, crept into her stance. She didn't want to believe whatever she'd been told, and if given a reason, she wouldn't.

He could let her think what she would. They could continue on as they'd been. He'd done worse.

Liam opened his mouth—to tell her the truth or a lie; he never knew. Because before he could speak, a scream split the night.

Brilliant, terrified, and close.

Together they ran toward the sound, leaving behind forever the option of choice.

Liam reached the water's edge first. The screams continued, but he saw no one anywhere near.

The water, the mountains, they magnified and distorted. The sounds that had seemed to come from here were in fact coming from—

"Over there." Kris pointed. A lone woman bobbed in the water, crying out as she surfaced, gurgling as she went under.

"Shit." Kris kicked off her boots, pulling her sweater over her head at the same time.

"No," Liam said, and she paused, one arm out of the sweater, one arm still in.

"She's drowning. We can't just stand here."

"It's too cold and too far. Ye'll die."

"Not before she will." Kris threw the sweater to the ground, the stark white of the T-shirt beneath shining against the dusky sky, then started on her pants.

"No," he said again, eyes on the heavens. "Wait for it."

She looked up, brow furrowed. "Wait for what?"

He hadn't wanted it to be this way. If he was going to tell her his truth, he would have preferred to do so in a less shocking manner. But he didn't have any choice.

Liam sprinted for the water, leaping from the shore as the sun burst over the horizon.

And he changed.

* * *

Liam went up as a man, came down as something else, seeming to pour forever from the air.

Gray, seal-like skin, a long, long neck, a bulky body, an even longer tail. He hit the water with a plunk, and the resulting spray became a geyser, soaking Kris from head to thigh.

She didn't stumble back. She stayed right where she was, gaze melded to the creature as he sped across the loch in the direction of the still-bobbing, no longer shrieking, woman. She appeared exhausted past the point of survival. Without help, she would soon sink below.

"He's Nessie," Kris muttered, from lips that felt like wax.

She'd known, hadn't she? She'd come searching for Liam to make him admit just that. Yet still she stood staring and shaking, while her mind circled ways to explain away what her eyes could plainly see. The human brain's power for rationalization never ceased to amaze.

Nessie—no—*Liam* reached the woman in no time. Kris recalled reports of the monster's incredible speed despite her great bulk. What else that had been reported about her—make that *him*—was true?

The creature sunk below the surface like stone, straight down, an impossibility that had also been reported before. However, the ripples formed by that huge body seemed to drag the woman down as well. Kris cried out as she disappeared from sight.

Had Kris been wrong? Had Nessie— Kris cursed. Had *Liam* pulled the woman under? Once he was a monster was he truly a monster? If so, then why had he saved her?

An instant later, the beast surfaced. The woman, obviously spent and nearly unconsciousness, clung to his back. The thing that was Liam slowly turned toward Kris and began to move.

Kris scanned the area. Was this woman another victim of the copycat serial killer? Or had she merely fallen in, then could not get out?

The latter seemed too far-fetched. How lame would you have to be to trip on the shore, fall into the water, thrash around until you were too far out to make it back on your own, then scream for help at a time of day—or almost night—when there was little chance of getting it?

This whole situation smelled worse than the oldest salmon in the loch.

All questions were put aside when Liam reached the shallows. Instead of dumping the woman's body from his back, then nudging her toward the shore as he'd done the last time, he actually pulled himself onto land.

He was massive—the body of an elephant, the neck of a moray eel, and the head of a boa constrictor combined. When Kris moved forward to take the woman, she felt dwarfed, both frightened and humbled. This creature had existed for centuries. The things he had seen and done, the people he had encountered, all that he knew . . . she couldn't get her mind around it. Nor the idea that she'd touched and kissed and—*admit it, Kris*—loved this being in his human form, was too much for her mind right now as well.

Something about her feelings, her responses, tickled the edge of her brain, and if Kris had had time to think, she might have drawn it out. But when she went to her knees in the mud and damp grass next to the woman, every thought but one fled her head.

"She isn't breathing."

Kris had taken CPR, but it had been a while and she'd never had to use it. Still, she found the steps coming back.

Clear the airway. Position the head. Pinch the nose. Mouth over mouth and exhale, one one thousand, then again, two one thousand. Check to see if she'd started to breathe on her own.

No. *Dammit!*

Chest compressions. One and two and three and—

Kris reached thirty, breathed for the woman twice more, and went back to the compressions. By the time Kris thought to look for Nessie, the creature was gone.

The woman suddenly drew in a great, gasping breath and began to choke. Kris turned her on her side, and lake water poured forth like a river.

"What-what—?"

Kris pressed her back on the ground, which was cold and wet but all they had. Together they shivered violently enough to shake loose a few teeth. Kris would have given the woman her sweater, but it lay in the mud, as soaked as her hair.

"Stay still," Kris said. "You nearly drowned."

"I—" The woman lifted her hand to her head and winced. "Someone hit me."

"That seems to be going around," Kris muttered.

She glanced toward the road, hoping a car would happen by. The sun was up, but it was early yet.

"Then they were carrying me, but it was dark, and I couldnae see."

Sounded familiar.

"Then I was in the water, and it was cold and deep and I couldnae get anywhere no matter how hard I tried."

Kris remembered feeling the same way when she was in the loch, then—

"Nessie came," the woman whispered. "Did ye see her?"

Lies *did* get easier the more they were told. Kris had no problem at all meeting the woman's eyes and saying, "No."

* * *

Just when Kris thought she'd have to leave the poor, shivering, in-and-out-of-consciousness woman alone in the mud while she went for help, Alan Mac and all his cronies arrived like the proverbial cavalry.

After giving her the same *seriously, you again?* glance, Alan Mac took over. The woman babbled about Nessie, but no one seemed to think this was odd. They all went about their business of helping the victim, securing the scene, then spiriting her away.

Luckily the EMTs, or whatever they were called in this country, had brought blankets. Kris grabbed two and tried to make her escape. But Alan Mac appeared at her side and took her arm. "What happened?"

"How did you know to come here? And with all of . . ." She lifted her chin to indicate the cavalry. "Them?"

He didn't answer.

She turned her gaze to his, and she knew. Somehow Liam had gotten word to him. Perhaps Liam could shift back and forth at will, although why then . . .

Kris frowned at the slowly rising sun. Why had he said, "Wait for it"? Why hadn't he jumped into the loch and saved the woman immediately?

Because he couldn't. So how had he brought Alan Mac here so fast? Perhaps Liam was a talking lake monster.

Kris choked. This was all so ridiculous. Though nonetheless true.

She considered accusing Alan Mac of being a guardian, but that probably wasn't the best idea. He guarded Nessie, had protected her—*him*—for who knows how long. What if protecting the monster included making sure that anyone who'd seen him change never saw that, or anything else, again?

Kris considered the chief constable. Did she really think he'd toss her in the deep to keep Liam safe?

Yes.

"The woman said Nessie saved her," Kris blurted.

"Aye," Alan Mac agreed, gaze intent on Kris's face. "And what do you say?"

Kris shrugged. "I found her on the shore. She wasn't breathing. I did CPR; then you showed up."

"Mmm," Alan Mac said. "I ken there is a bit more to it than that."

"Said someone hit her on the head, dragged her to the water. Next thing she remembers, she was drowning."

Alan Mac cursed. "I have to get back. I'll drop ye at the cottage."

Kris considered saying she'd walk, but her legs were still trembly, along with the rest of her. A September dawn in the Highlands was not the time to be soaked to the skin. If her lips weren't actually blue, they soon would be.

So she climbed into his car, which smelled like old tennis shoes and bad coffee. Kris would have opened the window if she'd had the energy.

"What else is my victim going to tell me?" Alan Mac asked.

Kris sighed. Cops liked to have witnesses repeat their stories, see if anything new shook out, but this was tiresome. She was a reporter. She knew what he was up to.

She rapped her knuckles against her head. Then made her hand dive downward. "Splash," she said, and used both hands to indicate just that.

Alan Mac rolled his eyes. "And then?"

"According to your victim, saved by the monster."

"Yet ye saw nothing."

Kris met his eyes. "Nothing but her."

After the sun set, Liam climbed from the water and found the clothes he kept hidden for those times he waited too long and changed before he was able to disrobe. When that happened, the clothes he'd been wearing just disappeared.

Magic was like that.

"I told ye t' leave her be."

Though he was still dripping wet and completely naked, Liam didn't start when the voice came out of the shrouded darkness of the forest. He'd known someone was there. He'd expected him to be.

Alan Mac stepped out as Liam put on his pants. "She knows."

"Of course she knows." Liam zipped the zipper, the sound a perfect punctuation to the sharpness of his words. "She saw."

"But—" Alan Mac frowned. "She looked me right in the eye and swore she saw nothing but the woman."

Interesting. Liam had to wonder why Kris would lie about this, considering her aversion to lies.

"She saw," Liam repeated. "I shifted right in front of her."

"Are ye daft?" Alan Mac threw up his big hands. "Now I'll have t'—"

Liam was across the distance between them in an instant, one hand around the much larger man's throat. "Ye willnae."

"My vows," Alan Mac began.

"Bugger your vows." Liam leaned closer and squeezed. Alan Mac's face began to redden. "Ye willnae touch her. She is mine."

He shoved the man away. Alan Mac stumbled and nearly fell. His fingers rubbed at the mark on his neck as Liam calmly picked up his shirt and put it on.

"Those vows were composed in times long past," Liam continued. "They arenae . . ." He searched for a word.

"*Right* anymore. Ye cannae kill someone because they see me change. I forbid it."

"Yes, Uilebheist."

Liam sighed. Until recently no one had known his name. They'd all called him Uilebheist. Gaelic for "monster."

He hated it.

Certainly he'd been a monster once upon a time. He had killed. He had enjoyed it.

But since he'd become the beastie known as Nessie, a monster in form by day, a man by night, he was a true monster no longer.

Which made it both ironic and annoying to be called that. But he'd allowed it because . . . what difference did it make what they called him? And really, he'd deserved nothing less.

He still didn't deserve to have a name, a life, to love. But it had been nice, for a little while, to pretend.

"Ye told me she came to do a show on this place, on you."

Alan Mac seemed to have conquered his momentary fear. One of the reasons Liam liked the man. He was honest, at least with Liam. He'd lie like a lazy dog to everyone else on the planet. But Liam trusted Alan Mac both to protect him and to tell him the truth.

He'd like to think the constable was his friend, but that wasn't the case. Alan Mac had little choice in the relationship. Which made it not friendship but bondage. Liam wished he could release the man, but only death would do that.

"What can she do?" Liam asked. "Her camera is at the bottom of the loch."

He never had determined just who had shoved her off. It could very well have been one of his guardians. There was a reason no good footage of Nessie existed, and they were it.

"She came here to expose ye as a hoax."

"People do that by the dozen," Liam said. "Since I am not a hoax, they dinnae succeed."

"What if she—"

"What?" Liam threw up his hands. "Tells the world that she slept with the Loch Ness Monster? What d' ye think will happen to her career then?"

Alan Mac's eyes widened as understanding dawned "Ah," he said.

Liam headed for the road.

"Where are ye going?" Alan Mac hurried to keep up.

"I have to talk to her."

"What? No!" Alan Mac laid his hand on Liam's arm, then quickly snatched it back when Liam paused, looked at the man's hand, then into his face. "If ye just . . . disappear she'll leave."

"I doubt that," Liam said, though maybe the constable was right. Regardless, he could not let Kris go without at least trying to explain. He owed her that.

"Ye cannae tell her."

Liam could do anything that he wished. He was the Uilebheist. Once people had treated him like a god. Sometimes, they still did.

"Dinnae worry about Kris," Liam said. "Worry about whoever is killing women and trying to blame me. If we dinnae stop that, we'll soon have another visit from Mandenauer or one of his minions. Perhaps this time they might even know how to kill me."

Liam's heart lightened. He'd been hoping someone would discover that for centuries.

CHAPTER 25

After yet another long, hot shower, fresh, dry clothes, and a pot of coffee, Kris opened her computer. She spent hours fighting with the Internet, which seemed determined to waver in and out and keep her from uncovering any information about the kelpie of Loch Ness.

In the end she found little more than what her brother had already told her. She had to wonder if someone—a guardian?—had erased all traces of the tale.

To the majority of the world—those who weren't *Jäger-Suchers,* "secret" Interpol consultants, or nut jobs—legends were merely that. Tall tales believed by superstitious ancients. Legends weren't true; the creatures described in them weren't real. They were the fairy tales her mother had read, kept alive for fun and the occasional Disney movie.

So why the great purge?

Eyes burning, Kris laid her head on the back of the couch. Next thing she knew, the room was dark and someone was knocking on the door.

Figuring the caller was her brother, or Alan Mac with more stupid questions, she hit the lights and stumbled across the floor, rubbing her eyes with one hand, pulling the door open with the other. Then she stood there with her arm frozen in the air next to her face.

Liam's hair was wet. Now she knew why. She still couldn't move or speak or think straight.

"Can I come in?"

She should slam the door, scream, shoot him with silver.

No! The thought horrified her—because she didn't want to kill anyone, any*thing*? Or because silver didn't appear to have any effect on him at all?

"Please," he murmured. "I'll tell ye everything."

Kris stepped back and let him walk through the door.

A waft of cool air followed; it smelled like rain on green trees, the moon in the middle of the night, and she yearned.

Annoyed with that yearning—he'd lied to her all along; he wasn't even human, talk about a date from hell—Kris gave in to the urge to slam the door. She expected the sharp *clack* to make him start, but it didn't.

Why would it? He had nothing to fear. He was an inde-structible lake monster.

Kris laughed, though the sound that came from her mouth was more of a waterlogged sob. Liam glanced at her, concerned, even took one step toward her, and she amazingly took one step toward him before she could stop herself.

What was it about the man that made him so hard to resist?

The thought that had nagged at the edge of her brain earlier tumbled free, and Kris lifted her hands to her temples and pushed. No matter how hard she tried, she couldn't make the realization go away.

"I didn't understand why I felt like I did about you," she murmured. "Why I kissed you the first time I saw you. Why I wanted you so badly, when that's not like me. I don't trust anyone that fast." She laughed and now it was bitter; she was bitter. "You seduced me. It's what you do, what you are."

"Kris—"

"Don't lie to me anymore!" she cried. Then, horrified when tears pricked hot against her eyelids, she blinked until they went away. "You're a kelpie. You seduce, then kill. So why was I special? Why am I still alive?"

He took a deep breath, letting it out long and slow. "I no longer kill," he said.

"But you do seduce."

"I didnae try." He spread his hands. "But I am what I am."

"It was an accident?"

"I havenae seduced a woman since I became this."

Kris snorted. "Right. I just jumped you because my slut gene kicked in. Must be the balmy Scottish air."

"There is—," he insisted, then when she practically hissed at him corrected himself, "*was* something between us. It wasnae like anything I'd ever felt. I *have* never felt." He lifted a shoulder. "Lust. Desire. Aye. But anything more, never. And that's why . . ." He looked away, pursing his lips.

"Why what?" she demanded.

"Why I let this go on as I did. I dinnae deserve happiness, but I couldnae resist it with you."

"You are so full of—," she began. "You wouldn't know the truth if it reared up from the loch and bit you."

Why she was surprised to discover that he was a man, just like any other man—even though he wasn't—she didn't know. She *expected* lies to spill out of every mouth that she met. So why then, when she'd discovered Liam had lied, did she want to curl up and die?

"Cry," she muttered. She would curl up and *cry*. She would wish to die for no man. Hell, she'd wish to cry for no man, either. Not anymore.

He gave her a strange glance, and she realized she'd said that out loud. "Never mind. You're telling me you haven't been with a woman in centuries."

"I swear—"

"Bullshit," she said matter-of-factly. "You might not be human, but you're still a man, or at least you have all the parts, and no sex for a millennium or two isn't possible for your breed."

"I couldnae," he said. "I had hurt so many and, in the night, they haunted me." His eyes met hers, and she felt again that odd shimmy in her chest. Must be too much coffee. "I was never at peace. Until I found you."

She wanted to believe him so badly she ached. She knew he was lying, and still she wanted to forgive, to take his hand and let him pull her into his arms.

"Just tell me your story," she ordered. "Leave my stupidity and your tricky dick out of it."

His brow furrowed at her words, but instead of questioning them, he began to speak. "I came into being when the earth was new. I am of the fey."

"You're a fairy," Kris said. "Right."

"Not as ye think of them now, no. *Fey* is an ancient term meaning 'bewitched' or 'enchanted.' I appeared right here, on the loch as I am now, full grown and knowing my place. I was Unseelie, a malicious being; I took joy in what I was and what I did."

"Seduce and kill."

"Aye. I was a monster. I was born one."

"Not born," Kris said. "Not really."

"I dinnae know what else to call it. I was delivered to the earth, and I remember nothing before I was me."

"Enchanted, bewitched," Kris murmured. "By a great big witch, or maybe a god."

"Maybe *the* God."

"You think God would unleash something like you?" Kris asked, then paused. She was constantly amazed at the things put on the earth by whatever force had put them there. A seducing, shifting, serial-killing kelpie?

Why the hell not?

"Go on," she said.

"I was two natured."

"Aren't you still?"

He nodded. "But then I wasn't human."

"You still aren't," she muttered.

His face tightened—a flinch—before he continued. "I looked like a man, but that was just glamour. Magic to make me appealing."

"Are you magicing me now?" Kris demanded. That would explain why even though she knew what he was, she still couldn't stop staring at him. He was just too damn pretty.

"No need. I am human," he insisted. "At least beneath the moon."

"Beneath the moon," she repeated, another piece clicking into place. "I've never seen you in the sunlight."

"Ye have." He lifted his chin to indicate the loch. "At dawn ye'll find me there."

"Monster by *day,* man by night?" she murmured. "That's a little backward."

"'Tis part of my punishment, my curse. Human beings live in the light. But not me. Never me."

His voice was bereft. She couldn't blame him. Never was a very long time.

Kris straightened. He might say he wasn't working his

voodoo on her, but something was going on. Why else would she have any sympathy for him?

"You drowned a witch's daughter," she said. He'd drowned a lot of daughters. Hundreds, maybe thousands. But the last one was the one who had changed everything.

"Aye. I didnae know, of course, who she was."

"Would that have stopped you?"

"Doubtful. Though the curse was terrible. *Is* terrible," he clarified. "But no more than I deserved."

"She cursed you to be Nessie by day and a man by night," Kris said. "What's so damn bad about that?"

"She gave me human understanding. Morals. A conscience. Once I killed for the joy of it. Now . . ." The eyes he turned to her brimmed with agony. "I remember everything I did. All the time."

Kris began to see the beauty, and the horror, of his curse.

Liam put his hands to his head and pressed as she had done earlier, as if he could make the memories, or perhaps the voices, stop. "Every woman. Every word. The begging, the pleading, my laughter. How it felt to touch them, to know what I would do to them in the end and to want that end as much as they wanted me." He dropped his hands, now fists, against his thighs, pounding to the beat of each word. "I was a monster."

She couldn't argue.

He took several breaths, forcing his fingers to uncurl before he continued. "I'm moon cursed."

"Seems to me that beneath the moon you aren't cursed; you're . . ." She waved her hand to indicate his beautiful face and gorgeous body.

"She cursed me to eternal torment beneath the moon. To understand the pain I gave, and feel it myself for all time. When I'm Nessie, I can think, but not like this."

"Why bother with Nessie? Why not just curse you to live in human form, tormented and immortal?"

"Forever is a long time. Time heals, they say, though I havenae found that. But what if someday enough has passed, and I put my sins behind me? I could have a life. The life denied her daughter by me."

Understanding dawned. "But you can never have that life if you're a huge, slimy lake monster whenever the sun shines."

"Aye," he said.

"Nice curse." Very clever.

"There is something about being confined to the scene of yer crimes," he continued, "walking the same land where ye did such horrible things, swimming in the loch where those bodies still lie, charged to protect what ye made a graveyard, that makes it all seem like yesterday."

"You can't leave?" Kris asked.

His gaze became distant. "Ye know the few land sightings of Nessie?"

"What about them?"

"Sometimes the memories, the loneliness, the *voices* became too much, and I would run. But as soon as the sun bursts into the sky, I flop to the earth and roll around like a one-legged cow." His lip pulled back in a disgusted snarl.

And the curse became cleverer and cleverer.

"You're a shape-shifter," Kris said. "Yet silver doesn't hurt you?"

"I was cursed to *eternal* torment. If silver can kill me, there's nothing eternal about it."

Sympathy flared again. To be in agony, to know it would never end . . . She was surprised Liam hadn't snapped and started killing people just so Edward would—

Kris caught her breath. Had he?

"I can see every thought cross yer face," he murmured. "I havenae begun killing again; this I swear."

"Oh, well, if you swear," Kris said. "Then you must *not* be lying."

"I'm not. I was standing next to ye when we saw the woman drowning. I saved her as I saved you."

He had. And since he couldn't leave—or so he said—he hadn't been mimicking legendary beings in Botswana. Although there could be two killers—

Kris's head began to ache.

"Does Mandenauer know?" she asked.

"Who I am? No."

"About your curse? That you can't be killed?"

"Also no. I always hope that on one of his visits he'll attempt the right way to end my existence. If anyone can do it, he can."

"He's tried to kill you?" Kris asked.

"Now and again he's caught a glimpse, taken a shot. I am good at hiding. Mandenauer is equally good at seeking."

"But you haven't— You said you didn't . . ." Kris paused, then blurted, "If you haven't killed anyone, why does he want you dead?"

"I *have* killed. Centuries ago, 'tis true, but I killed nevertheless."

That didn't seem right. Didn't everyone, everything, deserve a second chance?

And here she was thinking favorably about him again. Him and his damned mojo were messing with her mind.

Liam was a killer. Just because he hadn't killed recently didn't mean he wouldn't do so again. Maybe he'd reformed, but would that reformation cause all the women he'd drowned to suddenly arise?

"Mandenauer hasn't made the Loch Ness Monster a

top priority," Liam continued. "Which might be why whoever is killing women is trying to blame Nessie."

"Why?"

"To force him to increase his efforts and end me once and for all."

"Who did you piss off?" she asked. "Besides me."

Liam's lips twitched, though his eyes remained sad. "Hard to say. Dougal's never cared for me." He lifted one shoulder. "But he doesna know that I am the monster."

"Who does?"

"Only those with my brand."

"The tattoo. Your guardians."

"Aye. Alan Mac, the Camerons, Jamaica, Johnnie MacLeod."

She'd missed the pub owner. "Where's Johnnie keep his tattoo?"

"Ye dinnae want to know."

Probably not.

"Jamaica," she began. "She's a witch."

"Aye."

"She said she no longer practiced, but I had to wonder once I looked up Obeah if she was perhaps—" Kris stopped. It sounded foolish even in her head.

"What?" Liam appeared completely confused.

"Sacrificing people to—"

"Obi?"

"Or you."

"Me?" Shock spread over his face. "No. I would never— *She* would never. Jamaica came here broken, horrified by what she'd done. I dinnae think she could kill again, even to save herself."

When Kris thought back on what she'd seen in Jamaica's eyes as the woman related her past, she had to agree. "I guess I can check her off the list of suspects."

"You thought Jamaica was the serial killer?"

"Right now, I think everyone's the serial killer."

Silence fell, but it didn't last long, since Kris—as usual—had more questions. "It's not like you need a guardian to protect you from silver bullet–wielding *Jäger-Suchers*. What do they do?"

"They make it seem like I belong. So no one suspects, aye? I have a room in one of the Camerons' properties. I work at MacLeod's on occasion. Alan Mac is helpful if someone ever questions my background."

"You better have him do something about a passport and a license. When my brother checked you out, he didn't find any. Nowadays, everyone's got a number."

"I'll tell him."

Kris tightened her lips. Why was she *helping* him?

"Where did you get guardians?" she asked. "The witch certainly didn't post them to keep you safe."

"No, she didnae," he agreed. "Hundreds of years ago I saved some children from drowning. Their families, in thanks, promised to guard me all of my days."

"Same families?"

"Aye. One dies, another takes their place."

"What if one leaves?"

"They dinnae."

"Because they can't? Like you?"

"They arenae cursed. They *can* leave. They just . . ." He spread his hands. "Dinnae."

Loyalty. A concept Kris admired, even if it was loyalty to an eternally cursed monster.

"None of them have any idea who might hate Nessie enough to end her?"

"It could be anyone, Kris. If we believe that our killer is the same killer that's been using legends as a signature, then this isnae personal."

"Random killer," Kris muttered. "They're always *so* easy to find."

"I'll find him. Ye need t' stay out of it. Go home, Kris. Where ye'll be safe."

The idea of flying off to Chicago, leaving behind a serial killer and her broken heart, should have had Kris throwing everything into a bag and catching the first flight out of Inverness; instead it made her struggle to breathe. She didn't want to go; she couldn't.

"I'm not leaving my brother to face this alone," she said.

"Yer brother doesnae need yer help. In fact, havin' ye here can only hurt him."

"Why?"

"Did ye notice he's stoppin' by daily? If not to protect ye from the big bad man who's bedding his baby sister, then t' make sure ye dinnae end up in the loch. If ye werenae here, he could concentrate on his job."

If she weren't here there'd be no one to swear that Liam wasn't a monster. Well, he *was* a monster. Just not the monster they were searching for.

And why did that matter? By his own admission he was a killer. If he got caught in the cross fire while the others were hunting a serial killer, would that be the worst thing?

Yes, if after killing Liam they then stopped looking for the real culprit.

"I'm not going anywhere," she said.

"I didnae think so."

Kris should probably tell her brother and/or Edward everything. At least then there would be no "accidents" with the silver bullets, although from what Liam said, bullets would be as worthless as feathers.

Kris tilted her head. If she told them that Liam was unkillable, what would they do? Proceed to find a way to kill him, since an immortal self-professed "monster" would not be something either one of them was prepared to leave alone?

Perhaps they'd take him from the loch and put him in a great big glass "Nessie bowl" where they could study what made him tick for . . .

"Eternity," she whispered. Maybe she'd keep what she knew to herself. For now.

"I know ye can't forgive," Liam said, "and I dinnae blame ye. I didnae mean to lie, but it's—"

"Habit."

"Would ye have believed me if I told ye what I was when first ye arrived?"

He had a point. She'd have written him off as a lunatic. Still—

"After you saved me in the loch, after I said I'd seen Nessie, that I wanted to prove she existed and I wanted . . ." She paused remembering that she'd asked him to help her. Talk about inviting the fox into the henhouse. "You could have told me," she finished.

"Aye," he agreed, and that was all. He made no excuses, and she liked that. There was no excusing a lie, and trying to do so only made the untruth glare ever brighter.

"You should go. I need—" She rubbed her forehead. "To think."

As if thinking would make her mind stop whirling and her heart stop hurting. But having him here wasn't helping, either. Having him here made her remember every kiss, every touch, every thought and hope and dream, followed by the knowledge that they had all been a lie.

And that she would never kiss or touch him again.

"I'll be close by."

"You always are." Which should be creepy but somehow wasn't.

Then he was gone, leaving behind a great big empty Kris wasn't sure she'd ever fill.

The middle of the night and Kris surfed the Net. Probably something she'd be doing a lot of in the middle of the night from now on.

When she couldn't sleep. When she was long gone from here. When she woke up missing him.

"Idiot," Kris muttered. "He's a moon-cursed lake monster. What kind of future did you have?"

Another water-soaked laugh erupted. How was that for a star-crossed romance? Next time she'd pick a man who didn't shape-shift.

Kris shook her head. She couldn't believe she was having this conversation with herself. But then, could she really have it with anyone else?

"He said he'd never seen Nessie," she muttered.

To be fair, he *hadn't* seen her. He *was* her.

"He seduced me."

How horrible. He'd encouraged her to have great sex. He'd made her scream. What a bad, bad man.

"Not a man."

In that case, at least he wouldn't leave her like almost everyone else she'd ever loved.

Love? Kris rubbed her face. She didn't love him. She *couldn't* love him. He definitely didn't love her.

But Kris remembered Liam's face when he touched her, and there'd been something there. Something that had made her insides flutter.

She'd felt things for Liam she'd never felt for anyone else. She'd told him things she'd never told anyone else. If she was honest, and considering her policy on honesty she'd better be, she didn't want to run away and never see him again.

But she still wasn't sure if what she felt was real, and if her feelings had been brought about by magic, weren't they just another lie?

Her e-mail binged. Kris clicked on the icon. When she saw the e-mail address, she leaned closer.

JAMAICA@JAMAICABLUE.COM

"Where have you been?" Kris murmured, and opened the e-mail.

HEAR YOU'RE LOOKING FOR ME. COME TO THE STORE BEFORE I OPEN. JUST YOU AND ME. WE NEED TO HAVE SOME GIRL TALK. I'LL BE THERE AT 5. BEHIND ON THE PAPERWORK.

Kris glanced at the time. Only a few hours to go.

What could Jamaica have to tell her? Kris didn't think the woman would break her vow and reveal Liam's true identity, not that it mattered, since Kris already knew.

However, once Jamaica heard that, then maybe she'd be able to shine new light on Kris's dilemma. As a guardian, the woman must know a lot about the being she guarded. Perhaps even if he could make someone fall in love.

Kris dozed on and off, jerking awake every twenty minutes, afraid she'd see the sun shining in, discover the day half-gone and her opportunity to "girl talk" with Jamaica gone. Which meant at 5:00 A.M. Kris already stood outside the coffee shop.

No one answered her knock, so she pressed her face to the glass. A circle of golden light spread from the back room. Flickering shadows gave the impression of someone moving to and fro—Jamaica doing paperwork.

Kris tried the door, which wasn't locked. Probably not the brightest idea with a serial killer on the loose. She'd mention it to Jamaica.

In the gloom, she dodged chairs and tables. It wasn't until she stood a few feet from the office that she heard the strange sounds.

Heavy breathing. Splashing. Then the screams.

She took the final steps into the room at a near run, then stared at the television, transfixed. It only took an instant for her to recognize the incident on the loch playing across the screen. The woman going under, bobbing up. The figures on the other side, too far away to really see.

"What the hell?" she murmured as something big hit the water and moved quickly across.

Even though she knew Nessie was coming to help, Kris shivered. From this angle, it didn't appear that Nessie was helping the woman at all. From here, it looked like Nessie was killing her.

A shuffle sounded behind her. "Jamaica, where did you—" Kris turned.

It wasn't Jamaica.

CHAPTER 26

Liam had planned to keep watch on the cottage until his presence was required in the loch. But after a few hours spent staring at the light in the window, he realized just how pathetic he was and took a walk.

Why had he allowed himself to fall in love with her? Liam kicked at a dead branch in his path. As if he'd had any choice in the matter at all.

So intelligent, so interesting, so brave, and yet so wounded. The way she'd looked him right in the eye and insisted—to him!—that there was no Loch Ness Monster. Yet when presented with undeniable evidence she'd not only changed her goal but also become fascinated with everything about Nessie. About him.

She would tilt her chin just so, and her lips would tighten as she tried to hold in the pain, but her eyes swam with the memories of love and loss and betrayal. Memories she had shared with him. To be trusted like that had made Liam feel truly human.

He'd thought himself miserable before. But now he would experience the agony of loving with no hope of being loved in return. Who could love a creature such as he?

He had blood on his hands that would never wash free no matter how many days he swam in the loch.

Even if by some miracle Kris loved him back—perhaps if she hit her head one too many times and completely forgot the meaning of the words *liar* and *murderer*—her loss was inevitable, as she would die and he would not.

Too bad the witch who had cursed him wasn't still alive to witness his pain. She would love it.

Liam wandered, but the loch and the trees and the bright shiny moon did not give him an instant's peace, so he came back to Kris.

By the time he returned, the window was dark and she was asleep. He glanced to the east. Just a few hours until dawn.

Suddenly a car pulled up. Her brother got out, then pounded on the front door, shouting her name. He rattled the knob. The door held.

Until he kicked it in.

Liam ran across the road, up the walk, and into the house. He knew even before Marty, staring at her open computer, said, "Fuck!" that Kris was gone.

"What happened?" Liam asked.

"There's an e-mail from Jamaica telling Kris to meet her at the coffee shop." He headed for the door.

Liam put his hand to the man's chest. "What is so wrong with that?"

"Jamaica Blue is in a hospital in Inverness."

Liam's blood, which had run cold since that cursed night beneath the moon, suddenly ran even colder. "Why?"

"Someone beat the hell out of her, then left her for dead. The doctors have no idea why she's still alive."

Liam knew. Jamaica had powers. She'd sworn never to use them again, but when the situation was dire vows would be broken, blood would be spilled, sacrifices made.

"Who?" Liam murmured, the softness of his voice belying the turmoil within.

"If I knew that, I wouldn't be here; I'd be kicking his ass until he occupied a bed in the room next to hers."

"Why are ye here?" Liam asked. It didn't follow that Jamaica being hurt would send Marty to his sister.

Marty's gaze was tortured. "Because the last thing Jamaica said before she lost consciousness was, 'Save Kris.'"

Kris awoke with a nasty headache. If she got conked on the head any more she was going to wind up with brain damage.

Except she hadn't been hit. Not this time. This time she'd been drugged.

Which was *so* much better.

She was cold. No longer inside, but somewhere near the water, as she could smell the loch and . . . pine trees.

Kris opened her eyes. It was still dark. She hadn't been out that long. Unless she'd been out an entire day and most of the night. But she didn't think so.

She lay on the ground. Her hands were bound, but her feet weren't, so she sat up, and then wished she hadn't. Not only because of the increase in brain pain, but also because as soon as she did she saw that she wasn't alone.

"How are you feeling?" Dougal Scott asked.

"Are you crazy?"

Fury flashed in his eyes, and Kris wanted to bite her tongue. Obviously he was crazy. He was a damn serial killer. Pointing that out, however, probably not the best idea while bound and helpless.

"I wasn't sure you'd come," he said, getting over his anger fairly quickly. "If you'd be up in the middle of the night again and see the e-mail in time."

"I—" Kris broke off. "How did you know I'm up in the middle of the night?"

"Your lights. I could see you moving about behind the curtains."

He'd been watching her. No wonder she'd felt so . . . watched.

"What if I hadn't seen the e-mail?"

"I'd have come to you." He shrugged. "But it was easier if you came to me."

"Why are you doing this?" she asked.

"I need them off my back."

"Them?"

"The *Jäger-Suchers*. Interpol." He took a few steps toward her. "Clever to send you. I didn't suspect. Not until I found your silver knife."

Hell, she'd known that was going to bite her on the ass.

He tilted his head. "But are you *J-S* or Interpol?" He continued before she could deny being either one. "Doesn't matter. I was mad." He wagged a finger at her. "You fooled me. I thought you liked me. Still, I shouldn't have used your knife on that girl." His face fell. "I never meant for her to be found. But she got caught in the damn lock. And that put a crimp in what I've been trying to do."

"Which is?"

"Don't play stupid!" His shout echoed over the silent loch. Would someone investigate? Should she hope they did or that they didn't?

He appeared to be waiting for her to answer. Considering his hair-trigger temper, she decided to humor him. "You wanted Nessie blamed for the killings."

"If they kill the Loch Ness Monster, or capture it, they won't be looking for me anymore."

"You've been killing people all over the world using the MOs of the local legends."

Made sense. He'd been studying those legends for most of his life. He had a damn display in his museum. But—

"I thought you didn't believe in Nessie."

He made a derisive sound. "No, *you* didn't believe in Nessie. I just wanted to get in your pants. I decided that was the quickest way. Then you decided to fuck the monster, and I decided you should die."

"Why would you want to kill people?"

"Magic's in my blood. Sacrifice brings power. But no matter how many I killed, the power never came to me. I couldn't access the magic."

"If sacrifice didn't work, why'd you keep killing?"

"I liked it. I may not control the magic—yet—but the rush after I kill . . ." Dougal breathed in, and his chest expanded as if that power he wanted so badly, the power he'd killed for, had come to him at last. "Having command over life and death makes me feel—"

"Crazy?" Kris muttered, then wished she'd kept her mouth shut when his eyes glittered with both madness and fury. How could she ever have thought his eyes were gentle, intelligent, and attractive? Hadn't she learned by now that there were more ways to lie than with words?

"Would a crazy person be smart enough to use the local legends as a cover?"

In Kris's experience *crazy* didn't mean "stupid." It usually meant "freakishly smart." However—

"The authorities knew what you were doing." They just hadn't known *who* was doing it. "They followed you to Drumnadrochit."

"I wanted them to. I needed a place where a real legend lived."

"In the other places there was no monster," Kris guessed. "Except for you."

He cast her a narrow glance, then nodded. "I needed something I could blame, and they could kill."

"Why Nessie?"

"I knew the Loch Ness Monster existed. My family was here when the legend was born. Or at least when the curse was."

Kris's head ached. Her mouth tasted like dirt. Her mind wasn't working as quickly as she'd like, but eventually she caught up. "You're the witch's ancestor."

"Aye," he said sarcastically. "That I am."

"I don't understand," Kris managed. "Why would you want Nessie dead? Isn't the monster cursed to eternal torment?"

"He doesn't seem too tormented to me. Why would he be? He gets to fuck you."

"He?" Kris asked. "Wouldn't Nessie be a woman?"

Dougal's expression revealed how lame he thought her attempt to throw him off that scent.

"I know that *Liam*," he said the name with a sarcastic twist, "is Nessie. All my life I've heard over and over how that horrible *thing* murdered our golden daughter. How there must always be one of us here to make sure it was tormented for all time. I accepted the charge. I'm the last of my line."

Kris tried to wiggle out of whatever he'd used to bind her hands. She couldn't make it budge a centimeter. No surprise. Dougal'd had a lot of practice binding his victims.

"Imagine my shock," he continued, "to discover the monster wasn't tormented but treated like a god. The locals, as well as the tourists, worship the thing. Even my own *granaidh*, who'd also been *charged*, allowed it to walk freely among them like it was as human as it appeared. The creature has guardians to protect it." His lip curled. "But they won't once they see the film of their precious Nessie drowning a woman."

Kris blinked, remembering the video that had been playing at Jamaica's. "Your victim is alive. Nessie didn't hurt her; Nessie saved her, and she will say so."

"That isn't the video I'm talking about." Dougal's eyes glittered madly. "It could have been if she'd *died*. Why did you have to know CPR?"

"Sorry," Kris muttered.

"I wanted to show you what he was. I thought then you'd kill him, or have Edward do it. But you're as dazzled by the creature as everyone else. I can barely get people in this village to say hello to me on the street, but that thing they revere." He glanced toward the video camera and tripod partially concealed by the trees. "Not for long. You'll be my new star, and *you'll* die like you're supposed to."

Kris had kind of figured her death was on his agenda. Why else would he trick her and drug her and drag her . . . ?

She glanced around. They were at a remote portion of the loch, backed by a craggy hillside, surrounded by thick trees, the water lolling past a tiny exposed portion of shore, barely big enough to land the small boat they'd arrived in. There were a hundred places like this up and down the loch.

"He'll never find us," she murmured.

Dougal glanced at the steadily lightening sky. "Give him time."

Marty and Liam arrived at the coffee shop very close to dawn. Even though Liam knew he was pushing it, that he could easily shape-shift right in the middle of Jamaica's shop and pretty much break everything into a thousand pieces, still he ran inside.

Kris wasn't there; he knew that, too. But they had to follow every clue, even if those clues eventually led to her body.

Fury coursed through him. He would kill whoever hurt her. He would enjoy it the way that he used to. And if that turned him back into a creature unable to value human life, one the *Jäger-Suchers* would certainly destroy, then so be it.

A piece of paper lay on the ground. At first Liam thought it had drifted from Jamaica's overburdened desk. He picked it up, nearly put it back without reading it. But the large block letters caught his attention.

DUNWAR.

He shoved the sheet at Marty and ran.

The Interpol agent was fast. He caught Liam as he reached the water. "What does this mean?" Marty demanded.

"'Tis a point on the loch. Remote. The quickest way is by water."

Marty looked around helplessly. "We need a boat."

Liam's gaze went to the sky. "I don't," he said just as the sun burst free.

Kris had to do something. Dougal planned to kill her, blame it on Nessie, then go about merrily murdering hither and yon once Marty and Edward believed they'd taken care of the problem.

He'd screw up again, no doubt, and have them both back on his trail. But in the meantime, she'd be dead and so would Liam. Kris wanted to avoid that.

Reasoning with him was out. Dougal had lost all reason long ago.

So . . . She'd just have to kill him before he killed her.

He'd need to get her in the water somehow. Maybe she could drag him in, too. Hold his head below the water with . . .

Kris yanked again at the bonds on her hands. With what? Her teeth?

"Time for a swim." Dougal motioned to the loch with his gun. "Get in."

"I'm not going to be able to swim with my hands tied."

"No," he said with a smirk, "you won't."

"Won't that be suspicious?"

"A serial-killing kelpie bound your hands? What a wicked, wicked creature." He flicked the barrel at the water. "Go."

"I . . . uh . . . No." She stood. "You want me to drown. You're not going to shoot me."

"No?" He lowered the weapon and fired. Dirt flew up a few inches in front of her. Kris couldn't help but scoot back.

Dougal followed. "Get in."

Kris lifted her chin. "I won't."

Bam!

Earth exploded centimeters from her right toe. She stumbled into water just past her ankles. Kris tried to inch forward.

Bam!

Water sprayed to her left. This time she held her ground, gritted her teeth, refused to move, though she did flinch. *Bam,* right. *Bam,* left. Right. Right. Left. Left.

He reloaded so fast and fluidly, she only managed a single step forward before he shot again. Three in succession—to her right and left and right. Dizzy, ears ringing, she swayed.

And the water erupted as Nessie broke the surface.

The creature brushed past Kris, heading for Dougal, teeth bared. Dougal's eyes bulged, the whites flaring in the bright morning sun. He fired, emptying his clip into the gray seal-like skin.

Nessie flopped into the shallows like a beached fish and lay still.

Kris's mind froze as solidly as her feet already had in the icy waters of the loch. She stared at the massive bleeding dead lump that was Nessie.

"Huh." Dougal looked at his gun.

"Th-th-that's—" Kris's teeth began to chatter.

"Unfortunate," Dougal finished.

Kris had meant to say *impossible,* but obviously not. From what she could see, Nessie had already stopped breathing. Perhaps a descendant of the witch who created the monster was the only one who could end the monster. Who knew?

Kris's whole world shifted, and everything became clear—an instant too late.

Seduction was one thing, love completely another. Great sex could not make you feel something you didn't truly feel.

Like the love she felt for Liam Grant.

"Well." Dougal slapped in a third clip. How many did he have? "I can work with this. Drown you, say she did it and I had to shoot her. Too bad about the video. I would have enjoyed it later, but sometimes you have to improvise." He tossed the gun aside, grabbed Kris's arm, and began to drag her into the loch.

Kris struggled. Not that she cared about drowning. Not anymore. Liam had died saving her. He'd died believing she hated him. She'd wondered if she would ever feel again the way she felt about Liam. Now she knew that she wouldn't, and the luster of life dimmed.

However, she wasn't going to let Dougal get away with blaming her death on Nessie. And the only way to ensure that was to live.

So Kris fought. She dug in her heels; she struggled and screamed. Dougal yanked and scratched and cursed.

Then he slapped her.

Behind him, the eyes of the Loch Ness Monster opened.

On land Liam was slow and ponderous. But in the water he was king. So he played dead, and he waited for that murdering bastard Dougal Scott to get but a little closer.

Crack!

The distinct sound of flesh meeting flesh caused Liam's eyes to snap open just as Dougal hit her again.

Liam's neck snaked out, his body already rolling into the water as his jaws closed on Dougal's thigh, biting deep, tasting blood. Together they thrashed, but the man was no match for the monster. Dougal's scream cut off as he was pulled beneath the surface.

"Liam, no!" Kris cried, but it was too late. The instant Dougal had marked her for dead, he had marked himself as well.

Together Liam and Dougal sank into the frigid depths of Loch Ness.

CHAPTER 27

"Kris!"

Her brother ran out of the woods. His gaze went to the water. But only a few swirls, a few bubbles, remained. Still, one look at his face and Kris knew he'd seen the whole thing.

"I won't let you hurt her," she said.

"Kris—"

"I've never asked anything of you in my life, Marty, but I'm asking this. Don't call Edward. Just let Nessie stay Nessie. Let Dougal stay dead. Make up whatever the hell you have to. Forge whatever you have to forge; I don't care."

He lifted his hand to her face. "Dougal hit you."

Kris shrugged. She was getting used to black-and-blue.

"I'd have killed him, too," Marty muttered. She looked at him suspiciously. "You really think I'd turn Liam in to Edward?"

Ah hell. He knew.

"How do you—?"

"Dougal left a note telling us where he was. I'm not

sure why. . . ." He looked around, saw the camera in the shadows of the trees. "Hmm," he said, brain obviously percolating. "Anyway, Liam became Nessie and got here a lot quicker than me."

"Not that much quicker," Kris muttered. "Did you break the land speed record?"

"Nearly."

"Will you leave Liam alone, even though he just killed a man?"

"Dougal was more of a monster than I've seen in a long time. Creepy, sneaky bastard. I'd have had to hire the 'fix it' guy to kill him anyway. Way I see it, Grant just saved me the trouble."

"What about Edward?"

"I'll tell him I took care of the problem."

"And if he finds out you're lying?"

Marty winced. "Let's just hope he doesn't."

Kris felt terrible asking her brother to lie, and to Edward Mandenauer. But what choice did she have?

"We could tell him the truth," Marty ventured.

"Which is?"

"Benign lake monster. No reason to kill it. Like you said: Let Nessie stay Nessie."

"You think Mandenauer will go for that?"

Marty sighed. "Probably not."

"Then keep this to yourself."

"All right. But Kris—"

Kris stared at the water, waiting for the familiar dark humps to appear, but they didn't.

"You can't have any kind of life with him."

Kris forced herself to look at Marty. "Why not?"

"He's a monster."

"You just said yourself—Dougal Scott was the monster. Liam's just . . ." She glanced back at the loch. "Liam."

"Hell!" Marty muttered.

"What?" Kris's gaze flicked around the clearing; she peered into the trees, half-afraid she'd see Mandenauer coming out of them.

"You're crazy about him," Marty said. "No going back now."

"No." Kris watched the water again. "There isn't."

"What are you going to do?"

"Love him," she said. "It's all I *can* do."

Marty cleaned up the scene. He seemed pretty good at it. Really, there wasn't all that much to take care of. He retrieved a few shell casings, along with Dougal's camera and tripod.

"I doubt anyone's going to come along anytime soon. If they do . . ." He shrugged. "It's not like we have a body to dispose of."

"What about Dougal's disappearance?"

"He's a serial killer. No one's going to care."

"No one knows that."

Marty's face hardened into one she didn't recognize. No longer the brother she remembered or even the man she was coming to know, but the Interpol agent who dealt with crap like this every day. "They will when I get done. I'll say I pieced the truth together, then confronted him. He flipped, tried to kill me; I shot him, and he fell into the loch."

Kris had thought to keep everything quiet, but loose ends were better tied up. It wasn't as if they'd be blaming an innocent man for crimes he hadn't committed, and the victims deserved justice; their families deserved to know what had happened to them.

Together Marty and Kris made their way to his rental car. It wasn't an easy trip. Through the trees, down a nasty slope, across a craggy hill, Kris was leaning on her brother heavily by the time they reached what constituted a road in this part of the loch.

He helped her into the passenger seat and she must have fallen asleep, because the next thing she knew, Marty had rounded the bend near the cottage. Alan Mac sat on the porch. Kris groaned. All she wanted was to go back to sleep.

"Don't worry," Marty said. "The constable will be so inundated with the work this mess is going to cause, he won't have time to bother you."

"He'll need a statement."

"I already took it." Marty stopped the car. "All you have to do is sign. Once I type it up."

Kris put her hand on her brother's. "Thanks."

"I'm not going to disappear on you, Kris." His eyes, so like her own, were earnest, and for the first time in a long time she believed every word that he said. "I promise."

"What the hell?" Alan Mac pounded a huge fist on Marty's window.

Marty winked, and they got out of the car.

As Alan Mac was a guardian and would no doubt hear the truth from Liam anyway, Marty told it. Together they got their stories straight while Kris continued to stare at the loch. She couldn't help herself; she needed to see Liam. But he didn't appear.

The constable assured Kris that Jamaica would be okay. She'd come out of her coma and named Dougal Scott as her attacker. He'd have been in big trouble even if he hadn't kidnapped Kris.

"Why would he leave her alive?" Kris wondered. "She'd seen him."

"She should have died." Fury suffused Alan Mac's pale face. "Anyone other than her would have."

"Magic?" Kris guessed, and he nodded.

"Idiot had no idea the power he was messing with. He's lucky she didn't incinerate him."

"That would have required a sacrifice."

"Something she would never do again." Alan Mac looked away. "I wouldnae have been so generous."

Kris heard admiration in his voice. She tilted her head, narrowed her eyes, then smiled. Maybe something more.

"Without a sacrifice, how did she have the power to save herself?" Kris asked.

"Blood magic," Alan Mac said. "Less powerful, but effective enough to keep her breathing until someone else could."

"Blood?" Kris began, then understood. Jamaica had used her own. There'd no doubt been plenty of it. "Ass," she spat.

"Aye," Alan Mac agreed. "If he wasnae dead, I might have killed him myself."

"I don't understand why he hurt her," Kris continued. "Dougal knew Liam was Nessie. He didn't need Jamaica to tell him."

Alan Mac snorted. "As if she ever would."

"Then why?"

"She suspected Dougal was up t' no good, and she confronted him. But crazy folk are wily, and he—" Alan Mac's voice broke. He remained silent a moment, cleared his throat, and continued. "She should have come t' me. But the woman takes her guardian duties seriously."

"She took the same vows you did," Kris pointed out.

"That's exactly what she said."

At last Marty and Alan Mac left. Kris tried to sleep but was unable to. Even when darkness fell and the night stretched on and on, she sat at the window with her gaze on the water.

But Liam didn't come.

As dawn threatened, she left the cottage and went to the loch. Sooner or later he'd show up.

She'd be there when he did.

Liam watched Kris watch the water. He hadn't planned to go near her again. She'd nearly died because of him. If she had, he wasn't sure he'd have been able to go on.

Although he had no idea how not to.

But when she came to the shore he found himself drawn from the trees where he'd always blended so well with the shadows. Perhaps if he let her tell him to his face that there was no chance for them, maybe then his foolish heart would cease to yearn.

Liar, he thought. He was no more able to stay away from her now than he'd been able to the first night they'd met.

She looked up as he approached. Liam stumbled, from both the beauty of her smile and its existence. Shouldn't she be frowning, shouting, perhaps throwing things?

"Kris?" he whispered.

"You saved me." She took a step toward him, but he stiffened and took a step back.

"I killed a man." He clenched his fingers into fists. "I enjoyed it."

Kris tilted her head. "You think that makes you a monster?"

"I didnae have to be *made* a monster. A monster is what I am."

Not even a rustle sounded from the grass as a third voice disturbed the gloaming: "Tell me more."

Kris cursed, her gaze going past Liam. "Do you ever knock on a door, walk up a road, wait for a damn invitation? Or do you always lurk about, then appear from nowhere with a gun?"

Liam didn't need to turn to know that Edward Mandenauer had come.

This time for him.

Kris's heart was pounding so fast she nearly missed the old man's response.

"I hardly appeared out of nowhere. And if I didn't lurk, I'd never find out anything at all." His gaze went to Liam, who still had his back to Edward, eyes on Kris. "For instance, the identity of a monster that has just killed a man."

She saw the intent on Edward's face and threw herself in front of Liam as the gun came up.

"Kris." Now Liam turned, picking her up bodily and hoisting her out of the way. "He can't hurt me."

"No?" Mandenauer's bushy white brows lifted. "How very interesting."

"He's done nothing wrong," Kris said softly.

"Killing a man and enjoying it is not wrong?"

"He ended a serial killer."

"Kudos," Mandenauer drawled, faded gaze still on Liam as if he were the last slice of dessert at a chocolate buffet. "It is not the killing I mind so much as the enjoying of it."

"Dougal Scott was a serial killer," Kris said. "We may never know how many people he murdered. He beat Jamaica Blue nearly to death, and he planned to kill me, film it, and blame Nessie."

"Diabolical." Edward still didn't lower the gun. "Unfortunately, I cannot let a monster that has killed remain on the loose. He may have developed a taste for it."

"He didn't," Kris said.

"Nevertheless—"

"I won't let you hurt him."

Edward managed, just barely, to keep his lips from twitching. "My dear, you won't be able to stop me."

"I won't have to. His curse does that."

The old man's eyes glittered. "How so?"

"He was cursed to eternal torment. If he can be killed, not very eternal."

Liam continued to hover, tense and ready, between Kris and the ancient *Jäger-Sucher*.

"Remarkable." Edward stared at Liam as if he were a fly in a web. "We will have to find a place to study you. A more controlled environment."

Liam sighed. "All right."

"Like hell!" Kris stepped in front of him again. Again he moved her out of the way. "He's not putting you in a fishbowl. He's not going to experiment on you like he's *Mengele*," she spat.

Edward's eyes narrowed.

"I am a monster, *mo bhilis*. I have killed. Not only today, not only Dougal, but hundreds and for centuries."

"Shut *up*, Liam," she said, but her words held no heat. She heard the truth in his voice even before he admitted it.

"I've wanted to die for a long time now."

She turned, taking his hands, staring into his face. "Even now that you have me?"

Hope lit his eyes, but it faded fast. "Believe that I love you. But ye'll never know for sure, and neither will I, if what ye feel for me is true or a result of my magic."

"I feel it; doesn't that make it real?"

He shook his head.

"Come along now," Edward ordered.

"He can't. It's—" Kris glanced past Liam's shoulder, and her eyes widened.

"Liam," she whispered. "The sun."

CHAPTER 28

Liam spun, then stood blinking in the bright light of a sun he hadn't seen with human eyes in centuries.

"I thought you were moon cursed," Edward said.

"I thought I was, too."

Kris took Liam's hand again. For the first time, his wasn't noticeably cooler than hers. This time their skin temperature was the same.

She peered at their linked fingers. "What happened?"

"I dinnae know."

Kris turned to Mandenauer. "Ever hear of anything like this?"

"Curses *can* be broken." His already-wrinkled brow wrinkled even more. "Usually the one who cast the curse is needed in order to remove it."

"What if they're dead?"

"You raise them."

"Raise them," Kris repeated. "Huh?"

"Voodoo. Magic."

"Maybe Jamaica—" Kris began.

"No," Liam interrupted. "I forbid her to break her vow for me. And she's hurt, weak. She couldnae."

Mandenauer pulled out a cell phone and pressed a single button. Someone on the other end must have answered, because he began to speak without benefit of "hello." "Have you found another way to break a curse beyond having it removed by the one who originated it?"

He listened, then shut the phone without benefit of "good-bye." "According to my expert on curses, some can be removed by wiping out the line that did the cursing." He turned to address Liam. "In other words, every ancestor of the witch that cursed you must die."

Liam grimaced and said, "I wouldnae," at the same time Kris murmured, "Uh-oh."

Edward brought up the gun again.

"I would never take another life to ease my own," Liam insisted before Kris could speak.

"Dougal," Kris managed, both fear and hope in her eyes. "He said he was the last of his line."

"Convenient," Mandenauer murmured.

Liam ignored him. "How could they all be gone?"

"They must be." Kris lifted her chin to the eastern sky. "You're you."

Liam studied his hands, his arms, his legs, as if he expected them still to disappear as he morphed into a seal-skinned lake monster. "I dinnae understand."

"There is much in this world that is not understood." Mandenauer put up the gun. "Which is why I find it so remarkable." He actually winked at Kris. "I may never leave."

"Is this permanent?" Liam asked.

"I have never known a curse to skip a day," the old man observed. "Have you?"

"No, sir."

"You're mortal now," Mandenauer said. "Be careful. It takes some getting used to."

Edward turned and strolled toward the trees. As soon as he walked into their shadows, he seemed to disappear.

Liam stared at the sky. He couldn't seem to get enough of the sight of the sun.

"I love you," she murmured, then waited for Liam to repeat that her love wasn't real. Except she knew the truth.

Love was love. If you felt it, it existed, no matter how the emotion had come about.

He lowered his gaze, and her heart took one large *thump,* then began to whirl. He gathered her into his arms, and he kissed her, his lips now as warm as his hands. And while she'd liked their chill, she discovered she enjoyed the warmth just as much.

His eyes, too, were different. Certainly they still held sadness, a few shadows, and probably always would, but they were brighter, lighter. They seemed to look forward instead of forever back, and his next words proved it.

"Marry me." Not a question, more of a command.

"You believe I love you?"

"I do."

"What changed your mind?"

He indicated the sun with a jerk of his chin. "Ye still feel the same way about me now as ye did when the sun slept?"

"Exactly."

"That I'm standing here on two legs in its light means I'm no longer Nessie, nor the kelpie that seduced. Any spell ye may have been under is broken. I'm a man. And a man cannae make someone love."

"No, he can't," she agreed.

"Then ye'll marry me?"

"I'll think about it."

Confusion flickered over his beautiful face. "I thought ye loved me."

"I do. But, Liam—" She took a breath, let it out slow and long. "Where will we live? What will we do? How—?"

"Not now," he interrupted. "I'll spend a lifetime"—wonder spread over his face—"an actual lifetime, making amends for what I once did. But for now—" He kissed her again, putting a stop to every question but one. "Will ye let me make love t' ye in the sun?"

Later, after they'd run laughing across the road, carrying pieces of their clothing, pulling grass out of places grass should not be, Kris lay in bed with her head on Liam's shoulder.

"I'm glad you're you," she said. "But kind of sorry about Nessie. The tourist trade will take a nasty hit."

"I doubt it."

Kris drew back so she could see his face; there'd been something in his voice. . . .

"I never said I was the only thing down there."

Read on for an excerpt from Lori Handeland's next book

CRAVE THE MOON

Coming soon from St. Martin's Paperbacks

"You got another letter from moldy, old Dr. Mecate."

Gina O'Neil glanced up from grooming a horse to discover her best friend, Jase McCord, holding up a brilliantly white business-sized envelope. She knew exactly what business it contained. How could she not, considering the obstinate Dr. Mecate had sent her at least half a dozen others just like it?

It would behoove you to allow me to dig on your property.

What in hell was a behoove?

Proving my academic theory would increase the cachet of your establishment.

She had the same question about cachet.

I would be happy to advance remuneration.

Who *talked* like that?

"Helloo." Jase waved the envelope back and forth, his wide, high cheek–boned face softened by the chip in his front tooth that he'd gotten when he was bucked from a horse at the age of eight. His face, combined with his compact but well-honed body, made him look like a marauding Ute warrior, which was exactly what he would have been if born in a previous century. "What should I—?"

Gina snatched the envelope from his hand. "I'll take care of it." In the same way she'd taken care of all the others.

Direct deposit into the trash can.

Gina turned back to Lady Belle, and Jase, sensing her mood, left.

Nahua Springs Ranch was not only Gina's home but her inheritance. Once one of the most respected quarter horse ranches in Colorado, Nahua Springs had become, after the death of Gina's parents nearly ten years ago, one of far too many dude ranches in the area. Nevertheless, they'd done all right. Until recently.

Recently she'd begun to receive as many letters from bill collectors as she did from Dr. Mecate. Certainly his *remuneration* would be welcome, considering their financial difficulties. Unfortunately what he wanted from her was something Gina couldn't give.

If she opened the letter, she knew what she'd find. A request for her to let him search for Aztec ruins on her property.

She couldn't do that. What if his search took him there? What if he found . . . it?

She couldn't let that happen.

Gina crossed to the open back doorway, drawing in a deep breath of spring air as she stared at the ebony roll of the distant mountains and the spring grass tinged silver by the wisp of a moon.

Giiiiii-naaaa!

Sometimes the wind called her name. Sometimes the coyotes. Sometimes she even heard her name in the calls of the wolves that were never, ever there.

The singsong trill haunted her, reminding her of all she had lost. She'd come to the conclusion that the call was her conscience, shouting out the last word her parents had ever uttered in an attempt to make sure she remembered, as if she could ever forget, that they had died because of her.

Everything had both started and ended in that cavern beneath the earth.

"Kids will be kids," she murmured, echoing her father's inevitable pronouncement whenever she and Jase had gotten into trouble.

Let them roam, Betsy. What good is having this place if she can't run free like we did?

Gina's parents had been childhood sweethearts. Boring, if you left out the star-crossed nature of their relationship—Betsy the daughter of the ranch owner and Pete the son of the foreman. Everyone on the ranch had considered them as close as brother and sister. When Betsy's father had found out they were closer, he'd threatened to send her to college on the East coast, right after used his bullwhip on Pete.

The reality of his coming grandchild had ended both the threat of a whipping and any hope of college. Not that Betsy had cared. She'd loved the ranch as much as Pete had, as much as Gina did now.

Gina and Jase *had* been kids that day, heading straight for the place Jase's granddad, Isaac, had warned them against.

At the end of Lonely Deer Trail the Tangwaci Cin-au'-ao sleeps. You must never, ever walk there.

According to Isaac, the *Tangwaci Cin-au'-ao* was an evil spirit of such power that whoever went anywhere near it died. Basically, he was the Ute Angel of Death, and he lived at their place. What fifteen-year-old could resist that?

Certainly not Gina.

She'd become obsessed with the end of Lonely Deer

Trail. She'd crept closer and closer. She'd taken pictures of the flat plain that dropped into nowhere, yet a tree seemed to grow out of the sky. And when that sky filled with dawn or dusk, the tree seemed to catch fire.

How could anyone not want to explore that?

Jase hadn't wanted to go, but she'd teased him unmercifully. In the end, he'd given in, as she'd known he would. And to Jase's credit, he'd never once said: *I told you so.*

Not when the earth had crumpled beneath them.

Not when they'd tried to climb out and only succeeded in pulling an avalanche of summer-dried ground back in.

Not when they'd been buried alive, unable to move, barely able to breathe.

Not even when they'd both understood they would die there.

Because if Gina's sleep was disturbed by the ghostly, sing-song trill, if on occasion the wind also called her name, if she felt every morning in that instant before she awoke the same thing she'd felt in that cavern—the stirring of something demonic, the reaching of its deformed hand in a mad game of *Duck, Duck, Goose*—pointing first at Gina, then at Jase, before settling its death-claw on her parents, well . . .

That was probably *I told you so* enough.

Mateo Mecate stared at the hieroglyphics until they blurred in front of his overworked eyes. He might be one of the foremost scholars in Aztec studies, but the letters still sometimes read like gibberish. He shoved them aside, removing his glasses and rubbing a hand over his face.

According to the calendar, May meant spring. As usual, Tucson wasn't listening. The temperatures had been pushing ninety for a week.

The door to Matt's small, dusty, scalding office opened,

and his boss, George Enright, stepped in. His gaze went to the papers on Matt's desk, and he frowned.

"Mateo." Enright's voice held so much disappointment, Matt expected him to cluck his tongue, then shake his head, or perhaps his finger, in admonishment. "This has to stop. I've put up with it thus far because of the respect I had for your mother. But the time has come to move on."

Enright was the head of the anthropology department at the University of Arizona where Matt was a professor of archaeology—his specialty, like his mother's before him, the civilization of the Aztecs.

Nora Mecate had been a descendant of that great civilization. She'd been fascinated—some said obsessed—with proving a theory she'd gleaned from ancient writings passed down through her family for generations. She spent her life—no, she *gave* her life—trying to prove it.

"You could become the chair of this department when I retire. But you need to abandon your mother's ridiculous theory. You're becoming a laughingstock." Enright lowered his voice. "As she was."

Matt stiffened. Any academic who refused to face facts became an amusing anecdote at the staff water cooler. Matt had noticed a lot of the graduate students staring and whispering lately.

Not that such behavior was anything new. For some reason the women around here liked to fashion him a Hispanic Indiana Jones. He wasn't, but that didn't stop them from pointing and giggling and showing up during his office hours with foolish questions they already knew the answer to.

Matt wasn't interested. Not that he didn't occasionally date—if the willing women he took to dinner, then back to his bed, then never saw again, could be considered dates—but his life was work, and he had little use for anything else.

"I have one more location on my mother's list of possibilities," Matt said.

Enright lifted his artificially darkened brows. Everything about Enright was artificial—his gelled, black toupee, his high gloss manicure, even his right hip.

When Matt did not elaborate, Enright sighed. His breath smelled of the Jack Daniels he kept filed under *W*.

"The semester is nearly done, Mateo. By fall, be ready to move on."

"Move on?" Matt echoed.

"Choose a different avenue for your research or choose another university." The door shut behind Enright with a decisive click.

Matt glanced at his mother's notes. As he shuffled them, searching for something he might have missed during the eight thousand other times he'd shuffled them, he could have sworn the scent of her—oranges, earth, and sunshine—lifted from the pages. Sometimes, when he touched them in the depths of the night, their whisper was her voice calling him in from childish explorations across every dig they'd ever shared.

He'd enjoyed a charmed childhood. What wasn't to love about living in a tent, searching for buried treasure and never once—until he'd come here—stepping foot in a school?

Nora had been the only child of the very wealthy Mecate family. When she'd chosen to become an archaeologist, more than a few inky-black Mecate eyebrows had been raised. She didn't *need* to work for a living; she most definitely didn't need to dig in the dirt. That she wanted to had been beyond the comprehension of many, including her father.

However, only poor people were crazy. Rich people were eccentric, and the more eccentrics in a rich family, the greater their prestige. The raised eyebrows had lowered before too long.

When Nora had turned up pregnant—not a boyfriend or a husband in sight—no one had bothered to exert their eyebrows at all. That Mateo would be a Mecate, and carry on that precious name, had gone a long way to bridging the gap between Nora and her father.

She'd dragged Matt with her all over Mexico and the southwest. She'd taught him everything she knew about how to research and explore. Then she'd died on a dig the summer before he left for college.

"Hell," Matt muttered, tracing one finger over his mother's chicken scratch scrawl.

While still a young woman, Nora had translated the ancient Aztec writings she'd uncovered in the musty library of the family estate and discovered something amazing.

The reason the Aztecs never lost in battle was that they'd possessed a secret weapon, what Nora referred to as a super-warrior, a being of such incredible strength and power that she believed him to be a sorcerer. That warrior had been buried somewhere in the American southwest. All she had to do was find the tomb.

Scholars would have accepted her searching for remains north of the Rio Grande, even though most believed the Aztecs had not ventured farther than Central Mexico. But the tomb of a supernatural warrior? A sorcerer?

No one but Nora believed that.

Certainly when Matt was a child, his mother's tales had captivated him. He'd accepted them completely. But as time went on, Matt's enthusiasm for a supernatural warrior waned.

However, Nora's research on the tomb itself was solid. There was something buried at an as-yet-undiscvoered site north of the Rio Grande. Perhaps nothing more than a very large, freakishly strong, and more deadly than usual Aztec, but if Matt found that tomb and those remains, he could vindicate his mother's theory. Or at least those parts it was possible to vindicate. Then she would no longer be a laughingstock.

And neither would he.

His mother had translated a list of half a dozen possible sites from the hieroglyphics she'd found. They'd explored all of them—save one—and to date they'd found nothing but rocks.

Detractors pointed out that the Spanish had destroyed most, if not all, of the Aztec records—flat, accordion-like books known as codices, fashioned from deerskins or agave paper. Any texts that survived had been written under the strict supervision, and often with the help of, the Spanish clergy.

Therefore, the writings Nora Mecate had based her life's work upon—*Super-warrior? Sorcerer? Indeed!*—were nothing more than a hoax perpetrated by some laugh-a-minute priest in the fifteenth or sixteenth century.

"Because priests back then were known for being extremely 'ha-ha' kind of guys," Matt muttered.

Matt had been studying the documents himself ever since Nora had died. He could find nothing wrong with her geographic translations. He had found no other viable sites.

Therefore, Matt had one last chance to prove her theory. If the final location yielded nothing new, he'd have little choice but to give up his mother's dream—which would be tantamount to admitting she was a crackpot—and move on. However, he'd encountered a problem with the remaining site.

Matt pulled a glossy, three-fold brochure from the center drawer of his desk. The front panel revealed majestic mountains—four shots—spring, summer, winter, and fall—green, blue, gold, brown, white, purple, and orange abounded. Horses gamboled. He turned the brochure over to see if bunnies hopped and cattle roamed.

Instead, he found an artsy portrayal of a cowboy in silhouette, head tipped down, hat shading his face. However, the outline of the body was every ride-'em-cowboy-wanna-be's dream.

Inside lay the propaganda—several gung-ho paragraphs superimposed over a sepia print of what he assumed was the main house, which, despite the "old time" feel of the photograph, had obviously been updated and well maintained. According to the text, gourmet food complemented an authentic western experience.

"Yee-haw," Matt murmured, rubbing the slick brochure between thumb and forefinger before removing another older, less slick, more crumpled paper from his desk.

He wasn't an expert on photography, but he was still fairly certain the person who'd taken the pictures for the brochure was the same person who had taken the image he'd uncovered on the Internet about a year ago. The one that matched the final descriptive translation for the burial site of Nora Mecate's super-warrior.

Somewhere on this dude ranch lay his last chance to vindicate both his mother's, and his own, life's work. Sure, he'd had his assistant leave a dozen unanswered phone messages, followed by as many unanswered e-mails. Then Matt had taken over and begun to write letters, reiterating the request for permission to dig. He'd yet to receive a single response. It infuriated him.

Deep down he knew that his single-minded devotion to proving his mother's theory, or as much of it as *could* be proved, was based on guilt. He'd stopped believing in the super-warrior long ago. He'd started to wonder if his mother was the kook everyone thought her to be.

Grow up, Mom. I did.

Even now, Matt winced at the memory. She'd died still believing and he'd—

"Gone on," Matt murmured. He hadn't really known what else to do.

So, if Gina O' Neil, owner of Nahua Springs Ranch, thought her silence would make him go away . . .

Matt booted up his computer and clicked the tab for *expedia.com.*

She'd soon find out how wrong she was.